7/14

INLAND

Also by Kat Rosenfield:

Amelia Anne Is Dead and Gone

kat
rosenfield

NLAND

Dutton Books

An imprint of Penguin Group (USA) LLC

DUTTON BOOKS
Published by the Penguin Group
Penguin Group (USA) LLC
375 Hudson Street * New York, New York 10014

USA * Canada * UK * Ireland * Australia
New Zealand * India * South Africa * China

penguin.com

A Penguin Random House Company

CIP Data is available.

Printed in the United States of America

978-0-525-42648-6

10 9 8 7 6 5 4 3 2 1

Designed by Vanessa Han

for my parents

INLAND

People that build their houses inland,
People that buy a plot of ground
Shaped like a house, and build a house there,
Far from the sea-board, far from the sound

Of water sucking the hollow ledges,
Tons of water striking the shore—
What do they long for, as I long for
One salt smell of the sea once more?

People the waves have not awakened,
Spanking the boats at the harbor's head,
What do they long for, as I long for,—
Starting up in my inland bed,

Beating the narrow walls, and finding
Neither a window nor a door,
Screaming to God for death by drowning—
One salt taste of the sea once more?

~Edna St. Vincent Millay

THE COAST

CHAPTER 1

15 YEARS AGO

IT IS NOT YET SUNSET when the tall young woman who lives on the cliffside makes her way down to the beach. Sure-footed on the wooden steps, worn smooth by sand and weather. She treads lightly, her feet naked and white against the earth, leaving only the barest impressions as she steps over the driftwood remains of a tree and around the jagged cluster of rocks, where the small, pale body of a crab floats idly in a tide pool and its brothers sidestep hastily out of the way.

The beach is empty in all directions, the only sign of life a trio of seagulls wheeling high arcs overhead. Other days, summer days, there are people here. Children playing in the shallows; a young man and his dog sprinting through the surf; the elderly couple who lives down the beach, wearing matching Windbreakers, strolling hand in hand. Their names are Peter and Polly, but she doesn't know this, nor do they know her name. Theirs is a passing acquaintance. They only smile and wave, nodding their white-topped heads in polite recognition at the woman with broad shoulders and striking blue eyes and waist-length tumble of hair, so wind-blown and wild that only its own weight can keep it under control. Some days they see her on the beach, on her way to or from the water, and pause to say hello; others, she is in, swimming, when they pass by. On those days, they've learned not to bother with greetings. She never looks back at the beach, never seems to notice them, not even if they stand at the water's edge and call out across the waves. Peter, who used to work as an electrician and still prides himself on figuring things out, tells his wife that he thinks the young woman must wear plugs to protect her eardrums, that she probably has tubes in her ears.

"I'm sure you're right, dear," Polly says, and they walk on down the beach. But later, when she's alone, Polly will think to herself that she's not so sure, not at all. She has seen the young woman's face peering out from the water, as still and blank in the sunlight as a silver coin. Even from twenty yards away, there is something unsettling in the way she gazes back—as though from across a great distance, and without seeing anything at all.

———

There are days, too, when she doesn't appear, and the couple wonder out loud to each other where she is, if she might be ill. It never occurs to them that she's not like them. Like most creatures of the earth, Peter and Polly keep time by the sun, enjoying the way its last rays warm their backs as they make their way back down the beach. They like to watch comfortably from their porch, a bottle of wine between them, as it sinks below the horizon in a blaze of pink and crimson.

The woman, though, keeps time by the moon, and the way it holds the oceans in its inescapable thrall, bringing them up to cover the coast and then rolling them away, back and back, to expose the briny mudflats, the gleaming beds of deep blue mussels, the slick and slippery rocks crusted over with barnacles like small, brittle teeth. She comes when the tide is highest.

Today, the beach is empty. Peter and Polly have long since passed by, and no children play in the surf. Autumn has cooled the water, chilled the evenings, driven away all but the most intrepid swimmers. But she has never minded icy water. When she peels off her dress and steps into the waves, it is like cool silk brushing her skin. She places her palms on the surface, and breathes deeply of the sea.

"I'm here," she says softly. "I'm yours. Yours as I have always been, as I always will be."

The answering voice seems to come from everywhere, rising up from the depths of the water, ringing out from inside her own head. She doesn't look around, not anymore; after so many trips to the water's edge, she knows that no one can hear it but her.

You are mine.

"Yes," she says gently, lovingly. Her fingers stroke the undulating surface, leaving tiny furrows in their wake that vanish as fast as they appear. Her voice is a purr. "Yes."

The child is mine.

"Yes. She will love you as I love you, always."

The man is nothing.

"Nothing," she breathes, and the word sends a chill through her heart. She steels herself, and says it louder. "Nothing. He is only a man. A means to an end. He gave me the child, but I have given him nothing, and nothing is what he is."

It isn't the first time she's said these words. She has been saying them for years, offered them up willingly every day, ever since that first moment when she stepped into the waves with the sun glinting like fire off her wedding band. She speaks them like vows, from the depths of her heart, a promise she has always intended to keep.

She can still remember when she meant it. When she believed every word that crossed her lips, because she believed so deeply in herself, in her own brilliance, in the solution that seemed foolproof and sure. She had done her research. She had taken her time. She knew the rules, and so she had carefully picked a man with whom she could follow them—a man she was sure she could never love. She had selected him, and then seduced him, all with a surgeon's skill and clinical detachment. This passionless bore of a professor, all hard facts and cool logic. He was the kind of man with whom it was impossible that she'd fall in love. In fact, she'd strongly suspected him incapable of the emotion himself. Of deep feeling of any kind, for that matter. He was too cold, too staid, too set in his ways to let another person into his stony heart. He was buried in his books, his rocks, his papers.

Entirely safe, just as she'd planned. Just as she knew he would be.

She'd also believed, truly, that she was as perfect for him as he was for her. It had always been her intention to find a man who would be to her just what she needed, no more, but it had been her good luck to find one for whom she was sure that she would be the same. She could tell just by looking at him that this man, long past the age at which most men married, had no true need of a wife, no deep yearning for a woman to share his life. You could see that in the way he lived, alone, no family or friends close by, his few social connections merely professional. There was no loneliness in him; he did not ache to love, or be loved. It wasn't in his nature. But he would appreciate what she had to offer: a well-kept home to come back to at night, a companion when he was lonely. A nubile, young body to warm his bed. And in return, he would give her the things she desired: a ring, a home, and—most importantly—a baby. Her daughter, her baby girl. The marriage, the man, were merely vessels for the child she'd always longed for.

Her husband could have her body, but not her heart. Never her heart. That was how it would happen, because that was what she'd planned. Because her heart had been claimed by another. It always had been, and would be forever. It was as she had promised, that first night on the shore, still in her bone-white wedding gown.

I'm here. I'm yours. Yours as I have always been, as I always will be. I will never leave you, and when the time comes, I'll come willingly.

A gust of wind lifts her hair from her shoulders, sending a shudder down the length of her spine.

The rising tide rolls in, as it did on the first day and each day since, churning in lace-froth eddies around her ankles. The sand drags away beneath her feet, as it always has.

She makes her way into the water, as she always does.

And she thinks, as she has so often lately, that she wishes she could go back five years, to the day she first approached him with a smile on her lips and her hair tumbling free and wild over her shoulders, and slap herself hard across the face. She wonders, bitterly and not for the first time, how she could have been so stupid, so reckless, so shortsighted and full of hubris.

And she prays, desperately and not for the first time, that she still has some secrets left. That the way she feels for her husband, the way she'd been so damned sure she'd never feel, is hidden somewhere watertight and out of reach. That she is as good a liar as she always believed herself to be, now that it matters more than ever.

She has so much more to lose.

There are shadows in the water. She reaches for them as they reach for her, walking out against the rising tide. Her eyes close as the waves break against her hips, as she breathes in deeply, as she bends her knees and sinks down deeper, as she feels the lick of water beneath her chin. She swims, as the sun makes its last golden gasp across the sky.

Only the vanishing light tells her how much time has passed, as she turns back toward the shore. The sea crashes and seethes, rushing past her to kiss the shoreline, hissing through the narrows between the hulking rocks. The waves call her name as they strike the beach, with all the urgent passion of a lover's breathless whisper. It is always this way, when it's time to leave. It is always this way, when the one who loves you is powerful, and jealous, and loathe to let you go.

"When the time comes, I'll come willingly," she whispers again. "And so will she."

But it isn't time, not yet. It will be years—her body beginning to show its age, her daughter nearly a woman—before she trades in this little life for the endless one that comes after.

The wind dies away, leaving the chill of early evening to shudder across her skin. She turns and swims for shore, stroking gracefully through water that grows calm as she glides over the surface. Her pale legs trail behind her, long and strong, until her fingers brush the rough bottom and her feet settle again on the soft, gritty sand.

Overhead, a gull screams in triumph as it lets loose a tightly closed shell to shatter, glittering, against the rocks. It swoops down in the last, fleeing light of the day to pluck its dinner from among the shards. The sky above is ablaze in red; when she steps dripping from the water and looks out to the horizon, it is across an ocean the color of lava, gone glassy and still, the gentle swells rolling in lazy rhythm.

From a place far off, above the beach, comes the creak and slam of a thin screen door. A porch light is flicked on; a man, tall and slim and standing in inky silhouette on the porch of a weathered house, calls her name.

"I know who I am," she whispers. *"He is nothing to me."*

But the words hold no comfort, and no truth.

From the shadowed house above the beach, she can hear her daughter crying.

CHAPTER 2

NINE YEARS AGO

THERE IS SOMETHING IN THE WATER. *A shadow, something dark and long and strong and sinuous. It slides beneath the shimmering waves, and I turn to watch as it comes closer, moving fast, an opaque patch that surges silently forward and slips under the keel of the boat on one side.*

I see it first. I see it, and I look away.

She is in the water, too; she is always in the water. Treading lightly, feet pedaling and pushing against the endless azure nothing below. She has been telling me, like she always does, that it's so lovely. So light. That I can't imagine how wonderful it feels. That the sea is like a cushion, a bed made out of sun glimmer and spray. She is beckoning, coaxing me to leave the little daysailer and come swim beside her. She tells me we'll float there together, two tiny dots of life on the rippling surface, with light glinting off *our slick-shiny hair and our feet fluttering like pale wings in the blue.*

I am only half listening. The shadow has disappeared beneath the boat.

There's nothing else. No splash. No sign. No portent cloud come to cover the sun. There is only the shadow in the water, and there is no time left.

When she sees it, she says only two words.

The first is "Wait."

The second, full of panic and water and the sudden, swelling noise of the sea, is my name.

The shadow has disappeared.

When I turn back, I am watching my mother drown.

In the movies, drowning is the most undignified of deaths. People scream, and flail, and thrash around. They make waves, clawing at the liquid surface and finding no purchase, until their waving arms lose strength and their mouths fill at the corners and they sink, feetfirst and fingertips last, beneath the rippling water.

That's not how it happens at all.

—

Back on land, there were questions. Why were we so far from shore? Why would my mother, surrounded on all sides by endless, directionless water, strip the sails and leave the safety of the boat? Why hadn't I thrown out a life jacket or a rope when I saw her struggling, or held out one of the long, light oars that were still suspended, untouched, in their space beneath the gunwhale?

My father, his mouth screwed tight with grief and anger and incomprehension, cast a shadow over my hospital bed. He stood next to the slim, silver IV stand, just as ramrod straight and rigid. Just as cold. He kept the shades drawn, keeping the world out and the fluorescent lights on, until I lost track of how many days I'd been there. No sun to mark the time, only the doctors and nurses and question-askers who came and went in a parade of quiet sameness. Everyone who entered my room was the same shade of blue-white pale, lit in the same sharp relief, the same hollow shadows carving their brows and jaws.

"You're not making sense, Callie," my father said, after the last one had left.

"There must be something you're not remembering," he said.

"Tell me the truth. Tell me."

My favorite doctor, the one with crispy, salt-streaked hair and the scent of coconut oil on his clean, dark hands, would usher him out of the room when I started to cry. In the hallway, he would lay his palm on my father's shoulder—a bronze beacon of warmth in that white, cold world—and bend in close with whispered advice.

"I know it's hard," I heard him say as the door swung slowly closed. The words slipped through the shrinking gap, settling in the room, sinking into the chair where people would sit with their pressed lips and endless questions.

"I know it's hard," he said. "But a trauma like this, at this age . . . it may be better, for her and for you, if she doesn't remember."

My sun-kissed doctor believed that my memory was incomplete on purpose; that my mind was healing itself with a story that made no sense, washing itself white, blotting out what I'd seen and burying it in a place where it couldn't harm me.

I was glad when the questions stopped.

It was easy, pretending to forget. Faking it a little more each day, and more still, until even my father believed that the truth about what happened that day was lost forever. Buried in my unplumbable mind. As hopelessly irretrievable as my mother's body, undiscovered and slowly unmaking itself somewhere in the depths of the Pacific.

It was easy—easier than trying to explain, through my cracked and sun-blistered lips, how this wasn't the first time that Mama had slipped out of the boat when the wind went down. How she could stay there, forever weightless in the water, no matter which way the current was moving us. That everything they'd ever believed about drowning was wrong.

Because there were no waving hands, no screams. She was simply there, and then not there. She disappeared beneath the surface without a splash or shout, and not so much as a bubble marked the spot, and the water where she'd been was as smooth and unbroken as dappled glass.

"You're not making sense, Callie," my father had said.

"I'm sorry," I said. "I'm sorry."

What I didn't say was: Yes, I am. I am making sense. I am making sense, if you just believe that this is how it happened.

The wind disappeared.

There was a shadow in the water.

And when it moved beneath our boat, the sea opened its yawning blue mouth and swallowed my mother whole.

THE MOUNTAINS

CHAPTER 3

THE SUBSTITUTE GYM TEACHER is eyeing me suspiciously. We've met once before, but he doesn't remember. I can't even blame him; I wouldn't remember me, either. I haven't been in school for three weeks.

"Last name is Morgan, you said?"

"Yes, sir."

"And you're sure it's this class."

"Pretty sure," I say, and he cringes. My voice is ragged and dry. They say that scar tissue has built up in my larynx, the souvenir of too many intubations. Too many hospital visits, too many times when my body has needed outside assistance to do the supposedly simple job of breathing on its own. When I talk, people flinch as though they want to lay a fast palm on my back—to knock loose that painful scrape from my throat. As though, if they just hit me hard enough, I'll cough it up onto the carpet.

I don't talk often.

"I don't have a file for you. And nothing about an exemption, either."

"I haven't been in school. It might have gotten lost."

His eyebrows go up another notch. They started climbing the moment I walked in; I can mark their movement by the number of folds in his forehead. He's entirely bald, this man: shaved to the shiny limits, a head like a cannonball. The tag on his binder says MR. THICKE, and he is—built wide and strong like a bulldog, with taut, firm skin and a coiled spring of a body. Someone who's moved all his life with the ease and fluidity and strength of a well-oiled machine. Someone who has never, I can tell just by looking at him, never struggled just to breathe.

I struggle. I wheeze and I pant and I drag the air in, clawing at it with ragged gulps, while it fights to stay out of my lungs.

Mr. Thicke looks at me, at the soft, unmuscled mass of my body, at the inhaler in my hand. I cough, and he winces.

"All right," he says. "I'll have to check with the admins, but in the meantime, go on and sit this one out."

I'm not sure which one of us is more relieved.

—

I can count the number of gym classes I've taken on one hand, and they've all ended the same way: early, prostrate, with my head against a cot and the bitter taste of albuterol coating my tongue. In the past six years, I've come to understand that exercise is a luxury for the healthy. Even the doctors don't push it. Even they, I suspect, don't want to see what I look like in sweaty, ungainly motion.

It's not a pretty sight. I'm not a pretty girl. Not even average, even on my Real Person days—the ones where I successfully get out of bed, and eat cereal, and make it through all eight periods without an attack. I'm nothing like the girls I glimpsed when I passed through the locker room to see Mr. Thicke, the ones who were giggling and shimmying into swimsuits, with lean legs and taut stomachs and skin that still looks kissed by the summer sun.

I can't swim. Can't run. Can't even move, not like they do. My body is pale from disuse, soft and limp and with the flabby consistency of unbaked dough. I have hollows under my eyes and pits in my skin, cracked lips and a rough face. Last year, the corpse of a drowned dog washed out of the sewer near our house after a week of hard rain; the first thing I noticed was how much its bloated, misshapen gut looked just like mine.

When I point to my gravelly ass and loose white flesh, the doctors remind me about priorities. They say that there's plenty of time to be pretty, but first I have to be well.

"I'm not getting any better," I say.

"You're doing fine," they say.

My father says, "Do as they say."

It's only us, now. My father and I, navigating our old Subaru like a two-hand ship, moving in one-year increments toward the center of the country. Following orders, seeing doctors, installing ourselves in university housing with the efficiency of frequent movers. They all look the same: classy, cared-for, conveniently located for a visiting professor's walk to campus and with two bathrooms, not one. A private space for the man's sick, pale whale of a daughter and her rattling boxes of pills. We moved first to get away—from the house, the shore, the memory of my mother. Now, we move toward the promise of wellness. Toward this doctor, that study, this university with full health coverage and then some, attached to that research hospital with access to cutting-edge technologies.

We live in desert places, arid climates, landlocked states with broad, flat horizons and the dry, unsaturated air that is all that my lungs can handle.

It's been this way, every day and every year, since she died. Since the day that I left the hospital, when he carried me in a blanket to the car and laid me in the backseat and drove me back to our seaside house, now full of closed cardboard boxes and bare surfaces and empty walls.

He'd been packing away our old life while I healed, giving it away to neighbors and charity, preparing to move us east.

With no rugs, no photos, no furniture, the sound of the Pacific was louder than ever; the surf, always a soft rushing sound track as it washed the cliffs far below, was so urgent and deafening that it sounded as though it was going to crash through the door. The lines in my father's forehead deepened with every wave.

In my parents' room, the bed was stripped bare and the closets were empty.

He'd given away her clothes.

That my mother was gone, I could understand. They'd told me in the hospital, gently breaking the news. As though I didn't know. As though I'd already forgotten, as though I wouldn't spend the rest of my life closing my eyes and watching her vanish beneath the sea. But I'd still expected to find her there—not alive, not in person, but I thought that something, some piece of her, would still be there. In that house, our house. In closets, on tabletops, in the shelves crammed full of books and scattered with shells. In the sea-smell of the sheets, and the damp-curled papers that lay on her desk.

When I fell against the doorjamb, the ointment they'd rubbed on my sunburn left a greasy spot on the wall.

The next morning, he caught me digging through a charity box and shook me hard. I'd pulled out Mama's books, the three nearest the top, and clutched them weakly to my chest.

"You have to stop this," he said, then fell to his knees. He pulled me in, held me as close as I held the books, stroking my hair. When he said it again, his voice was the battered, beaten whisper of an old man. "Please, Callie, you have to stop this."

"I don't want to go. This is our house."

"You don't understand this now, but I'm doing this for you," he said. "We're going to have a new life, honey. Staying here, with all this stuff, doesn't make sense. We have to move on. It's better, for you and for me, if . . ."

If we don't remember.

He didn't say it out loud. But three days later, with the last bag packed, my father took us inland.

The following year, I collapsed at school with one lung flattened and sagging uselessly in my chest.

———

The air has gone thick in the office. My throat is beginning to close; I clutch my inhaler and will my lungs to fill, pull hard, sucking and gagging while white spots cloud away my peripheral vision. The side of the chair that I'm sitting in punches against the limp flab of my stomach as I sag toward the floor. Halfway there. There's a tabletop under my forehead, cool plastic against my face, Mr. Thicke's binder, a makeshift pillow.

Somewhere, I can hear the sound of long limbs carving water, the shrieks of the girls who breathe so easily and have all the time in the world to care about being pretty. I listen, crumpled in the airless space, wheezing and waiting for it to pass.

I miss another four days of school.

When I come back, Mr. Thicke is subbing my chemistry class.

"Last name is Morgan?" he says. There's not even a glimmer of recognition in his eyes.

"Yes, sir."

"I don't have a file for you."

CHAPTER 4

MAMA'S BOOKS ARE DOG-EARED, the pages pliable from frequent turnings and softened by the sea. Even inland, with so many years between us and the Pacific, I still remember the feeling of water in the air. The moisture got into everything. Warping the worn wooden floorboards, making the wallpaper curl, lacing our sheets with a cool, salty dampness that even the sun could never bake away. The books, with their swollen bindings and bloated pages, spring open of their own accord.

So many moves, the constant packing and unpacking and loss in transit, has left no room for memory. In our landlocked lives, this is what I have left of the sea and of my mother. Two of them are textbooks, hers from another life; they have her notes in the margins, underlinings and exclamation points, scribbled references to related studies, and Latin words that I don't understand. I used to read them in the hope that I'd somehow feel closer to her—that whatever she found so compelling in these dense, impermeable paragraphs would touch me, too—but a hundred readings later, I know better. The books don't speak in her voice. The words hold no meaning for me, the pictures even less. They're only sketches, black-and-white and boring, showing you every which way just what the inside of marine animals look like.

My father has never mentioned them, not since that morning when I dug them out of the charity box and refused to let go, but his eyes go cloudy when he sees me reading. I know he knows them; they were hers, when she was his. Vestiges of the path that led her to him, so many years ago, on the ivy-covered campus where they met.

"*It was a scandal*," she used to whisper, grinning, and Dad would shake his head and smile and pretend to be embarrassed. "You should've heard them gossip, Callie! The straitlaced professor, falling for a student? A scandal! And when he married her, well, they all nearly had a heart attack."

It was my favorite story, our own little routine, and I knew the words by heart. He'd press his lips together, and she'd whirl across the room like a dervish and ricochet off the furniture, making the tabletop lamps shudder and tremble.

She'd tumble into his lap and he'd try to scowl, but the smile would break free and spread across his face while his arms came up around her.

"What was it they said, Alan?" she'd coo, burying her face in his neck.

"That nothing good could come of it," he'd reply, and then they'd both look at me, and he'd cock an eyebrow, and say, "but Callie looks pretty good to me."

And Mama would say, "That's only because she's sitting still," and we'd laugh, bright and clear and hard, like it was the first time she ever said it.

That's how I want to remember them: together. Happy and easy and laughing at their private jokes, their favorite joke, the long-ago story of the stir they'd caused by falling in love. He had been a bachelor, serious and solitary, coming up on forty with nothing to distract him from his rocks and his books and his flyaway papers; she had been his student, full of questions and boundless energy, more than enough for the both of them. She was only a few years older then than I am now, but I am nothing like her. My mother was beautiful, graceful like walking water, all elegant long lines and tapered fingers and skin that was dewy and smooth. If we met now, I think, she wouldn't recognize me.

They were married that summer, on the beach below the house that would be ours. On the wall by the door, there was a photo; it showed her pulling him into the water, knee-deep and with her white dress blooming on the surface all around her, both of them laughing in a halo of sea-spray and golden light. A moment of bliss and beauty and newness, a portrait of a couple who had thrown caution to the wind and who couldn't care less. Nobody who saw that picture, nobody who looked at those faces, would have tsk-tsked about the age difference, the impropriety, the scandal of their romance. Nothing that beautiful could ever be wrong.

I haven't seen that picture since. Not hung on the wall in our series of rented houses, not hidden in a drawer, not safely stowed in those boxes that follow us from place to place but never seem to get unpacked. It's vanished, and so has he. That man in the water is gone. In my father's eyes, there's not so much as a trace of the one who laughed and loved so easily, who rolled up his suit pants and followed his bride into the churning sea. That man, the one I called Daddy, is as lost as she is.

Maybe it's best if I don't remember.

Inland, nobody laughs. Not him, and not me, either. It's better for me if I don't find things funny. Laughing means coughing, more often than not. It's better if I press my lips together and keep my breathing even.

Instead, I flip through the pages of the bloated, boring books. I trace her notes with a fingernail. I wonder what she saw in here that was worth the enthusiastic scribbling and the sharp exclamation points. And I wonder, too, what she saw in him that made her put it all aside. She abandoned her studies the following year, content to simply sit in our high house, on the cliff and above the sea, and wait for him to come home each day. First alone, and then with her baby. Together, we would watch the waves and wait.

My father looks unhappy when he sees me with the books, but he won't take them from me. There is no danger in *The Physiology of Pinnipeds* or *Studies in Marine Evolution, Volume 4*. The other, though—the slim one, with the old-fashioned binding and the single, well-worn page in the center—I don't dare read in front of him. Even as a child, as I stubbornly held them close while he shook me by the shoulders, I instinctively turned its title toward my chest so that he wouldn't see it, or the photo tucked inside, or the page with a crease in the corner.

This book is different.

It's not like the others. It hasn't been kissed by the sea. It still closes, tight and flat, as though it was kept in a dry, close place, rarely read and rarely touched. The cloth binding is worn and threadbare, and the gold-stamped title on the cover has grown dull. When I opened it the first time, the photo tucked in as a bookmark had fluttered to the floor: a faded picture of two little girls in skirted bathing suits, standing in the surf on an empty beach. They're looking over their shoulders, squinting into the sun and smiling. Beside them, a tall woman with long hair and slim hips is turned away from the camera, gazing out to sea. A light scrawl of pencil on the back reads, *M & N with Auntie Lee.*

One of the little girls is my mother, and it's her initials that are the last to mark the flyleaf. "M.M.," for Maera Morgan. The others, "D.M." and "Λ.M.," are a mystery to me. The second M is present every time, in different hands, as though the book was passed down along with the name. It's my name, too; that, at least, was a piece of my mother I'd never lose, even after she'd vanished from our lives.

"When I was your age, before Nessa was born, my parents had a little boy," she said, the first time I asked about it. She was smiling, she was always smiling, but her eyes were sad and serious. "His name was Andrew. He would have been your uncle. But sometimes things go wrong, and Andrew died when he was just a few days old. If he'd lived, he would have carried on the Morgan name. But now, it's up to me to make sure it keeps going. So you, my daughter, will be a Morgan. And unless your father and I have a boy someday, you'll just have to make sure that your children are Morgans, too."

My father, who still smiled back then, looked at me with mock-seriousness and said, "Of course, given the alternative, naming you after your mother wasn't a difficult choice."

Mama made a face and said, "There's nothing wrong with your name, Mr. Twaddle."

"Excuse me," my father said, "but that's Doctor Twaddle to you."

And I am still Callie Morgan. If I were to write my initials inside, my M would line up beneath hers.

I've long since removed the picture, put it safely in a frame by my bed, but the book falls open to the poem all the same. The edge of the page is worn, the corner creased. It's not hard to imagine that my mother, like me, turned to this page again and again. That she traced each line with her finger, letting the words carve a familiar path on her tongue, until, like me, she no longer needed to open the book at all. The poem is a short one, its rhythm easy, rushing forward and then receding with the gentle cadence of waves on sand. I can picture her sitting in our house, high above the Pacific, reciting it in time to the sound of the surf. Maybe she even read it to me, while the boards creaked and the wallpaper curled and the sea pounded on and on.

> *People that build their houses inland,*
> *People that buy a plot of ground . . .*

I've never felt my mother in the other books, the heavy ones that caught her interest and held her excited scrawls in the margins, until the day that she put them aside for love. I've never sensed her in those pages, though I sometimes saw her read them, tracing her old notes with a fingernail and furrowing her brow at what she'd left unfinished.

But this book—though it has no margin notes, though I'd never seen it in her hands, though I can't remember its slender spine peering out from any of the shelves that lined our walls—this book is different.

She's there, between those lines. I can hear her in the breathless pause at the end of each phrase, the moment of calm before the rhythm rushes back in. I can see her, sitting on the porch in the gray, salty dawn that was full of the sounds of water. And though my initials aren't written on that first page, though there's nothing to mark this book as mine, I know, somehow, that it's meant for me.

Because I know. I know what it is to drown with no water in sight. To wake up at night, strangling in a tangle of sweat-drenched sheets, clawing at walls so close and unforgiving that for a moment, I know I've been buried alive and left to die. Not even the sudden click of the light can stop the scrabbling of my fingertips in that airless panic. Not even my father's hands, thrusting the inhaler into my mouth, and his voice, screaming at me to be calm and to breathe. On those nights, even as the air finds its way back in and my heartbeat subsides to a throb, even as he peels the hair back from my sodden forehead and tells me it's okay, I know the truth.

I am not going to get better. One day, the air won't come. One day, I'll scrabble at the beige-bland wall while my throat clogs with that senseless, scentless, stagnant dark. I'll die in this room, or one just like it, and there will be nothing he can do. I will drown in this arid inland night, the sea just a distant memory.

And when I do, I will wish with my last fluttering thought that I had followed her into the blue.

CHAPTER 5

THERE ARE MORE LEFT ASHORE in the Morgan family. That's our legacy: more stranded survivors, more mourners, more people throwing dirt onto coffins that hold nothing but trinkets and empty air. Even we, my father and I, stood above a hole in the ground and tossed our handfuls of earth onto the box that didn't have my mother in it. Just to have something to bury, just for the finality of watching the coffin disappear. The ones left ashore get left with nothing. The ocean doesn't give back its dead.

Nessa says that there are Morgans scattered up and down the coasts of a dozen countries, near and far, north and south. She says that we're drawn to the sea, answering a voice as inescapable and patient as any faithful man's call from God. My granddad was a Navy man, she tells me, sure-handed and strong, who would've stayed aboard another tour if not for the daughters waiting for him in their clapboard house on the bay. There is a cousin many times removed, a renowned painter, whose seascapes hang in galleries in London and whose studio looks out on the Celtic Sea. There are swimmers, sailors, divers. There are lobstermen, fishermen, marine hunters, and aquatic biologists. Even Nessa, always a drifter and still so young, has found her calling in the surf, teaching children to paddle out on their oversized beginner's boards and stand up proudly on the waves. She says that when the sea has given our family so much, it only stands to reason that it takes some of us, too, at the end.

Nessa. The only living person in the world who I miss. The only one who will ever miss me.

We left her behind on the second move, the one that took us over the border of eastern California and put the dry, dull landscape of the Mojave Desert in between us. She had driven out to see us off, surprising me as I struggled to cram the last of my belongings into a bulging cardboard box. She'd swirled into my room, all whirling blue linen and bright, clinking bracelets, her sun-streaked hair tumbling over both our shoulders as I leaped squealing into her arms. Nessa's visits were always planned-out, the result of endless phone calls and bitter negotiating and shameless begging on both our parts. We pleaded and cajoled until my father was too exhausted to do anything but agree—just as long as it was a short visit, just as long as she had somewhere to stay, since we weren't set up for visitors.

Not this time, though. This time, there had been no plan. The look on my father's face, as he stood dark and silent behind her, said as much. She'd called in sick to work and left before dawn, she told me, breaking the speed limit all the way there. Racing across California in her boxy old Volkswagen, the one with a bent fender and a surf rack on the roof and grains of sand buried in the upholstery.

It wasn't until years later that I understood: when we moved inland, no amount of pleading could bring Nessa to our doorstep. We had moved beyond a line she would not cross.

That day was the last time I saw her. We said good-bye in the heat of the afternoon, outside the house with a FOR RENT sign already sunk in the yellowed yard, where I clung to her waist and sobbed, "Come with us, come with us."

"I can't, baby," she said. "I wish I could, but I can't." Her long fingers stroked my hair, untangling it, smoothing it against my sweaty neck. She has the same graceful hands as her older sister, the same bronzed skin and calloused palms, the same tapered fingers with the same smooth, oval nails.

When I closed my eyes, I could almost imagine that it was my mother holding me, my mother's hands cupping my cheeks. I cried harder, pressing my face into the draping linen of her skirt, feeling it grow rough and wet while she made comforting sounds.

Shhh. Shhh.

I knew he had appeared behind me when her back stiffened and all the music went out of her voice. I kept my face in her skirt, hearing only the creak of the warped porch boards as they shifted beneath my father's weight.

"This is wrong, Alan," she said haltingly.

"It's not your business, Nessa," he replied, directing his gaze toward a spot near her feet. Since my mother's death, he couldn't bear to look at Nessa, this woman whose eyes were as deep and treacherous—the same almond shape and azure shade—as those of the wife he'd lost.

"Not my business?" Nessa snapped. "Callie is my family, too! And do you think *she* would have liked what you're doing? Do you think *she* would have thought it was right, taking Callie away from everything she knows, everything familiar? And think hard before you lie to me, because I know for a fact that Maera made you promise never to do this. She wanted Callie raised right, by the ocean, with people who love her."

My father flinched when she said the name, and his dead, heavy gaze moved from the sidewalk to the old porch rocker. His voice was flat and cold.

"I'm her father," he spat back. "Which means I love her, in case you've forgotten. And you're right, it's not what Maera wanted, and if you think it's easy for me to break that promise to her . . . well, I wouldn't expect you to understand. But she's gone, and somebody has to do the right thing here. Somebody has to pick up the pieces."

She laughed at that—not a real laugh, but a humorless, toneless bark.

"Pick them up and take them a million miles away," she snapped.

My father turned away.

"I have to do what I think is best," he said. His voice floated back to reach us as the door creaked open and he disappeared into the dark, clean interior of our soon-to-be-former house. "Callie, say good-bye and come inside."

Nessa had been glaring, daring him to meet her eyes. Now she sighed, swallowed hard, and looked away to the west. She muttered under her breath, eyes on the horizon. For a moment, she looked much, much older than twenty-four.

"This is wrong," she said again, more quietly. Her hands began to move again, combing through my hair. "God knows how your daughter will suffer before you see how wrong it is."

Over the rattle of the little VW's engine, she embraced me for the last time. I'd dried my eyes long enough to say good-bye, swallowing down my sobs in an effort to prove that it was all okay. When she lifted one of her own jingling necklaces over her head and placed it around my neck, I did my best to smile. The chain was a linked line of golden fire in the afternoon sun; the sea-glass pendant, smooth and opaque, played its light green glow against the white of my shirt.

"That's to help you remember," she said. A deep line had appeared between her brows, and stayed there even as she tried to smile. "Until you come back."

"He won't bring me back."

Her smile disappeared, and for a brief moment, a shadow seemed to move in the deep, troubled blue of her eyes.

"He has to," she said. And then the darkness lifted, and her forehead smoothed, and her smile—the real one, the one not full of worry—came back. "And if he doesn't, I guess I'll just have to come steal you."

But she didn't. She hasn't. And though I used to wish that she'd come to take me back—hard wishing, with my eyes shut tight and the cool, smooth green of the sea glass in my hand—I don't do that anymore. I no longer want to be rescued; there's no home for me, not there and not here. I belong nowhere, and I don't want Nessa, the only one who will ever miss me, to see the shuffling, wheezing creature I've become.

I still wear her sea-glass necklace—buried in my worn T-shirts and baggy robes, where my father can't frown at it the way he frowns at everything. And her letters find me every month, long after she stopped bothering to call our ever-changing succession of phone numbers, long after I gave up teasing her for not having an e-mail address. I like it better this way. It would be easier, but it would also be a shame, to have her voice come filtered through a screen; to lose the way her handwriting swoops across the page, all flair and flourish. The way the paper smells, like sunscreen, salt, and perfume.

She writes to me about my mother. My father, too. She tells me how they met and married. How they made a life. How my mother loved the sea, how its voice filled our house with sound, how there used to be a time when the two of them found happiness in hearing it. She reminds me of what we used to have, and paints with her words all the things she believes could still be mine. She writes to me about a tiny beach town south of LA, a stucco cottage, a day spent teaching children to paddle out on their bobbing boards, to watch the ocean move. She says that if you're patient, a wave will come to take you home.

She tells me to hold on, to be strong, to believe no matter what that things won't always be this way. And because I love her, I give her what she wants. I write about the future; I use the word "hope"; I spin the pathetic highlights of my lonely life into something that looks nearly normal, and trust that she won't read between the lines.

I pretend that I believe it. That somewhere, far away in the center of the sea, my homeward-bound wave is being born.

"Aunt Nessa says the ocean has a voice," I said once.

It was a mistake; I could see it in the way he looked at me, like I'd said a bad word. It had been a good day. I had made it through school, had come home feeling well enough for dinner, and the two of us had made a roast: chopping vegetables side by side, letting the deep, rich aroma of browned beef and red wine fill the chilly house, passing the meal in warm and quiet comfort. There was a dish of crisp green beans on the table and a pint of ice cream waiting in the freezer, and he had smiled when he told me it was there. But now he stiffened, staring at me over the rim of his water glass and then placing it carefully to the side.

"Aunt Nessa does a lot of drugs," he replied, and cleared his place.

The ice cream went uneaten.

———

I keep her letters, all of them. A growing stack of small rebellion, hidden in a book. I know better than to mention them now. But I keep them, and the trinkets in them. She sends me shells with scarlet ridges; a shard of printed pottery that made its way to shore; a piece of driftwood like a bony finger, knobbed and polished smooth, bleached white by the sun.

"We'll see each other again," she writes. "Remember where you come from."

In the crease of every folded sheet of paper, there are tiny grains of sand.

CHAPTER 6

AWAY FROM THE UNPREDICTABLE COASTLINE, in the wide, flat expanses of the Midwest, everything begins to look the same. The neighborhoods we settle in are identically designed, abutting college campuses that boast the same broad lawns and low brick buildings. Even the houses are alike; they're squat and nondescript, perched like small beige boxes on their parcels of yellowed grass, evenly spaced and all painted the color of eggshells. Moving from and to these places doesn't feel like going anywhere at all, and sometimes I wonder if we've packed a truck and driven for hours only to come back to the same house we'd left, on the same street, where the same neighbors watch our comings and goings with curiosity.

For nine years, we've drifted in this sea of sameness. My bedrooms are always painted a restful shade of neutral. The schools, when I am in them, all smell of the same cheap tomato sauce and are tiled in the same institutional green. The hospitals are their own world: all fluorescent-lit, chemical white, with chrome accents and movable plastic parts on the beds.

This is Laramie. We've been here six months. Before this came one year in Elko; before that, two years in Grand Junction. There's more beyond that, a half-dozen houses in the past nine years, but it's all the same to me: four walls, a small window, the glow of my laptop, and the pills on the nightstand. The beige paint on the walls, the clean, dull carpet that covers the floor. The box houses and peering neighbors. If not for our address written on Nessa's envelopes, I'd never know. To have a sense of place, you need connection. An anchor. Something, or someone, whose very presence says "You are here."

Connection, in my airless, four-walled world, is harder and harder to come by.

I stopped trying to make friends after the fourth move. It was almost a relief; I'd never been good at it, had always lingered and hovered near groups of kids in the hopes of attaching to one who walked too close, latching on like an unnoticed burr and coming along for the ride. It rarely worked, or when it did, an attack and a missed week of school would leave me back where I'd started. My almost-friends, seeing me coming, would look at me curiously. Not with malice, but confusion, the way you squint at a stranger who stands too close and shouldn't know your name.

Drifting was easier. Attached to no one, comfortably alone, unnoticed and undisturbed.

Sarah Garrison was the last "friend" I'd had, the last to seek me out and make me her personal project. The golden girl of Grand Junction, who swept me into her social sphere with the same self-satisfied display as if she'd been scooping up a wounded animal from the side of the road. I was the broken-winged bird in need of nursing; she was my selfless savior, blond and bubbly and wanting to help, eagerly rescuing me from the social purgatory of the chronic invalid.

I like to remember how it was, early on. Comfortable—a different kind of comfortable from the one I was used to, alone in my room with my headphones on and my laptop open, the keyboard growing hot under my hands. It was friendly. Cozy. To have someone to sit with, to talk to, to make this place stand out forever as the one where, for a little while, I was just like every other girl with a backpack and a bobbing ponytail and a best girlfriend at my side. Even if her very presence, her silk-smooth skin and her easy movements and her healthy, shiny hair, were always a reminder of the things I couldn't do. Even if she insisted on walking me to every class, and made too big a show of carrying my books, and took a little too much pleasure in informing perfect strangers just how many pills I took each day. Even if I once caught her doing an impression of my last bad attack, with bulging eyes and flailing hands and an exaggerated *hnnn-nnngh, hnnnnnngh* sound to mimic my breathless gagging, while a dozen people laughed long and hard and loud.

You are here, I thought, and smiled through tightly gritted teeth. When Sarah stood and said too much about the details of my body's defectiveness, I would watch her lips move and drown out her voice with the strength of it. *This is home. You are here.*

Because being someone's pet is still better than belonging nowhere, to no one. Nobody tells you how lonely it is to be sick, how reality shrinks down to you, and the space around your bed, and the sound of your whistling breath.

For a while, with Sarah as my anchor, I wasn't so lonely anymore. She was the tenuous string that tied me to a normal life, a sense of belonging, an uninterrupted string of weeks when I slept well, and woke up rested, and felt my breath come easier. I was sick less, tired less. My self-appointed advocate, Sarah proudly collected class notes and homework assignments on the few days I missed, presenting them to me and waving away my thank-yous with practiced selflessness. She visited me in the hospital, joked with my doctors, held my hand with all the elevated, professional affection of a Mother Teresa or Florence Nightingale. She was especially solicitous when there was someone else to see it—fluffing my pillow, giving me a shoulder to lean on, all patient smiles and only the occasional backward glance over her shoulder to see who might be watching.

Until the day came, six months after my father had said, "This Sarah girl has been good for you," and three months after the doctor said, "We may be seeing an improvement," when Sarah grew bored with being giving. The novelty of her role wore thin, and then wore off, until I was no longer an exotic charity case, but simply the slow, doughy, boring, and unlikable thing that I had always been. She was impatient, annoyed, always walking too quickly as I coughed at her heels. That spring, she joined the track team; my next hospital visit, I made alone. I couldn't even blame her.

"This is so boring," she moaned as I lay panting on the couch with a bad TV movie playing in the background. "Why can't you ever do anything?"

I saw her less after that—and then only from a distance, running with the track-girl pack, ponytail bobbing behind her as they all ran past, a flash of chatter and laughter and long, lean legs. Until the day, sometime later, when she raised her hand in the middle of a final exam, in the wide-open silence of our crowded classroom, and—sweetly, smiling, without so much as glancing my way—said, "Excuse me, Mrs. Manning? Could Callie take this test in another room? If I have to listen to her wheezing for one more minute, I'm going to go insane."

You are here, I thought, desperately, as my throat began to constrict and the sound of snickering filled my ears. *You are here.*

When I arrived back at school the following week, empty-handed and left behind, Mrs. Manning coolly told me that if I knew I was going to miss so much class, the least I could do was get a friend to take some notes for me.

Clinging to an anchor, as it turns out, is also a good way to drown.

Since then, there's been no "here." No connections, no rescuers, nobody looking to salvage my limping carcass from the side of the road. Nobody takes my hand, or asks me out, or urges me to participate. My father, after the disaster and aftermath of Grand Junction, is kind enough not to ask if I've made any friends at school. I drift with his permission.

The neighbors know I'm here. I can tell from the way they peer at the house, the exposed slice of their eyes winking out from a body bundled tight against the cold, slowing their steps to catch a glimpse of the professor's indoor daughter.

"My daughter isn't well," he tells them. He's doing it now, caught on his way home from work by a passing neighbor; I can see his shadow where he stands politely on the porch, waving away the well-meaning old woman who showed up with a smile and a pie. Her lips purse with concern: in a moment she'll start clucking, and then she does, all fluttering hands and bird-like head, bobbing her worry and sympathy. Nessa's letters sometimes ask if I've met new people, if I'm making friends. When I write to her next, I'll tell her about this woman. I'll pretend that I saw her right up close and not from behind a drawn blind, spoke to her face-to-face instead of eavesdropping through a window.

"We met our neighbor," I'll write. "She brought a pie." And I'll make up a name—Myrtle, a good old-lady name—and an afternoon of conversation, and a granddaughter my age who sounds very nice and might stop by from time to time.

But Myrtle, or whatever her name is, has already gone. We'll eat her pie later, perhaps, but we'll never be friends. There is no granddaughter, and there are no afternoon visits. And when I come outside, she'll look at me like they all do, with the same sideways stare that people use to ogle amputees, the homeless, the people who have babbled conversations with voices only they can hear. I'm none of those; my damage is all on the inside, but they don't know, and their sidelong eyes crawl over me to find the defect.

They don't know yet that they'll never get close enough to see it.

CHAPTER 7

MY ROOM IS FULL of doctors. Doctors who look like doctors.

After a while, you learn that there are two types of doctors: the ones who wear their profession like a uniform, and the ones who don't. The doctors who do are numerous and unmemorable: a dark suit under a white coat under a blank face, holding my chart like a shield. You could switch their clothes, their shoes, their heads, and never know the difference. They pass through like LEGO people wearing lab coats, stiff and all the same, regarding my stats with interest but never looking at my face.

I've learned not to mind. Here, I'm a person of interest, an unsolved case. All symptoms and no cause, and certainly no cure. I have the elusive celebrity of sickness; when they roll me down the hall, people automatically know my name.

"Collapsed lungs and chronic fluid buildup," one says. Nearby, the other doctors put pens to paper. One angles his pad just enough that I can see the words "pulmonary" and "pleural" and "undiagnosed." The speaker is pointing at my chest—his stubby index finger hovering just next to the place where the needle goes in, close enough to touch me, but with no intention of doing so—when Dr. Frank barks from the doorway.

"Party's over!" he says, and they scatter. Dr. Frank is a doctor who doesn't: doesn't fit the mold, doesn't toe the line, doesn't disappear into the crowd of white coats and stethoscopes. He is long and lean, with sinewy hands and an extravagant mustache that twitches and jumps when he speaks, stiff on his lip like a gray wire brush. After my first Laramie hospital visit, after answering all the usual questions and letting them examine all the usual parts, I saw him from the window of our car—waiting to make a left turn from the parking lot as we drove past, down the road, into the orange western sun. He was behind the wheel of an ancient Chevy pickup, cigarette dangling from his lips, cowboy hat pulled low to shield his eyes.

The times I'd seen him since—smokeless and hatless, with charts in his hands and pens in his front pocket—it seemed to me that some essential parts of him were missing.

"Are you ready, Cal?" he says.

"Let's roll," I say, and he grins.

Rolling is what we do, down the hallway and through the swinging doors, into a bright white room. I lay back with my arms aloft and feel the brief pinch of local anesthetic, the warm, thick spread of numbness on my torso.

"Pain?" asks Dr. Frank, pressing a latex finger into the soft place between my ribs.

"Nope," I say. "It's fine."

"Well, no need to dally. You're an old pro at this one," he grins, and the needle slides home.

I prefer not to think about the days before this became familiar, or the dismissive doctor from three years previous who'd disbelieved me when I said it wasn't numb enough. The feeling of long, slender steel sliding into my rib cage was so terrifying that I'd passed out cold. I much prefer Dr. Frank, whose mustache twitches with concentration as he guides the needle in, who squints at the fluid he drains from my lungs as though it's a curious enemy. I'll even laugh every time, if I have to, when he brandishes the syringe like a fencing sword and calls it "The Big Sticker."

When it's done, he squeezes my shoulder before they wheel me out. His smile is broad as ever, but there's a line between his eyebrows. A crease made out of worry. It hurts to see it; my father has the same one.

He says, "I don't mind telling you, kiddo, I'd really like to figure out what's going on in there."

"Maybe you'll get lucky this time," I say.

He won't, of course; they've been sticking me three times a year since sixth grade, drawing out the fluid and examining its parts, and the only word we ever hear is "inconclusive." No cancer, no tumors, no disease from which you could draw a straight line to my fragile lungs and murmuring heart. But if someone were to find something, even if the something was bad news, I'd want it to be him.

"Sweet of you," he says, and the mustache twitches again. "You know, Doctor Salvatore and I have a running bet. If I can figure out why your lungs hate doing their job before he gets that rash of yours under control, he's gotta buy me a steak dinner."

I giggle, and the nurse swoops in and waves a finger in his face.

"What's the matter with you!" she chides him, and her long, long nail with its violet polish sways just beyond his nose. Her accent is musical, island-born. "You don't go shouting about a lady's skin rash when there's strangers all around! Shame on you!"

I try to follow the cue and fix Dr. Frank with a furious look, but I'm laughing too hard, and soon the nurse joins in, and so does he.

"And you wonder why I'm not married." He winks at her, then leaves.

They keep me overnight, for observation, like they always do. I touch the small, sore spot on my rib cage and lay back, one patient among many, a robed and blanketed body in a room full of uncomfortable furniture. The hospital is its own universe. A stark, white world full of wheeled beds and low sounds. If you lie still long enough, you'll begin to see that things are always moving: the rapid flutter of fluids in their tubes, the soft rise and fall of papers in the wake of an open door, the shallow pulse in the throat of the girl on a stretcher nearby. The air in here is dry and the nurses keep blinking, quick and constant, eyes flicking from the monitors to my face and back.

When I was younger, before this visit became just another routine, my father would sit stone-faced in the room's only chair, stiff and sleepless, his fingers laced together so tightly that the circulation stopped. With the white, cold hands beneath his chin, below the still and staring face, he was less a presence than an object. A marble sculpture, keeping watch. Portrait of a Desperate Father.

Now, he leaves a preoccupied kiss on my forehead and says he'll see me later. I should mind, but I don't.

"He's not going to stay?" says Jocelyn. My indignant roommate sits up in her bed, a slim hand on the rail, and rolls her browless eyes at Dad's departing back.

We've met here before, in this room, during my first visit with Dr. Frank. A hospital friend, one of few. This, the white and sterile world of illness, is where I find connection. The hospital friends are just like me, untethered and always tired, too strange and too slow and too absent from school to play the usual teenage games. We bond over our shared seclusion, waving at each other from our mechanical beds. There have been some for every city, every pediatric ward, every overnight stay. Other kids who know that normal life, and all its small sufferings, is a luxury in and of itself. I still remember their names. There was Paul, age fifteen, slim and pale and waiting to lose his spleen. He had white teeth and yellow eyes, dulled and jaundiced and wet. He read books in bed with a penlight.

Elizabeth, twelve, for whom a boiling pot of pasta had ended in the ER. Who smiled at everyone, waving at the ward with her clumsy, gauze-bandaged hands. At night, she'd wake up screaming when her pain meds wore off too soon.

Andy, age seventeen, tall and lean and insect-skinny, sucking at a tube in the hallway of the university hospital in Albuquerque. He'd waited until the nurses changed shifts before gesturing to our matching oxygen tanks and offering the conspiratorial smile of a fellow sufferer.

"What's your damage?" he'd whispered, the air whistling in his throat and then catching. I waited until he stopped coughing, watching the way his neck curved, his skin the color of light-brown leather and beading with the sweat of his efforts, sloping up until it was lost in a mess of rough, curly hair.

"A mystery," I whispered back, leaning in, allowing myself to smile. "You?"

"Cystic fibrosis," he said.

"That's not a fun one," I offered.

"Not so much," he agreed, but the grin stayed. "A mystery, huh? What's your name?"

I know it's not romantic, but we take it as it comes. Hospital friends, hospital life, is better than having nothing. And I never told anyone, but later that night, while a DVD played on the small television in the lounge, he slid in beside me on the rough orange couch where I sat alone, clutching the sea-glass necklace and struggling not to cough. We hid beneath a blanket, and his hands were soft and cold.

Jocelyn and I have shared a room once before, giggling into the night and laughing when the nurses run to shush us. But I won't see her anymore, and I'm glad. Here, when you begin to care for someone, you also begin to hope you won't cross paths with them again. You hope for health, for a cure, for secondhand news from the late-night nurse that your friend won't be coming back again; that she has joined the ranks of the well. When we met in this room earlier, Jocelyn clutched at my sleeve and whispered the good news that her tumors were shrinking.

Now, she notes the absence of my father and scowls.

"Did he ditch you before the anesthetic even wore off? Geez!" she says, indignant, and I try not to smile.

"He's got work to do" I say. "Papers, or something." My voice is matter-of-fact and not defensive, and Jocelyn slides back against her pillows.

"That's cold, man," she says, and her own father scolds, *Jocelyn*, and I realize for the first time that her family is here. They pop out of the background, materializing with the practiced ease of hospital professionals. The parents become experts at being not-here; when the doctors are at work, or if my father should come back, they'll fade away again. But now, they crowd around her bed, exhausted and uncomfortable and not going anywhere, thank you.

I ache for my own hospital entourage, but just a little. I would rather have my father disappear down to the cafeteria, rather sit alone while he sips bitter coffee and mauls his students' essays with a red pen, than watch him sit like human wreckage on the chair beside my bed.

I like the distracted father better than the desperate one.

"I don't mind," I say, and get three smiles in return.

When they draw the curtain around my bed to listen to my chest, I wave at Jocelyn and lie back in the muted light of what passes for privacy here. I become just another moving part in this machine made up of scrolling readouts, dripping IVs, swinging doors, and purposeful steps. Connected, if only for a moment.

It's not perfect, but it's familiar. It's something. Later, I'll fall asleep to the sound of Jocelyn's deep and even breathing, the rush and hiss and beep of monitors making a sound track for my dreams.

You are here.

CHAPTER 8

MY FATHER DOESN'T BELIEVE that the sea has a voice, but he takes its telephone calls all the same. For a month, the Gulf Coast has been calling. Twice a week, every week. An old colleague rings him up to beg. The sound of the phone is jangling and jarring, reverberant. No one ever calls here, and I snatch up the receiver at the first half ring. I've been out of school again, a two-week stretch this time, and the sound makes me feel like my teeth are shattering.

I've never met this man, but I know he's getting desperate; each time I answer, his voice has ratcheted up another half note in pitch.

"Uh, hello," he says. "It's Mike Foster again. Is Alan—"

"I'll get him."

—

Alan Twaddle, PhD, is more than the frustrated father to an invalid and the widower of a reckless woman. He is a legend, an innovator, an unmatched talent in geotechnical engineering. His brilliance had always been background noise in a life where other things seemed more important. When Mama was still alive, people asked why he hadn't taken his marvelous gifts to a place where people paid for them, abandoning academia and moving on. It was there for the taking: a blossoming career, a glowing reputation, a life of comfortable luxury for his wife and daughter. At the time, he'd smile at us over dinner and say, "I told them, what's the point? I've already got everything that a man could ever want."

But then, he lost it. And after she died, for a time, the phone calls grew frequent again. Fat-cat corporations, speculating miners and oil companies, begged his expertise. They need to know what lies beneath the earth, how to seduce it, how to worm their way in and then suck it dry. At the time, he told them no, and I was the reason why. Orphaned, helpless, clinging to the family I had left. I made a good excuse.

Now, he doesn't have one. Mike Foster's words spill out of the receiver uninterrupted, and my father only listens. Each time, he lets him go on just a little longer. Each time, his "No" has just a little less force.

And tonight, for the first time, he takes the phone into his study and shuts the door.

I know, of course, why they want him now. For weeks, I watched the tragedy unfold. Something had broken in the deep, dark blue, and the oil poured unchecked into the sea. Billowing, streaming, a river of million-dollar blackness cutting like a blade through the underwater world. In the late-night glow of my laptop's screen, the numbers ticked high, then higher. Death toll. Lawsuits. Damage. Miles of sea and seashore, lost to a torrent of insoluble catastrophe. I saw waves, cresting like liquid rust, pouring oil-slicked foam across the sand. Oozing pools of viscous brown, curling like Rorschach watercolor as the tide recedes. Animals, their airways clogged and fins weighed down by sludge, belly-up and gasping and covered in grease. Red, dead tides of floating fish, pale and with one glazed eye aimed skyward. They lie fin-to-fin like cobblestones, an iridescent landscape of wasted life.

The flow has stopped, but not the damage control. The public's wary eye is open wide, and everyone has something to prove.

———

Mike Foster doesn't just want my father's knowledge. He wants his name, to attach to his project and drop when necessary, to prove that he means business. That the men he works for are thinking of the future, of the children. They want to make amends. Green, clean energy is what the people want now, and Alan Twaddle, PhD, with his long absence from for-profit pursuits and his long history of publication, is more than just a talent; he's a mascot. A beacon. A poster boy for academic integrity and unselfish good works.

And, best of all, he's interested.

I can tell. The energy in our beige, bland house has changed. Even before tonight, with the study door shut tight and his voice rising with earnestness behind it, I had been finding small sketches scribbled on a Post-it note, or on the back of an envelope, or in the margins of the newspaper. A long vertex topped by pinwheel wings, bracketed by diagrams showing directional force. And bisecting that straight, slim length, a wavy horizon that can only be water.

When all is said and done, there will be a hundred, all in rows. Spindly towers that spread their three-pronged silhouettes against the blazing southern sun, rising gently above the water like strange white birds.

An offshore wind farm in the gulf.

The sea is calling, and my father is listening.

It's after ten when I hear the door open, the click of the light switch as the bottom floor grows dark. I burrow down in bed, faking sleep, listening to the soft sound of stocking feet on the dove-colored staircase carpet. He is muttering, still with the phone to his ear, lowering his voice as he nears my doorway.

"Mike, it's a great opportunity. I know it, and you know I know it. But my daughter—"

The man on the other end answers so forcefully that for a moment, it's as though he's right there in the room. Tinny, but clear, he interrupts with his final pitch.

"We understand that, Alan. I've looked into it—discreetly, don't worry—and the university hospital . . ." His voice grows lower now, as though he knows I'm listening. I strain to hear, tilting my head toward the door, watching my father's shadow bleed and amble over the carpet as he paces. He settles closer to the door and then the tinny voice is back, clear and loud: ". . . cutting-edge. She'll have the best care."

"But the move—"

"And," the voice breaks though, "it will be paid for. Everything, one hundred percent. You won't even see a bill."

My father doesn't answer, and the silence draws out, until Mike Foster answers for him.

"You can't tell me that all these years haven't taken their toll, financially."

I don't hear my father's reply, if he gives one. The sudden roar of blood in my ears, a surge made out of guilt, drowns everything out. I know, although he hasn't said so, that my life has not been cheap. It's in his face when the bills arrive, the way his mouth drags down tight at the corners before he can stop them. Five figures before the decimal point. Dwindling balances on poorly hidden bank statements. Once, back in Grand Junction, I answered the phone when a creditor called. I know enough to know that I am not just a daughter but a money pit, a black hole, an endless sucking lacuna of need.

My father has moved away from the door. I hear his voice, rising and falling, too far away now to be anything but noise. It has a rhythm to it, ebbing like the tide. My eyelids have grown heavy.

The air in here is thin and dry; I picture it rushing over barren mesas and brushing through sun-bleached slot canyons, passing over the long, dead stillness of the Great Basin on its way to reach my lungs. I feel it drag against my throat. It doesn't want to go down easy, and I swallow with an effort that tastes like chalk.

I am weightless, dreaming, floating far away, when my father's voice dips low in acquiescence and then stops.

I sense, rather than hear, his footsteps in the hall. He is standing in my doorway.

Quietly, he says my name. But when I stir my way out of sleep, peeling my eyelids back and turning my head to answer, he has already walked away.

THE RIVER

CHAPTER 9

THERE IS SOMETHING IN THE WATER.

It bobs in the shallows where water meets weeds, riding the barely there roll of the current. The thing is strangely shaped and out of place, a spot of orange plastic in a palette made of browns and greens. When I get closer, I can make out the curve of a tiny foot, a shock of waving, bright blond hair. A pair of painted eyes with unlikely azure lids glare blankly skyward, peering out above pinkish lips that are set in a permanent pout.

A Barbie, set adrift without her dream house.

Or her swimsuit.

I'm crouching to get a better look when fast footsteps thud against the dock and fifty pounds of chubby child flings itself against my back. I stumble and veer toward the edge, my feet thudding like ungainly clods, then catch myself against the short wooden post that anchors the dock in the riverbed.

"Bee!" I shout, whirling on my attacker, more sharply than I mean to, and the little girl drops away with a wounded look. Her lip begins to jut, a pink, pouting shelf between the pudge of her rounded cheeks. It doesn't quiver; she's angry, not hurt. I stand, face burning, guilty even as my heart pounds an adrenaline-fueled warning in my chest. She glares at me, eyes full of accusations. I swallow hard and consciously drop my voice down to a soothing pitch.

"Sorry, Bee, I didn't mean to yell. It's just that—" I take a deep breath, look back over my shoulder at the slow ooze of the river, the naked Barbie bobbing brightly in the water. *Bitch*, I think. *You make it look so easy.*

"I know!" says Bee, brightly, her pout disappearing in a happy flash of recollection. "Your daddy said you can't swim."

"It's not a question of what he says," I mutter, but Bee isn't paying attention; she's already back beside me, the brief rebuff forgotten, showing me the reason for Barbie's lonely abandonment in the soggy depths. A length of fishing line is looped around the doll's neck, invisible in the water, tethering her to one of the metal cleats that sailors might use to moor their boats. When we first got here, the sight of them—that familiar metal anchor with its overhanging lip—

filled me with sudden sadness before I could understand why. Before I remembered, all at once, that our sailboat's slip on the Pacific coast was studded with those same small, sturdy mounts.

It was one month ago when we arrived, in the dark, a damp, pitch-night in late July. A few hours in the air and another two on the road, as our chauffeur cursed his way through six wrong turns and my father cranked the cool air high, and higher. He doesn't like the heat. All those years spent inland were supposed to be for me, but I understand now that he might have always gone there, given the choice—to those dry, cool desert places, where the winter works with cracking viciousness at the earth and the sidewalks and your bleached, raw skin. He liked that arid harshness. Now, he growls at the air conditioners, twisting their knobs to the limit, making disgusted faces as a V-shaped sweat stain blooms below his shirt collar. He says that the wetness breeds bacteria, that amoebic life is sprouting in all that damp. His green-minded, earth-worshipping, carbon-counting coworkers would be horrified to hear that he showers at the environmentally unconscious rate of half an hour per day, until the bathroom is thick with steam. He tells me not to laugh at him for powdering his armpits.

I was warned, too, that the humidity might hurt. That my lungs might kick up a fuss, grow thick with mucus, shut down against the alien moisture in the air. The first time, stepping out of the car into the loamy, scented darkness, I choked on the thickness of the night. It was soupy, nearly solid, full of the thick and fetid smell of living, and dying, things. The sweetness of decaying leaves. The wet, warm smell of river water. The strange perfume of joe-pye weed and the low, dank notes of mildew.

It was too much, and I doubled over in the driveway, until my father hauled me into the wide-windowed house with its artificial climate.

"You'll need to stay indoors," he said. "And watch out near that dock. I don't have to tell you to be careful and stay away from the water, do I? It's not safe. I'll be working late most days. I don't want to have to worry about what you're doing here while I'm gone."

At the time, I'd simply nodded. And I did stay in at first, wandering through the chilled expanse of the house with its clean white walls and cool countertops, everything smooth and stainless steel, conspicuous in its expensive newness. The private retreat of an oil company executive, rarely used and all for us.

"It's the finest property we have available: quiet, private, a perfect haven to come home to at the end of the day," Mike

Foster had crowed, eager and fast-talking, anxious to see my father pleased. "We'll deliver your car later today, and in the meantime, there's a great little motorboat down by the dock if you'd like to explore the river. All gassed up and ready to go. Good fishing around here, you know. And there's a handyman to maintain the property, no need to mow the lawn or trim the trees; that's all taken care of.

"And best of all," he'd simpered, "no city traffic or polluted air to bother your little princess!"

He stood in the polished kitchen on the morning after our arrival, a thin and fidgety man whose darting eyes and shaky smile were a perfect match for the high, nervous voice on the phone. He was far too fussy and focused on my father to notice or care that the princess in question wasn't so little, was in fact sitting lumpily at the breakfast bar just past his elbow and wheezing with the effort of pulling herself onto the stool. The house was three times the size of our last beige box, with miles of plush carpeting and too many stairs.

"Thank you, Mike," my father said drily. "I'm sure we'll get used to the fishy smell."

Mike's smile faltered by several degrees; he reapplied it with conscious effort as he pushed a brochure across the countertop.

"This is Ballard, an excellent school, they'll be expecting your call . . . er, that is, if you plan to enroll her," he

stuttered. "I understand your daughter has, ah, some spotti-
ness in her academic record . . ."

"I have a three-point-seven GPA," I said, and this time,
Mike's smile disappeared in a wince at the scrape of my voice
and didn't return. "It's my attendance that's spotty, not my
record."

"Ah, of course, yes. Well, good then," said Mike, looking
everywhere but at me. "Well, you can enroll her as soon as
you're settled in."

"We'll see," my father had said, and resumed grimacing
out the unblemished expanse of the window.

The never-used appliances, never-slept-on beds, newly laid
laminate flooring without so much as a footprint to mar its
sheen. Until I realized the similarity, I couldn't understand
why I felt so instantly at home here. The white, the chrome,
the lack of human grease: inside, on that first day, our house
felt like a hospital. Only better; the soft white rooms were
comfortable, not clinical. Clean, but not sterile, and with re-
cessed lighting that made everyone's skin look soft and dewy.
Even mine.

But as July stretched into August, I began to peer outdoors.
I pressed my nose against the endless windows, leaving oil on
the glass. I looked to the shadowed drop-off, the dock's dark

wood steps, the tall trees and the openness beyond them. I began to open the door and cross the porch, venturing out a few steps and then farther as the sun dropped down behind the trees. And eventually, my bare feet found the wooden steps and carried me—along the dock, above the water, until I sat on its tip in the orange, fragrant evenings, and gently dropped a foot into the river. I found, after the initial shock, that the air is so very smooth. Lubricated, draping like liquid velvet over my outstretched arms and legs.

When I inhale, it slips down my throat as gently as a summer breeze.

This is part of the promised package: the house on stilts, the yard, the trees, the staircase and the dock, the small, bobbing motorboat beside it. Our piece of brackish riverfront in private isolation—follow it for fifteen winding miles, and it brings you to the sea. They're gifts of the funding company, along with my father's six-figure salary, a leather-seated Lexus, and the handsome, poised physician whose number we have programmed on speed dial.

"The best care," Mike Foster had said, and I'm getting it. My doctor's name is Sharp, and he is—incisive and quick and no-nonsense, with dark eyes that miss nothing. He wields his needle precisely, with the same practiced assurance as Dr. Frank but none of the joshing and grinning. Dr. Sharp is all pointed questions and focused attention. I saw him on the second day. I am taking a host of new pills, per his instructions. I hope, more than anything, that I won't be seeing much of him.

Because I like it here. I like the humid dampness in my sheets, where Mama's poetry book is hidden underneath my pillow. I like the smooth heat of the sea-glass necklace, resting against my skin. And I like this place. The fecund banks, choked green with weedy growth. The cypress trees that rise like sentries straight from the depths of the water. The pale stripes of sand on the river bottom, the waving, tangling hair of reeds and algae. And the dock, its limber legs sunk deep and fast. The posts are made from the trunks of young trees, slender but sturdy, dark and polished, and punctuated here and there by the twist of a sudden knot. My father cautioned against splinters, but they're as smooth as waterworn stone, buffed by the passing touch of a hundred different hands. At its farthest point, it sits surrounded by dark green water. Look down, and you'll see fat, slate-colored fish making urgent paths through the forest of underwater weeds. Turn back, and the wooden path seems to emerge straight from an enchanted bowery, draped with the sweet breath of honeysuckle and decorated with the dusky lace of Spanish moss.

I have never seen anything like it.

"I'm making her a mermaid," says Bee, pointing at the drifting doll. Barbie is on her back, her molded plastic breasts gleaming obscenely in the sun.

The girl is our neighbor, the child of a mother who works with my father but whom I never see. She's like him, a hater of the heat. I know her only by her silhouette; at night, she sprints from her carport to her front door with her high heels in one hand, trying to beat the first light lick of non-conditioned air. She doesn't even wait for Bee, who dawdles by the car until the soles of her shoes start to melt against the driveway, dangling a doll or a worn stuffed animal by one tenuous leg. I know that she's been playing in our yard when I find doll parts in the grass, little arms and hands and feet, a single googly eye, or, once, a Barbie head staring insolently up at me from the corner of our driveway. The doll in the water is the same one, which means that Bee's mother, safe in her palace of central air and chilled chardonnay, must have spent an evening performing a lifesaving recapitation procedure.

Bee spotted us our first week in, padding across the quiet drive to where we stood unloading groceries.

"Let me know if she bothers you," the shoeless silhouette called, and my father shrugged and looked at me, and I looked at Bee. Even in the deepening evening and the shadows of the overhung street, I could see missing teeth in her little-girl grin. I shrugged back at him.

"It's fine," I called across the street, but got no answer—just the satisfied click as her front door sealed shut.

Bee is the first person that I've ever known who's lonelier than I am.

"See?" she says, and grabs my hand. "She's a mermaid. She's beautiful. Did you ever see a mermaid?"

"I see one now," I say, and point at the Barbie. Bee laughs and tugs on my hand again.

"You're silly!" she giggles, and the sound echoes down the river. "She's not a mermaid, she's just for pretend!"

"Oh, I see," I say. "Well in that case, no, I've never seen a mermaid."

Bee bends down and grabs the doll's tether, leaning into the water so precariously that my heart jumps into my throat. I've reminded her too many times that if she falls, I can't come after her, but she says that she can swim.

"I did. I saw a mermaid," she mumbles, reeling Barbie in.

"Oh yeah? Where'd you see that?" I imagine a south Florida seaside carnival, women with flowing hair and sequined seashell bras, sucking discreetly on air hoses while they cavort in chlorinated pools.

"Just here," says Bee.

"Here, in Florida?"

"No, silly." She wheels around, the Barbie in her fist, and points downriver. "Here! Just right here."

I stand, looking out, peering into the shadows under the trees. Searching—not for mermaids, but for what Bee might have mistaken for one, the long, gray body of the manatee they've told us we might see. They swim upriver, they said, sometimes lost, sometimes in search of warmer water. I desperately want to see one, to glimpse as much as I can of the underwater world, while we're here and while I'm healthy. I never thought I would be so close to the sea.

There's nothing, though. I'm disappointed, and then disappointed in myself for being such a child. Bee comes to stand beside me.

"She'll come back," she says, and I shrug even though I hope she's right.

"Where was it, exactly?" I ask. She points again, and answers.

"Just there," is what she says.

And then: "It was right next to the dragon."

And suddenly, I'm laughing—laughing because of course there was no mermaid, and probably no manatee, either, and certainly no dragon. But there is this little girl. And the dock, and the silky air that exits my lungs in a lightweight whirl of sound that's so ringing and unsullied that I can't believe it's me who's making it.

CHAPTER 10

DR. SHARP WIELDS HIS PEN LIKE A WEAPON, not so much writing on the paper as punishing it. He stabs and slashes so furiously that if the needle were coming next, I'd be terrified.

Only it's not. There's no need for the needle, he says, and though there's no warmth in his words, I could hug him all the same. In my crackling paper gown, with the ice-cold stethoscope traveling over my back, I take a deep breath—a real one, with no coughing or wheezing or sandpaper drag—and feel briefly sorry for Dr. Frank, who had wanted so badly to be the one to help me. Who had bet a steak dinner against his ability to make me well.

But only briefly.

The pen is attacking my chart again.

"How about side effects? Have you had any nausea, headaches?"

"No."

"Mood swings? Trouble sleeping?"

This time, I pause before answering. "No."

"Anything unusual?"

I want to tell him that there isn't. I want to say that nothing's changed, not a thing, except the sudden, sensationless movement of the air through my lungs where before there was only struggle. But after all these years, I know better than to hold anything back. They've told me, time and time again—that if I do, if there's something strange and I choose not to tell, I'll be the one who pays the price.

I take a deep breath.

"I've been having . . . dreams."

His eyebrow moves up, but not his eyes; they stay on my chart, where the pen has paused against the page.

"Bad dreams?"

I shake my head, cautiously. "No, not bad. More like . . . vivid."

"And nothing when you're awake? No thoughts of suicide or self-harm?"

I shake my head again.

"Vivid dreams can be a common side effect of the beta-blockers," he says, and snaps my chart shut, without even making a note. "And your last attack, when was that?"

I look through my memory and come up empty, and then feel giddy: there's nothing to remember. It's been weeks, at least. I grin. Dr. Sharp doesn't.

"Callie, you need to pay attention. If you can't be responsible enough—"

"No no no," I protest, and do my best to set my mouth in a straight line, make my face a mask of maturity. I also think, petulantly, that I was wrong: well or not, I really do miss Dr. Frank. "I had one on the night we arrived. In July."

"And since then?"

"Nothing big. There've been a couple times, maybe? But not bad. Not recently."

"And the minor attacks, what triggered them?"

I flush. "Um. I don't know, I mean . . ."

He snorts, impatient, and I think again how glad I am that he won't be coming near me with anything sharp—not today, at least. And, I hope, never again. He seems to want our meeting over as much as I do.

"There's no need to hem and haw," he says, clipping off the words with disdain. "Here, I'll make it easy: Was it exercise? Stress? Allergy?"

"Stress, I guess," I say, and think, *But not mine.*

If I had hoped that my father would mellow here, that the warmth of the sun and the slow pace of the South might make him looser, relaxed, and more malleable, I'd been wrong.

The nearness of the ocean, the coastal breeze, the sound of the river as it slurps along our property line: he hates them all. At night, he glares out the window in the direction of the coast, as though warning the water to come no closer. My last attack had come on one of those evenings—just after dinner, when I asked without thinking if I might go to the beach. The immediacy of his response—"Absolutely not!"—had startled me so badly that I choked, first on my own spit and then on the dry indoor air.

"Callie, please," he'd sighed, head in his hands, as I scrambled for the inhaler. "After everything that's happened, I can't believe you'd even ask."

But that's just the sort of superfluous detail that Dr. Sharp doesn't need. Just like he doesn't need to know about my dreams.

They're not like the ones I used to have, the drowning ones, the wall-clawing nightmares that scared me out of sleep and into the airless world of my identical inland bedrooms. In those dreams, I was always lost in endless nothingness. In those dreams, I was always alone.

Now, when I close my eyes, there's somebody waiting for me in that liquid dark.

The air between us is always full of murk and mush and shadows, her face is hidden behind her hair. But she knows I'm there, and she knows I know that she is.

Who she is.

How did you know I was here? I'd asked, behind the safety of my eyelids. I asked without moving my lips. My words swirled inside my head and then all around us, echoing back at me from corners unseen. Out of the blackness, so did hers. An answer, drifting in space.

I'd know you anywhere.

My mother is always waiting for me. In the night, in my bloodstream, carried on the wings of Dr. Sharp's pharmaceuticals. Waiting, in the ether, to see me again. When the wreath of her tangled hair moves closer, and her long fingers with their oval-shaped nails float out to brush against my cheek, I close my eyes and breathe in deep.

Sometimes, when I wake up, my pillow is soaked with tears.

My father is quiet as we drive the hour home, chewing on whatever he's been told behind closed doors. The move, the uncertainty of a new place and new faces and new regimens of drugs, has evaporated his confidence in me. Whatever Dr. Sharp tells me, my father insists he say again in private, behind the closed office door that the two of them shut in my curious face. Now, he flicks on the radio—an unspoken kibosh on conversation—turns it up, and stares straight ahead at the hard-baked highway stretching away in the distance, while the sun slinks away at our backs. He stays like that all the way home—humming tunelessly, answering my questions in distracted monosyllables, lost in the world inside his head. He's too preoccupied to notice the strange silver car parked just beyond our driveway. Too preoccupied even to notice that the doormat is askew, that the key doesn't turn in the lock. That someone is already here.

The whirling dervish of my aunt sweeps me up before the door can even close behind me. I'm wrapped in it, buried suddenly in a jangling rush of fabric and bangles and long, long hair.

Nessa, I try to say, but the word is so huge and ungainly, swelled with feeling, that it sticks in my throat and I can only make a croaking sound.

"Callie!" she yelps, right into my ear, and I realize suddenly that she's no longer taller than me. The last time I hugged her good-bye, I had pressed my face into her stomach, against the crinkly linen of her swirling skirt, and heard her voice shushing from somewhere overhead. Now, her cheek is soft against mine and my arms wrap around her neck.

It has been almost ten years.

She sees it, too, throwing me out to arms' length and taking in the whole of me. Brittle hair, pockmarked skin, so much pale, pale flesh. The look of unhappy surprise is there only a second, not more than a momentary crease of the forehead and a dark, angry flicker in her eyes, but I see it; I was looking for it.

"Holy shit, you're practically a woman!" she cries, and grins so hard that her nose crinkles, hard enough to erase the last lines of disappointment from her face. She's different, too. Older, with creases at the corners of her eyes, courtesy of the California sun. The skin on the backs of her hands is looser, weathered, studded with splotchy freckles.

My father has appeared from behind me, scowling, as though Nessa's use of the word "shit" set off a silent alarm. Only that's not it, I know.

"Breaking and entering, Nessa? I guess I shouldn't be surprised," he says drily, and looks pointedly at me. "Although it's a bit strange to find you in our house, considering that I don't remember telling you that we were here."

I try to look puzzled and shrug, but my thoughts go straight to the mailbox—the one at the end of the street, drab green and rusted at every joining, where only two weeks ago I'd placed an envelope emblazoned with our new return address. I had loved writing that letter, two closely spaced pages and not a single lie between the lines. I told her about the house and the dock, the dappled river and thick, gray trees. I didn't even have to invent a neighbor—

not when I had Bee, with her pudgy cheeks and mistreated toys and stubborn insistence on the presence of mermaids in the river.

"You can take it up with the university," says Nessa lightly. "You may not like to tell me when you're moving, but your assistants always seem happy to fill in the blanks."

I do my best not to stare. The lie is pitch-perfect, a made-up bit of music plucked deftly out of the air. Only the pressure of her hand on mine tells me that she's covering my tracks. I squeeze back, and feel her slender bones move beneath my fingers.

Nessa says she was on the next plane out, that she was headed for the airport before she'd even reached the last line of my letter, barely pausing long enough to pack. I'm not sure I believe her, except that the evidence of her hurry is everywhere; she's got no underwear but the pair she has on, doesn't even have her toothbrush. We've barely said hello before she shoves me back through the door, silencing my father's objections with sheer momentum, and bundles me into the shotgun seat of her rental car. As the sky turns violet and the trees roll away in shadow overhead, she presses the accelerator and heads for the drugstore, to pick up all the things overlooked in the moments between the letter and the plane.

"I wish I'd known you were coming," I say. I pluck self-consciously at my clothes—drab and dingy, wrinkled and rumpled, scuffed and stretched. The kind of thing I'd have hidden away at the bottom of a hamper if I'd known that my glamorous aunt was about to appear, in the flesh, right next to me. I'd have combed my hair, painted my nails. I'd have worn soft whites and deep blues, with the sea-glass necklace lying lightly against my clean, smooth skin. I would have transformed myself, somehow, into the kind of niece she should've had—would have made myself look like my mother's daughter, and not a dull and unwashed invalid decked out in grimy grays.

"I couldn't wait, baby," she purrs. "I had to see you!" The grin has softened but won't leave her face; she keeps stealing glances at me, as if to check that I'm still here.

"You didn't have to wait nine years," I say, and wish right away I could snatch it back. Her smile falters just enough that I know the words had teeth. I had sometimes written to Nessa, suggesting she find her way out to Grand Junction or Indian Springs or wherever we'd chosen to unpack our lives. Her replies, pages and pages of looping, long scrawl, always said the same thing at the end: *I wish I could.*

I never asked what had happened, what he had said to her, that made her decide not to come. At first, I was afraid he had told her some terrible lie to keep her away; later, I was afraid that there had been no lie at all. That Nessa

knew the truth about what I'd become and couldn't bear to
see it.

"You know I would have been there if I could," she says.

The canopy of trees peels away, the road smooths
and softens, as we draw closer to civilization. They've
planted palm trees along the road, spaced so evenly that I
can time their appearance in the window down to a tenth
of a second. Neither one of us speaks, and I count thirty-five
palms—thirty-five, so still in the last gasp of light, with their
fronds punching the sky like a shadowed fist—before the
lights of the pharmacy loom up ahead and she leaves me,
wordlessly, in the running car. But when she comes back
with a paper bag, settling back in the driver's seat with her
long skirt hiked up above her knees and out of the way, she
squeezes my hand—all okay, all forgiven.

"Let's not worry about the past, okay? The important
thing is that we're together again, and you have to tell me
everything," she says. "Everything! Do you like it here? When
does school start? Do you miss your friends in Laramie?"

I take a deep breath. I'm wondering if I can do now what
I did in my letters, if I can pick my words just so, create the
skeleton of a not-quite-lie, and let her assumptions fill in the
rest. But as we turn the corner, and the humid air touches

my face, I never get the chance to find out. My tongue has other ideas. And when the words come out, the voice saying them is clear and unapologetic. The truth rings like a bell.

"I don't miss anyone," I say, "because I don't have anyone to miss. I don't have friends, Nessa. Not in Laramie, or anywhere else we've been. I said I did, but I didn't. There's no one. There's never been anyone."

When she answers, she doesn't look at me. I don't know whether to be stung or relieved.

With her eyes on the road, she replies, "I know that, baby. I know."

CHAPTER 11

THE BIOLOGY TEACHER IS LOOKING at me suspiciously.

"Last name is Morgan?" he says.

I take a deep breath, getting ready for the inevitable new-student tango and grateful that at least we're alone, the first bell not yet rung. It's been thirty-seven days since my last attack. I know this because I dutifully marked each one of them, slashing a proud, self-satisfied red *X* on the calendar while my father watched warily over his latest round of figures from the latest samples of the ocean floor. Thirty-seven days ago, he took my inhaler—"So if you have an attack, I'll know," he warned—and made me a bargain: one month of easy breathing, and he'd enroll me at Ballard without argument.

I'm not sure who was more shocked when the thirtieth day rolled around.

—

"Yes," I say. "Morgan, comma, Calypso."

He raises his eyebrows at my full name; I roll my eyes in return, the wordless stand-in for an embarrassed, *I know.*

"Creative parents, huh?" he says, and grins. "Well, I'd remember that one if you were on my list, but you're not. My apologies, we're not always the quickest with paperwork around here. And where are you coming to us from?"

It's the new-student dance, the one I've done a million times, but I don't know this version—the one where I'm not being studied like a lab rat, where a sudden coughing fit doesn't earn a deer-in-headlights stare from a freaked-out adult. In this version, there's no curious ogling or wincing as I speak; my biology teacher has no wariness in his eyes, just a disarming, wide-open smile sitting between his comb-over and his shirt collar.

"We lived in Wyoming," I stammer. Is my throat closing up? *Please,* I think, *please don't let me stop breathing just because someone was nice to me.* The teacher—Mr. Strong, it said on the door—looks down again at his papers, shuffling them again as though he expects my name might magically rise to the top, talking all the while.

"That's quite a trek. Quite a trek! Wyoming, huh? Horse country, isn't it? You ever ride horses up there? You look like the outdoorsy type."

It's not just the dance steps I can't follow; now, I don't even know the song they're playing. I might as well have stumbled into another dimension. Dumbly, I shake my head.

"Well, welcome to the dirty South," he says, and the smile keeps shining on, bigger, brighter. Behind me, the low rumble from the hallway becomes a roar as the metal *clang* of slamming lockers starts to come in staccato bursts.

"I'll write you in here, and we'll give the office a few more days to let your teachers know who you are, but you might have to give them a nudge, okay? Keep an eye on that, maybe stop in on Thursday to make sure you're in the system. And here's your syllabus."

The classroom door opens as he pushes a thick sheaf of papers across the desk, and a tumble of kids bursts through with shouts of greeting. They're all grinning and waving, and I suspect that Mr. Strong's good humor and easygoing grin make him the kind of teacher that everyone likes. A favorite.

"Don't worry, you haven't missed much," he assures me, with one eye on the entering, settling crowd, noisily filtering its way to seats at the high, Formica-topped lab tables. "And let's see . . ." He scans the room, then shouts, "Hey! Ben!"

At the back, by the glass case filled with formaldehyde-preserved floating things and a handful of sun-bleached skulls, a boy with red hair and glasses snaps to attention. He even salutes.

"Mister S!" he shouts back.

"This is—" He pauses, looking at me for input. And though I've met no others yet, I make it official: Mr. Strong is my favorite teacher, too. Not just here, not just now, but of all time and forever.

"Callie," I say. "Please. Thank you."

"Right!" He turns back: "This is Callie. She's an accomplished horsewoman from the wild Northwestern plains, and she needs some help settling in."

I prepare for the miserable minutes to follow. I know what comes next. The boy will take me in—eyes down, eyes up—and sigh, and irritatedly make only the tiniest bit of room, and studiously ignore me for forty minutes except for the grunted information about which page we're on. All while the rest of the class looks on with half pity, half relief that it wasn't them.

Only he doesn't. *He doesn't.*

Instead, there's a smile. A beckoning hand. Mr. Strong's send-off pat on the shoulder, and only a handful of curious stares as I cross the room.

"Hey, Callie," says Ben. He pulls out the high-legged chair and waits, patiently, as I heave myself up. And when I do, he holds out a hand for me to shake—small but strong, and pleasantly warm—and then gestures at my ponytail, pulled back against the humidity and hanging in crazed, curly coils down my back. "Nice hair."

"Yours, too," I manage to whisper.

As promised, I call home at lunch. She picks up on the first ring.

"Callie!" she yells, and even as I cringe away from her ear-piercing squeal, I can't help smiling. It has been weeks—weeks!—and for all my father's glowering and pointed remarks, he can't make Nessa leave. He'd have to put his foot down, evict her, kick her out with a flourish and threats of arrest if she ever came back. But he won't. He can't. The confrontation, with its inevitable madness and sobbing good-byes, a perfect repeat of the last one, is a door he won't open again. And for once, his dry and undramatic disapproval has met its match.

"Aren't they missing you at your job?" he'd said, irritation creeping into his voice, when he came home late from work two weeks ago to find my aunt and me substituting a box of Cinnamon Toast Crunch for dinner.

"Oh, and aren't you sweet to be concerned!" Nessa sang, all innocence and wide eyes, then smiled at him—the way that a cat might smile at a dog as it scampered up a tree and sat, smugly, just out of reach. "But surfers, you know, they're such a laid-back crowd, it didn't matter a bit for me to take a leave of absence. In fact, I can stay as long as I like."

The last sentence was less a statement of fact than a challenge, aimed right between my father's eyes. *I can stay as long as I like.* But he didn't meet it. Didn't flinch. Didn't say, *No, you can't.* Instead, he sighed, and shrugged, and wandered away, closing the door to his study, and eventually planting a dry, distracted peck on my cheek when I knocked to say good night. I'm starting to think that he can't bring himself to take her away from me. Not again. Not this time. And not when, and even he has to admit it, Nessa has made herself useful. For all her flightiness and swearing and refusal to wear shoes, for all the nights she vanishes into the darkness by the water and then comes back with the telltale, slightly sweet scent of marijuana clinging to her hair, she's someone who can be there—to keep me company, to take me places, to be at the door when I get home in the afternoons. Filling the space left by the woman who came before her, looked like her, had the same musical voice. She is only a little bit older now than my mother was. Though the resemblance makes me ache—and though I know it hurts him, too, maybe even worse than me—I'm glad of it. It feels like a second chance, a substitute taste of the life we might have had.

———

"How's it going?" she asks. "Tell me everything!"

"There's not much to tell," I say, but I know she can hear the smile in my voice. She snorts, impatient.

"Well, what's it like?"

I think for a minute, the phone pressed to my ear, while students swarm around me. Some of them look, registering the presence of an unfamiliar face, but nobody peers at me like something inside a glass case. Nobody points and whispers. In this moment, in the flip-flops and jeans and fluttery, flimsy top that Nessa insisted on buying me at the mall in Tallahassee, with my backpack slung on one shoulder, I'm one of them.

You are here.

"It's not like it was," I say.

And she says, "Of course it's not."

And it's not. I can even say it out loud, now, confidently and clearly. It's not the same at all. It's in the way I move through the hallways, buoyant with air that keeps me from heaving, or coughing, or crashing against the moving surge of students alongside me. It's in Ben's face, open and familiar, as he tugs my ponytail and then pushes my bulky backpack into safe port under the table with one deft swipe of his foot. It's in the way I've started hoping his hand will accidentally brush against mine, and can't stop myself from smiling and blushing when it happens. It even comes home with me, straightening my spine as I walk through the door, putting a Mona Lisa smile on my lips when Nessa asks me about my day.

Three weeks after my first day, we open our biology textbooks to the chapter on marine ecology, the flora and fauna that live beneath the sea. It's full of diagrams, small text attached to narrow lines that point to the inner workings of frogs, fish, whales, and I feel the barest touch of déjà vu.

"Every marine species on the planet has evolved, physically, to survive in its native environment," says Mr. Strong. "Can anyone give an example?"

I don't even know that I know it, until he points at me. I don't even feel my hand reach for the sky. It must be somebody else, someone with a voice that's throaty, smoky, but as clear as a bell, who says, "Seals can collapse their lungs completely in order to dive in deep water." It's somebody else who receives the raised eyebrows from the kids nearby, who notices the smile from the boy sitting next to her, who raises her own eyebrows and shrugs and grins back.

"Excellent, Callie," says Mr. Strong. "Really excellent, that's exactly right."

—

Later, I'll be pleased for other reasons. I'll realize where the sudden knowledge came from, and smile to realize that something in my mother's ancient books, paged through so many times and with so little understanding, ended up speaking to me after all.

But as I gather my things and walk the familiar route to my next class, this is what I know:

He looked at me, and he knew my name.

CHAPTER 12

IF YOU WAIT AT THE SHORELINE while the tide comes in, the surf will begin to bury you where you stand. Water rushing up and all around you, the sand shifting away like a sly living thing beneath your feet, burying you deeper and deeper still, even as the undertow slides with a come-hither tug around your ankles. If you only hold still for a moment, you become the anchor that the world swirls around.

You are here.

In the weeks since school began, I've held firm while life crashes over me and springs up on all sides. I know this place, these people. I know the halls by heart. Names, faces: they're all familiar. This place full of fluorescent lights and laughing kids is my every day. I know the exact soaring curves of the live oak that hovers beside the white concrete entranceway, how many steps between Nessa's car and the wide front door of the school. I know how many picnic tables sit in the courtyard at the center of the building, and which ones have been permanently claimed by territorial packs of high-school archetypes. I know that the girl with the appraising stare, the golden highlights, the designer sunglasses, and the angry-looking mouth is Meredith Hartman; I know that every day, her friend Kimberly Dunn leaves lunch early to purge in the upstairs bathroom near the teachers' lounge. I even know which stall she likes best: third from the left, nearest the window, where the room is overwhelmed by the wafting sweet scent of the grass they cut every week.

I know that in the five minutes before the first lunch bell, I can go to that same bathroom and take my pills without ever seeing another human soul.

For the first time, I remember my locker combination without having to carry a cheat sheet.

Some days, I think that it's this place that made the difference. That the heat and the sunshine and the waving palms have softened the people who live here, melting away their sharp edges and slowing everyone's pace. It would explain the loss of my paperwork, all the carefully faxed records that my father has always made sure followed me no matter where I went. My name and vital statistics arrived three days after I started; my transcript, two weeks later. But the fat medical file—the one full of warnings, allergic triggers, medication logs, and lists of all the things that sickly girls aren't supposed to do—never made it. I picture it getting caught on its way, slowing, and then stopping just beyond the Florida state line, thumping heavily somewhere by the side of the road and simply deciding not to show up.

Nobody knows where I was before this.

Nobody knows about the scars, the pills, the hospital stays.

Nobody knows the girl who stood in the dark on her first night here, trying and failing to breathe.

And best of all, nobody knows they don't know. Even my father, busy and distracted, keeping longer and longer hours with his team of researchers and hovering investors, never thought to make sure that my old life had caught up with me.

Sometimes, even I forget that girl. She is growing smaller in my mind and in my memory, like someone who I knew by sight but not by name, a familiar face in a hospital hallway. With two months and two thousand miles between her life and mine, I no longer feel her nearby. And though there are some days when I wake up short of breath and begin to panic, frantic, convinced that she's come back to ruin every-thing, there are others when I don't think of her at all.

Instead, I hold still and let the rising tide bury me by another inch.

Ben is waiting for me by my locker, unseen but for a dab of orange frizz just visible over the shoulders of two tall and broad-shouldered boys. I've learned to look for him there, and he never disappoints. This, I have learned, is part of Mr. Strong's magic: putting people together with the same effortless intuition that lets him hold a room of teenagers at attention for a full fifty minutes. He knew, somehow, that Ben's gregariousness would match my unconfident quiet. That his won't-take-no-for-an-answer insistence that I meet this person, hear this band, see this movie, would make quick work of the mistrustful walls I'd built during so many years of loneliness. And that my peculiar sick-person fluency in Internet memes, Wikipedia peculiarities, and all the best bad television—all the side effects of an isolated life— would find an eager listener in this boy who was interested in everything.

"Cal," he says.

"I really hate when you call me that," I say, even though I don't, not even a little.

The others are already in line, a strange pack of unlikely friends with Ben its unofficial leader. His friends, and so they're my friends, too. Mine. Suddenly, and just like that. Five hundred percent more friends than I've ever had, anywhere.

There's Mikah and Shanika, born ten and a half months apart but seated together in every class. Mikah, who takes pictures of everything, is braiding her sister's hair. Shanika, who already has the jutting collarbone and long, limber legs of the model she hopes to be, is complaining about the stress on her knees.

"Hurry up," she demands. "Or get a chair. I'm not standing here with my knees bent and my neck all crooked for another minute."

"You will if you want those headshots with your hair back," says Mikah, then adds, almost as an afterthought, "bitch."

Corey, who is allergic to everything, scans the printout hung on the wall and says, "There's nothing here I can eat." Nobody pays attention; he says it every day, and every day he comes out the other end of the line with three hamburgers, no cheese, no condiments, just the meat and the bun.

At the same time, Jana—a big girl, with a big voice, who's better at being exactly who she is than anyone I've ever met—looks back over her shoulder and says, "Forget what's on the menu, ladies. I'd like to take a nice, big bite out of Eric Keller."

She says it loud.

Mikah lets go of Shanika's hair. Corey turns beet red and presses himself against the wall. Across the cafeteria, Eric Keller looks up at the sound of his name, tilting his angular jaw in a way that makes half the girls in the room go weak at the knees, brushing a hand over his close-cropped blond hair, and raises his eyebrows as Jana grins and waves. Nearby, clusters of girls are starting to giggle. At the front of the line, Meredith Hartman turns back and fixes Jana's oblivious back with a blood-freezing glare.

"Congratulations, Eric!" Jana calls across the room.

Eric's eyebrows climb higher and a small smile appears on his lips—all remaining female knees in the room turn to mush—and he calls back, "What for?"

Jana pops a hip, bats her eyelashes, and yells, "For getting into those pants today! YOW!"

The whole room bursts into laughter, then applause. Eric rolls his eyes even as a big embarrassed grin breaks over his face. Meredith Hartman rolls *her* eyes and places her order in a huff. Corey squirms against the wall, as though trying to burrow into it, and says, "Christ on a cracker, Jana, do you have to be so loud?" Ben, clapping along with everyone else, winks and exclaims, "Of course she does!"

And I laugh quietly, taking it all in, as the sound crests and then subsides, as Ben gives my ponytail a flirtatious yank, as Mikah leans in close to my ear and gestures at the embarrassed Eric and says, "But seriously, that *ass*," and then collapses in another fit of giggling.

You are here.

And for the first time in a long time, I dare to dream of keeping my friends close. That I'll bask in the sunny after-noons, all through the seasonless year as October turns to November to April to July, one seamless golden life in which I finally belong. Daydreams. Hope dreams.

Tonight, after dinner, I leave Nessa midway through a nine-o'clock movie. Two well-muscled actors are running through a blaze of gunfire as I yawn loudly and tell her I'm head-ing to bed. We're alone tonight. My father phoned at seven, sighing and apologizing but with an undercurrent of excitement in his voice, to say that he'd be working late and starting early again the next morning. On nights like these, he doesn't bother driving home, choosing instead to sleep on a cot in his office. The last time it happened, there had even been a grudging thank-you for Nessa at the end, or as close to it as he'd ever been able to muster.

"I guess it's good that Callie has some company, so . . . well. Good night, then," he grunted, then hung up.

Nessa had stared at me, and I'd stared back at her, and then we'd laughed so hard that she spilled her cereal all over her lap.

"You've been turning in early a lot," she says. "Is everything okay? You're not getting sick, are you?"

"No," I say. Too quickly, too loudly. I sound defensive and her eyebrows go up; I can almost see the question mark in the air.

"Sorry," I add, and force a smile. "I guess I'm a little sensitive."

I kiss her on the cheek as she reaches for the remote, and make for the darkened hallway. To the bathroom to take my pills, and then to the sweet solace of my waiting dreams.

"You don't need to be, you know," she says, just before I cross out of the room. She's still looking at the TV, trying to be casual, but her voice is warm with pride. "You're looking better every day."

"Oh, go on," I joke, but I'm not looking at her, either. My eyes are on the window, where my reflection looks caught by surprise, where an open mouth and wide stare mirror my own. Sometime in the past two months, somehow, I seem to have grown taller.

It doesn't take long to drift away, to find my mother in the dark. Snuggled deep beneath the covers, buried in soft, opaque layers of sleep, I try to tell her: about Ben, about Bee, about the waving palms and the way the air feels moist. About football games. homecoming rallies, Halloween parties. I want to paint her a picture of the broad, bright hallways of my school, Nessa sitting on the couch with her feet tucked underneath her and the television on, the sweet scent of the trees that floats out of the dusky yard to remind us of the closeness of the water. I tell her what I saw there in the window, the girl who was me, but not-me, with a stronger gaze and straighter back than the shuffling girl in gray who used to look back at me from the mirror in Laramie.

For weeks now, I've spent my nights telling her how things have changed, while her fingers brush my shoulders in the liquid, drifting dark. I thought she would be pleased. I thought she'd listen, like she's always listened. Captive, quiet, smiling from behind her tangled hair while I tell her every secret that I've kept. Every other night, the dark has drawn close around us, heavy and warm and safe.

But tonight, something is different. In my dream, she flits in and out of the blackness, all pale hands and swirling hair, advancing and receding and then close, closer than she's ever been, gazing into my eyes more deeply than before. I can see the beauty mark on her forehead, a small scar on her cheek. I can see her eyes, pupils dilated, as lightless as the darkest heart of the deepest water.

Come away, she says, her voice echoing back, bouncing noiselessly against the curves inside my head, careening sharply within the confines of my skull. *Come home, come home with me.*

Mama, I say, *I can't.*

Come.

I can't.

You belong with me.

You left me.

And suddenly, the darkness changes. It begins to move, to swirl, to froth. This is no arid blackness, I realize. And of course, of course it's not. We are in the water.

She is always in the water.

Her face is inches from mine. Her eyes are huge and dark, so close that I can look into them and see that her pupils are not just large but without boundary, that she has no irises at all. Her skin is white, her lips are bloodless. She is so pale, and I shudder, and I think, *Of course she is.* The ocean drained the color from her cheeks at the same moment as it took the air from her lungs, the life from her body. Had I really forgotten that my mother wasn't truly here? She's dead. Gone. Drowned. And this time, when the light shifts and she speaks again, it isn't in my head but in my ears. A voice that groans like creaking wood, like a rusted lock, like machinery shuttered and left to rot.

I would never leave you, she says, and her mouth opens wide, and her hands fly like striking snakes to grip my shoulders. Hard. Hard, and close. In the glistening murk, her lips peel back. And though it's still my mother's face, her hands, her long black hair, her voice rasps out between two rows of teeth like sharpened knives.

I DIDN'T HAVE A CHOICE.

And in my dream, I scream. I scream loud enough to wake, to kick, to surge up through sleep, and to claw for purchase on the wall. I scream as I reach for it.

My fingertips touch nothing.

No wall, no sheets, no bedside lamp.

I open my eyes.

I keep screaming.

CHAPTER 13

I AM IN THE WATER. Chest-deep, T-shirt blooming underneath my armpits, with my legs disappearing into the blackness of the river and my bare feet kicking in empty space. Above me, nothing moves—the night is motionless, heavy, humid. The stars are hazy between the still, sagging leaves of the trees. Somewhere behind me, the motion-sensing light mounted above the garage door is still blazing in recognition of my journey across the lawn—it casts my shadow, spidery and monstrously long, across the oily water and onto the opposite bank. Weeds are tangled around my arms and woven between my fingers. In the dark and sluggish depths below, something brushes against my ankle. And though I'm fully awake now, from somewhere inside my head, I can still hear that whispering voice.

Come away. Come home. Come down.

I kick helplessly, my scream breaking and becoming a ragged, airless sob, flailing in the indifferent water as my throat begins to close. Black spots cloud in at the edges of my vision, I sink deeper, choking and coughing and struggling for purchase.

And then behind me, there is a shout.

A splash.

Two hands, quick and deft with strong and tapered fingers, grab my shoulders and haul me backward. Back, my feet pedaling and sliding on the uneven river bottom, back and back, until my head knocks against the familiar heft of the dock and my panicked hands fly out to grasp its edge.

At my side, Nessa spits out a mouthful of river water and her own wet hair and gasps, "Oh God, oh God," then fills her lungs again and grabs me by the collar, pulls me bodily from the water and hauls me onto the shore.

My head knocks against a tree root. My throat is knotted, locked, paralyzed. Weakly, my hands move up to brush away the thing that's on my chest. The heavy thing. The thing that won't let me breathe.

There's nothing there.

There's no air.

The last thing I hear before I pass out, in a voice full of terror and urgency, is my name.

—

Twelve hours pass before we break the silence.

I am sitting on the dock, toes kissing the river. Nessa is beside me, unspeaking. Behind me, a few feet back and furiously scribbling, is Bee. Silently, I remind myself to remember to replace the ballpoint pens and scrap paper I unearthed in my father's office; he can't know that I stayed home today, can't know what happened last night. I also wish, silently, that Bee would get bored and leave. At least the pen and paper were enough to make her stop asking us, begging and whining in a voice pitched high enough to shatter glass, to play hide-and-seek.

My aunt and I are twins in tiredness, with matching shoulder slumps and the same plum-colored circles beneath our puffy eyes. At seven o'clock this morning, we had both turned blearily to watch the first blush of color in the lightening sky, curled in silence at opposite ends of the cool leather couch while the last of the dampness evaporated from my hair.

"I'm going to call you in sick to school," she said. "And then, I'm going to bed."

At the time, I'd been too tired to argue.

Now, in the heat of the afternoon, she turns to me and finally asks. I knew it was coming, but I still feel sick as the words come out, unignorable and out loud.

"Was that the first time?"

I sag against her, as much with the sheer weight of my suspicions as with exhaustion.

"I can't be sure," I whisper, *"but I don't think so."*

All those nights I dreamed of my mother; all those nights I woke up to dampness in my bed and on my shirt and touching the ends of my hair. I had thought it was sweat. Or tears. Something that came from inside of me, not somewhere out there. How many nights had I slipped out of bed, down the porch stairs, and across the yard? How many times had I walked, unconscious, into the water?

She only nods. Behind us, Bee pauses in her scribbling. Nessa waits until the sound starts up again before she speaks.

"This is a problem," she says, her voice low. "I know it's not your fault, but I can't even think about what might happen—what could've happened already if I hadn't been out here. My God, Callie."

"I'm going to start locking my door at night," I say.

"He might notice."

Only months before, I would have agreed. But something has changed—in me, in him, between us.

"No," I say, "not anymore."

———

Behind us, Bee drops her pen on the dock and shouts, "Done!" then thrusts her finished masterpiece at me as I dutifully turn to look. She was drawing a mermaid, she'd told me—unlike most little kids, Bee's favorite subjects never seem to change, her enthusiasm never flagging—and I take the scribbled-upon paper, ready to exclaim over its originality, even though I'm sure it'll just be a crude variation on the emaciated Disney princess in her seashell bikini.

Instead, I find myself staring. The thing she's drawn is something else, and it isn't wearing a bikini. Long and white from head to tail, with skeletal stick-hands and an unsmiling mouth and a scribbled mass of green-on-black sprouting from its scalp. My memory flashes back to last night's dream, to that hungry gape and tangled hair, and I shudder as I hand it back.

"It's great," I say.

Beside me, Nessa strokes my hair and sighs.

———

When my father gets home, he doesn't even finish saying hello before his eyes seek out and settle on the damaged kitchen drawer. The one with a fresh, angry dent in the place where my aunt forced it open with a screwdriver in order to find my inhaler, the one piece of last night's drama that we can't hide.

"Did you have an attack?" he says, and his voice is that much more terrifying for its evenness, its quiet. As though he'd been waiting all this time for it to happen, as though it were just a matter of time until I started getting sick again.

"Let me explain—" Nessa begins, but he cuts her off.

"I'd like to hear this from my daughter," he says, and the set of his jaw goes tighter by a degree. The bottom drops out of my stomach at the way he's looking at me. Suspiciously, like someone he doesn't quite recognize.

"It's not what you're thinking," I say, and think, *That's true, at least.* Even in his wildest dreams, the thought of me sleepwalking into that black and sullen water has most likely failed to cross my father's mind.

"Did you have an attack?" he asks.

"Yes," I say. "But not like before, okay? I swear. It was something else. A panic attack, I think. Totally a mental thing. But Nessa didn't realize, she thought I needed the inhaler, so she broke it open."

Out of the corner of my eye, I sneak a glance at Nessa—to see if she's following my lead, to see if she sees the careful line I'm walking. The one where, if I choose my words just right, I won't have to lie to my father at all. Not really.

"A panic attack," he repeats, and I can see the tenseness go out of his jaw, see the veins in his neck relax back against the skin. The worry line appears between his eyebrows. "From what?"

"I had a bad dream," I say. Beside me, Nessa nods almost imperceptibly.

"And what happened?"

"I woke up and I was scared, I couldn't calm down. But it stopped. On its own." I shift my weight, thinking as I do that this is still technically true, even if I'm leaving out the intermediate steps of being pulled from the water and then passing out on the lawn.

"It's true, Alan," Nessa interjects. "She calmed down on her own. It's just my fault for panicking; I'll pay for the damage."

My father makes a *pffft* sound, rolls his eyes, and mutters, "I'll believe that one when I see it," but the anger and suspicion are gone from his voice. He gives me a last, long look.

"I'm sorry about the drawer," I say.

His hand reaches out and squeezes my shoulder. He sighs. "It's all right. I guess I'm a little on edge, myself. I'm going to take a shower and a nap." He looks from me to Nessa, then back at me. "Be ready for dinner at seven, both of you. And when I say 'dinner,' I mean actual food, not the all-cereal diet."

Somehow, I manage not to collapse.

—

It's after dark when I find my way out to the water again. There's one more thing that we still haven't talked about. One more secret I need Nessa to keep.

She's there, with a few wisps of sweet-smelling smoke drifting from her nostrils and out across the river, when the wood creaks slightly under my bare feet; she flicks her joint into the water as I approach, then shakes her head and laughs.

"I keep forgetting that you're not six years old anymore," she says.

I settle next to her, gazing out at the patchy, shadowed forest on the opposite bank. "After last night, you smoking pot on our dock would probably be the second-most-awful thing my dad could find out about."

She snorts. "A *distant* second. Those were some amazing verbal acrobatics, Callie. Really, inspired."

"At least it was all technically true," I say, and she reaches out to squeeze my hand.

"You're so like your mom," she says. "She was a good actress, when she wanted to be, but she never liked lying to people."

I don't answer. Next to me, Nessa drops my hand and sighs.

"It was so strange, last night. When you passed by me, in the dark, I could have sworn you were her." She reaches out again, this time touching the loose ends of my hair where it curls near my waist. "You look so much like her."

I swallow, thinking again of my dream—of the thing my subconscious has given me to fill in the blanks where memories of my mother should be, a collection of parts, fingertips and hair and freckles, pieced together with other things out of a nightmare.

"I don't remember what she looked like," I say. "I don't even know where he keeps the pictures of her. Maybe he doesn't even have them anymore."

"I'm sure that's not true."

Nessa rubs small circles on my back, and for a few minutes, we're quiet. Above, the trees are full of frog-song. A bat flashes across the dimming space over the river, and there's a splash from somewhere in the water as something breaks the surface and then sinks back below.

"Do you remember anything?" she finally asks. "About the day she died?"

I shake my head. "I don't know. Pieces, maybe. But there are things—I remember them, but I don't know if they're real. And some of them can't be real."

"They can't?"

I shake my head again, angrily this time. Remembering that moment in the hospital, the story I'd tried so hard to tell, the sharpness of my father's words. *It's better if I don't remember.*

Nessa stops rubbing my back and turns to look at me. Out here, with the light from the house throwing her face into ghastly contrast, her eyes are too buried in shadow to see the expression in them.

"You should trust yourself, Callie," she says. "You have more strength than you think."

I wonder how she does this. How she knows just what to say. Whether she knows what I've been thinking since I woke up in the water, and whether she knows, even before I say it, what I've followed her here to ask.

Behind me, a door slams; when I look back, my father is on the porch, peering out at the place where we're sitting, his arms folded across his chest. He stands without speaking for a moment—looking, I think, for the joint that my aunt is no longer smoking—then calls, "Callie, dishes, please!" and walks back inside without another word. For a moment, my heart races and my throat constricts, but I breathe, and it subsides, as I turn back toward the water. I breathe deep, and think, *In the scheme of things, one more secret won't make a difference.*

"Nessa?"

"Yes?"

"I want to learn how to swim."

CHAPTER 14

I AM GETTING GOOD AT KEEPING SECRETS.

I can line them up end to end, a succession of half-truths
and lies of omission, each one putting that much more
distance between my life and my father's watchful eyes.
The truth about that night, in the dark, by the dock; the
scent of river water in my hair, washed clean and covered up
by the time he gets home from work; the sneaking, almost-
silent click as I carefully lock my door at night. It was
three weeks ago that we installed it, down low at the base
of the door, a position that various websites claimed would
thwart even determined sleepwalkers. From dusk till dawn,
my room turns from a sanctuary into a prison, my aunt
from a giddy ally to a watchful warden. I spent the first week
waiting—for him to notice, to visit, to see the lock and ask
me why.

He didn't.

I've stopped listening for his steps on the carpet. I don't wait for the sound of his knuckles against the door. It has been weeks now since he came to say good night, since he stood in the doorway and noted the rise and fall of my chest, and said, "You're really looking better. Much, much better." Without the constant threat of illness to keep him close, we've drifted. Him, into endless sheafs of scrolling data, later and more nights away, the constant thrum of conversation behind his study door. And me, into solace, solitude. The privacy that experts say a girl my age needs now. I'm left alone.

Just like any other sixteen-year-old with no-more-than-ordinary problems. And working lungs. And a busy, important father with so much on his mind.

I wonder what they do, other girls, with their long hours alone behind a closed bedroom door. I imagine they look in the mirror, studying, scrutinizing, tracing thick lines of shadow on their eyelids or filling the fullness of their lips with color. Or indulge unspoken dreams of boys, bodies, the rough backseats of cars. Their fingertips tracing circles like they hope his will do, in the dark. Or do they do nothing—nothing at all, stretched on their backs in the ice-cold silence of All By Themselves, letting their minds drift away from people, places, future plans, to settle out there in the careless wherever for a much-needed rest.

I wonder if this is what I should do, too. Now that I'm one of them. Normal, or nearly there. The battle with my body used to dominate everything, a ceaseless struggle, begging without end for me to pay attention to its demands. Ever since the airless pain subsided, the inside of my head feels huge and empty. Illness was a constant companion. Without it, the evenings seem to stretch on forever. How do people fill so many hours? How do I? There's a sixty-minute spot on the couch with Nessa, a rerun of a show I watched while sick last year. There's a thirty-minute dinner—with its stilted conversation, my father only half there if he's there at all, paging through e-mails and data at the table while we talk over his head. There are ninety minutes of work, two hours on a busy night, assigned reading or essays or redundant sheets of math problems—and that's even though I do it in fits and starts, cramming it in between conversations with the friends I suddenly have. The girls, Jana, Shanika, and Mikah, have looped me in on their Thursday-night ritual of group-watching horror movies over video chat. Ben sends me messages most every night, rapid-fire windows that bloom on my laptop screen, riddled with transposed letters and missing periods. I love the way he thinks, so much faster than his fingers can move.

And still, there's time to kill behind my bedroom door. Time to breathe. Time to read. I lie between the cool sheets at night and let the words form, whispered, in the hollows of my mouth. I trace the lines in my mother's book—the old one, its pages untouched by water but marked with the initials of strangers. The one she left for me to find, the one for the ones who are left behind.

I wonder if other girls, when they close their eyes and curl in for a catnap, can hear the sound of rushing water in the ear pressed against the pillow. *Water sucking the hollow ledges, tons of water striking the shore.* When I push the long, damp rope of my hair back over my shoulder, I can smell the dark, wild scent of the river underneath the cover of shampoo.

These days, I don't even feel guilty anymore.

In the end, it was easier than I'd dared to hope: the first, furtive lessons in the river, my hair draping over Nessa's wrists as she held me on the surface. First with her hands pressed firmly on my back, then only her fingertips, and then nothing at all but the coolness of the water as it broke over my shoulders and against my feet, the sense of her palms floating somewhere just below my shoulder blades.

"Before you learn to swim, you have to learn that you can float," she'd said. "Even when you're tired, weak, when you get a cramp, you're still safe in the water. Lie back and breathe, and it will hold you."

It took me by surprise: the rhythm of floating. The way that my hips grow heavy on the exhale, hinging backward below the curve of my back, the bottoms of my feet slowly dangling toward the deep. And then the air, filling my throat and breast and belly, calling my body back to the surface. My hip bones pop briefly, buoyant; my sternum rises up to touch the world above the water. In the sun, the droplets glisten and glide on my long, white body like little living things. I have never felt so alive.

"You're a good teacher," I say.

"It's easy, here. Usually I'm doing this with someone half your age, in between waves rolling in," says Nessa, and stretched out beside me on the river's surface. She has been teaching me to stroke, slowly, scissoring my legs with a rubber-band snap and breathing in the hollow of my armpit; now, we rest side by side, fingertips touching. Her long hair fans out and drifts down, tickling my wrist. "Did you know that your body floats better in salt water?"

"That's what we should do, we should go to the ocean," I say, and suddenly, there's nothing I want more than exactly that. To drive at full speed down the county road, flanked on each side by its stiff forest of stick-straight pines; run across the sand, casting my shoes off with a kick; dive through the breaking waves and lie breathing on the undulating sea. Or, better yet, to skip the drive entirely—to plunge forward into the barely there current, slip beneath the river's surface, let myself be carried away. Down the narrow alley, beneath the cypress trees, through the marshy watershed and into the open gulf.

My pulse throbs in my wrists and ears, beating with insistent invitation. Urgent.

The sea is waiting for me.

Yearning.

Calling.

I've never wanted anything more badly in my life.

Nessa just gazes toward the sky, nodding in a faraway way, and then gives me a smile full of clueless patience. "We'd better not, baby. The ocean has undertow, rip currents. We'll go one day, but you're not a strong enough swimmer yet."

NO.

I don't say it out loud; the word snaps out of a dark place inside my head, with so much ferocity and anger that it takes my breath away. Nessa, of all people—my mother's sister, the one who lives for wild surf, who sent me seashells in the mail—she should understand that I don't want condescending platitudes and vague promises. She should understand that I've waited long enough, that I've done my time and then some, that the sea is mine, it's waiting for me, and I won't be patient. I won't. I wrench away from her touch, and snarl, "I don't want to wait. I want to go."

I should throw myself into the water right now, and let it carry me away to the sea.

Her eyes grow large as she looks at me, then downriver, as though she's read my mind.

"Callie," she says, and her voice is low and urgent. "Get out of the water."

"No!"

I've never seen her move so fast. It seems impossible, how quickly her hand snakes out to grasp my shoulder, hard enough to bruise, how strong her slender fingers are.

"Get out of the water!" she shouts. "NOW!"

The space inside my head—so full of the beckoning call of the ocean—seems to snap in the center, a jagged rift that splits my thoughts apart and sends them spinning away, replaced by confusion and panic. *Is this me, who's so desperate to lose herself in the open sea? Is that my voice, demanding to go?*

Nessa pulls on my arm again, and I tread clumsily in the water, and she's behind me, pushing me toward the dock and shouting again that I need to get out, *out,* and then something else that I don't understand, until she says it twice more and the torpor evaporates and I flail my way toward safety.

Later that night, we stand together in the gradual dusk—accompanied by the pattering, chattering back-and-forth movements of Bee, who'd cheerfully come up behind us to announce that *duh*, of course there are alligators in the river, and that one of them had even crawled into a lot down the street last year and eaten somebody's cat. We scan the shadowy coastline, slapping away hungry mosquitoes and looking for the telltale mottled heads of sneaking predators, while she prattles on.

"Gators run fast," Bee chirps. "But if you run away special, they can't catch you. Here, see?"

I turn to look as she flees, zigzagging on diagonals back along the dock and into the yard.

"Like that!" she yells. I give her a weak smile and hold thumb to forefinger—*Got it*—and she waves before running the rest of the way home. Still zigzagging away from an imaginary gator, while I turn my attention back to the dense and shadowed coast across the way.

"Do you see it?" I ask. "Was it really there?"

Nessa is quiet and grim, the color drained from her cheeks. She stares out at the water with a taut, haunted look, and shakes her head for the hundredth time.

"It's gone. But it'll come back." She shudders. "I think I'm done swimming in this river. And you are, too."

And she is, and so am I. Not even when, in the end, the sun goes down without illuminating the hiding place of any sharp-toothed or scaly creature. The scariest thing we see is a dead, unthreatening fish that bobs past, belly-up, on its way to the open sea.

But whatever Nessa saw or heard—whether it was something in the water, or maybe something in me—has made her frightened. Cautious. When she looks at the river now, her face is a mask of anxiety, her eyes flitting up and down the bank and the small hairs on her neck all on end. But her hand is warm in mine, and she squeezes it reassuringly even as she gazes at the river.

"It's okay, baby. There are other ways to swim."

CHAPTER 15

IT'S AMAZING, how quickly you can miss things. You only need to have something for a moment—just for a day, for an hour, for the length of time it takes to hold a single breath—in order to want it back when it disappears. I've been without my mother longer than I knew her, but the hole where she's supposed to be still howls with echoing emptiness. I can no longer remember the placement of the rocks on the battered coast of my childhood home, but my dreams are full of the crashing sound of surf.

And though I swam in the river only a dozen times, I ache to be back in that black, slow water.

But I didn't fight Nessa's choice. The truth was, even as I felt the loss of the river—*my* river, with its lazy current, its untraveled path to the deep blue gulf—sink into my bones and settle there, aching, it was tinged with an acid hint of fear. I imagined things hiding, sliding along the river bottom and kicking up clouds of rank, filmy mud, lurking just out of the reach of the light. Even the night creatures seemed spooked; the chirping frogs and unseen rodents, who usually rustled in the shoreline brush as the sun disappeared and the world dimmed down, were silent as the dark crept in. The yard was quiet, the reeds all still. With no sound to distract me and no breeze to cool my face, the heat was unbearable, unmoving. A strange, heady smell rose up from the slow, black water.

There are other ways to swim.

It wasn't hard for her to keep her word. Not here, where the world is full of water and pools can be found in every third backyard.

"Whoa, whoa, whoa. Can we just talk about the part where this crazy woman had you swimming in the freakin' river?" Shanika squawked as I explained that my swimming lessons were getting a change of venue. "Forget the gators and snakes, that's just gross. There are *things* in there. Amoebas and stuff. People don't go in there!"

Mikah crossed her arms and looked indignant. "That's not true! Uncle Joe used to swim in there."

"Uncle Joe was a hillbilly," Shanika shot back, and managed to match her sister's look of righteous annoyance until they both began to shake and then collapsed against each other in mutual hilarity.

"Whatever," said Jana, raising an eyebrow at the giggling pair. "Callie's got the hookup on a nice, clean, non-alligator-infested place to swim, hooray." She looked at me. "I just hope your aunt didn't have to, y'know, clean the swim coach's filter to get you pool privileges," she added, and then waggled her eyebrows suggestively until Corey choked on his hamburger, and everyone was giggling too much to talk.

They didn't know Nessa, and so they couldn't understand: she didn't need to trade a thing to get something she truly wanted. Not Nessa. She was, after all, my mother's sister, with the same deep blue eyes and bright laugh as the woman who'd once shattered the hard shell of the most determinedly impermeable of men. All she had to do was ask. When we passed the swim coach on our way to the pool, padding side by side in our matching black tank suits and hair roped into long, tight braids, he didn't even blink; just stared at her with his frog-like face and said, "Hello," and nothing else.

For the first few weeks, Nessa joined me there in the afternoons. She would wait for me in the shallow end, calling instructions while I paddled up and back, while the combination of stroking and kicking and breathing finally went from a clunky collection of hard-to-fit pieces to a smooth, intuitive ballet. I carved long lines up and down the pool's painted lanes, arriving back out of breath, lungs aching, with arms as limp as crepe.

"You're looking great, baby," she said, squeezing my shoulders. "Look at these muscles!"

I didn't answer, except by rolling my eyes and flicking water at her before pushing off again for another lap.

But something is happening. Has happened. Even I can't deny it, the way that my body seems to have lengthened, tightened, as though my fleshy knees and neck and the jiggling cheese on my thighs have been squeezed and lifted by invisible hands. The legs of my jeans are too short and have buckling pockets of fabric where the extra flesh used to be, and my waistband keeps slipping southward. But more than anything else, it's the way it moves: this body that never obeyed me, that bucked and stalled like a run-down car whenever I tried. Everything that made me flat-footed and ungainly in my old life is different in the water. My double-wide shoulders, my gangling arms, and the things I'm missing, too; the waist and hips and womanly curves that nature didn't give me. Even with my newly smooth skin and toned muscles, I will never be a teenage dream of sinuous, delicate femininity. Not on land. But swimming, even my large hands and feet seem streamlined. Flat and powerful, knifing and kicking as I relearn how to move below sea level.

Today, I'm alone in the water. Even the lifeguard has disappeared, leaving me free to flout the rules. I cut back and forth and under, deep and deeper, sinking like a stone to the flat, gray bottom and then cutting like lightning to the opposite wall. It's not the same as the river—no scent, no sounds, no playful movement underneath my bobbing head and shoulders as the current slinks by—but there's nothing hiding, either. The water is clear, sharpening some things even as it dulls others, turning the world above into a shifting, shimmering nowhere and its sounds into barely there whispers. I push up, breathe in, dive down. I like it better here, suspended in the depths like a butterfly trapped in a Lucite grave. There is only me, and this weird blue world, and the silver colonies of bubbles that collect on my skin before breaking away toward the surface. I can be alone down here for what feels like hours—a privacy beyond even the most firmly locked door.

I know my time is up when the overwater noise becomes the *thunk* of entering bodies. The first few swimmers jump in, one of them noticing me and startling. I watch his pale legs disappear up the ladder, as long and white as a cadaver's. In the low and eerie blue-light fluorescence down here, everyone looks a little bit dead.

I'm squeezing the water from my hair when someone speaks, just over my shoulder.

"Where did you swim before this?"

I turn around.

Eric Keller, dressed for practice in nothing but a pair of goggles and a strip of streamlined spandex, is standing there. And though I keep a straight face, keep my mouth closed and my gaze impassive, I have the vague sense that an alternate-reality version of me—the girl I might have been if not for the hospital visits, the draining needle, the endless hours alone and wheezing in my succession of beige, bland bedrooms; a girl whose first and only kiss didn't happen in a pediatrics lounge—would, at this moment, be having trouble breathing for the first time in her life.

"I'm sorry?" I say, because I have to say something. I will myself to look at his face, studiously avoiding the rest. He shrugs—I watch his bare shoulders go up and down, rising and falling above what seems like a mile of muscled torso, and think, *Oops,* and then, *If Jana were here, she might actually faint*—and gestures at the pool.

"You look good in there," he says. "I just wondered where you swam before you moved here."

My mouth isn't closed anymore.

"Oh. I mean, I didn't."

He raises his eyebrows, and I suddenly think of my first conversation with Mr. Strong and blurt, "Wyoming is more like a horseback-riding kind of place."

He shrugs again, and pulls his goggles into place. The mirrored surfaces hide his eyes, but he grins at me.

"Well, now you're here, maybe think about joining the team. You've got a real swimmer's build; we could use you."

Over his shoulder and on the other side of the room, the door to the girls' locker room opens; Meredith Hartman comes through and stops short, her face going from neutral to pinched as she sees us together. Her eyes are uncovered, and not hard to read. I can see the way they narrow, suspicious and annoyed, as she examines the distance between me and Eric—the way her mouth twists as she concludes that I'm way too close.

I should feel ashamed. I should take a step back. I should hate this, the feel of her eyes on me, the way I've always hated it; I should duck away, like I've always done when people begin to stare.

But I don't.

Something is changing. Something has changed.

I take another step toward him. I smile back, and say, "I'll think about it."

And as I do, there's a whisper in my head: cold, confident, a thought so alien I almost can't believe it's my own.

Let her watch.

CHAPTER 16

I AM IN THE WATER.

Under it.

So deep, I cannot see the surface.

I wonder how I could have ever failed to see what this place is, this cold and shifting darkness where she waits to take my hand. Where else would I find her but here, in the light-less deep, where her body sank and settled and slowly came undone? Where else would she be but drifting on the underwater current, carried by the will of the capricious sea? Her voice is everywhere and nowhere, singing in the ether, bleeding and blooming in my head. The darkness around us keeps changing, shifting, getting lighter and darker in blue degrees. She takes my hand. She shows me a world like nothing I've ever seen.

We are in a deep, midnight-colored nothing with no bottom and no top, drifting in infinite space.

Then a shift, the sound of surf, and we're swimming in aqua-colored waters, a shallow place, with pale, drifting sands and a gnarled shelf of rock, where small fish dart and hide.

We huddle together in a place without light, watching a field of jellyfish, a city of pink electric clouds with tendrils that dangle like golden filament.

We watch from a distance as huge, monstrous shadows glide through a wreckage of rusted ships.

In this world, there is no starting or stopping point, no destination. Down here, beneath the surface, the sea goes on forever. And so do we.

In the end, we always return to the coldest, darkest place, where I always seem to find her. We kick in perfect symmetry, side by side, hair floating behind us in undulating clouds. I can feel, rather than see, her pale, long hand as it brushes my hip or shoulder; the glint in her large black eyes when they appraise my body's movements.

Come home, she says. *Come home.*

Her hand is on my shoulder. Lightly at first, then gripping, slipping in its quest for purchase on my sodden skin, a hand that is sinewy and strong and so, so cold. I feel myself losing direction, steered deeper into the frigid dark, and twist away in panic.

I'm afraid.

The hand disappears from my shoulder and she whirls to face me, body snapping soundlessly like a long, pale whip. Stark and white and right in front of me, even as the deepening blue-black presses in all around us, and I realize with equal parts horror and wonder that the light I see is her. Somewhere inside her, an ice-white glow that seems to originate in her bones and then seep upward, brightest at the curves of her shoulders, the jutting breastplate, the pulsing, papery skin of her cheekbones, her forehead with its creeping spiderweb of veins.

My daughter, she says. *My daughter.*

I reach for her.

When my hand finds hers in the dark, the glow from my tapered fingers is as cold and strange as starlight.

"Callie!"

I startle awake with my hands overhead—hands like I've always had, no luminescent skeleton bleeding through—and lunge for the bedside lamp before I realize that it's daylight. Sunlight is streaming through the oversized windows, high-angled and bright and warm. Only my skin, clammy and damp and strangely slick, tells me I've been having a nightmare.

There's another rap on the door, and Nessa calls my name louder. I cross the room in three long strides to open it, noting with relief the loose tumble of hair on my shoulders and the feel of dry, soft carpet between my toes. The dreams may not have stopped, but at least I'm having them in bed.

When I open the door, my aunt looks unusually flustered—frizzy-haired and red-faced, with circles like bruises under her eyes. As though she slept poorly and woke early to walk hard in the sweaty outdoors.

"Callie, there's a boy out here. He says he knows you." Her voice is accusatory. "He says you're going somewhere with him."

My gaze flies to the clock—it blinks back insolently at me, changing as I watch from 10:01 to 10:02—and I groan while dashing for my dresser.

"Why didn't someone wake me?"

"Why should we, if you're inviting strangers here and not even having the courtesy to warn us?" Nessa snaps back, and my jaw drops. I've never heard her angry like this, and definitely never angry enough to suddenly make herself part of an insulted "we" that includes my father. I close my mouth, open it again, can't even stutter a response before she exhales with a huff and walks away. I hear the door to her room close with just enough force to feel like a final harsh word.

I race around the room, pulling my hair into a messy knot and swapping my stretched, rumpled nightclothes for clean underwear, yesterday's jeans, a hoodie that smells faintly of chlorine. I slip on my sneakers, three years old and just recently scuffed for the first time, and then—with another pang at the memory of her cold eyes and inexplicable irritation—Nessa's sea-glass necklace. Its weight is comforting even as I wonder what I'd done that was so wrong, and even as the last lingering cobwebs of sleep clear from my brain enough to think again about the strangeness of her sudden defection.

Why should we? she'd said.

We.

We.

The realization hits me at the same moment that my father's voice, barely a mumble through the concrete and drywall, floats back through the house.

I'm out the door and down the steps in what seems like a single panicked leap, the door banging to announce my arrival as Ben looks up with a grin and my father— *Home for the first Saturday morning in what? Weeks?*—snaps to attention and stares at me like he's never seen me before.

"For God's sake, Callie!" he gasps as I take the stairs three at a time and land heavily on the driveway. He's looking everywhere—from me to Ben to the still-reverberating door, back to me again, looking frantically up and down the length of me as though checking for injuries and looking still more frantic at the realization that I'm fine. That I'm more than fine, I'm different. How many times has he passed me in the kitchen with his eyes on his BlackBerry, stopping long enough to ruffle my hair but never really seeing me? How many times has he looked past me, through me, assuming that everything was still the same?

I force my lips into a normal-kid grin, a hi-dad-nothing-to-see-here smile, and pray Ben hasn't been here long enough to ask too many questions. Or be asked. I can picture him, grinning cluelessly and blowing my cover in one fell swoop, saying, "Hey, did you know the swim coach asked Callie to think about joining the team next year?"

"Dad," I say. "This is Ben. He's, uh, my lab partner. Sorry, I should have—"

"Alan Twaddle," my father says.

"It's nice to meet you, sir," Ben says, proffering a hand, and shoots me a look full of so much unspoken reassurance that I feel every muscle go limp with relief. He gets it, or thinks he does. "It's great to meet you."

"Likewise," says my father. "I'm sorry, Callie didn't mention . . ." He trails off, looking to me for an explanation, when Ben jumps in.

"Sir, I was interested to see that you joined the Maxx-Foster project this year, are you working on an anchoring mechanism for the windmills?"

I stare. Ben smiles. Alan Twaddle, PhD, sputters twice and then covers it with a cough, saying, "Excuse me, the pollen in this place," and Ben just keeps going: putting a thoughtful finger to his jawline and blithely unleashing a full paragraph of jargon, one in which the only word I understand is "sediment." And then my father has gathered himself enough to answer, and the two of them are off and running, not leaving so much as an opening for me to speak.

Which isn't so bad, when the only clear thought in my head has to do with how much I like the way Ben's forehead wrinkles when he's thinking really hard. And how much I like just about everything Ben does, even when what Ben does is ask about my family with what seemed at the time like simple polite curiosity, and then go home and geek out on my father's rock-related research.

"Forgive me," my father is saying, "but I'm a little surprised to find someone your age who's even interested in what we're doing in the gulf, let alone understands it at such an advanced level."

Ben shrugs and grins. "I'm kind of a nerd, sir."

My father chuckles.

There's a cough from above, and three chins tilt skyward,

three hands rising to shield their eyes from the climbing sun. Nessa is on the porch, her hair falling forward to brush the railing in front of her.

"Hello again," says Ben.

She ignores him; her gaze is aimed at me, just me.

"Callie, come here a moment?"

"Sorry," I say, "I'll be right back and we'll go," leaving Ben to explain our plans and knowing that at this moment, he could say we were off to a heroin-smuggling operation in Mexico and that my father, dazzled and disarmed, would probably only ask if I needed any cash for tacos.

But not Nessa. If he tried to engage her with California knowledge or surfing-related trivia—and, I think, he probably did—it's had no effect. She's crossed to the other side of the porch, looking out toward the river with her shoulders hunched protectively around her core. I approach tentatively, not speaking, until I'm at her side. Our shadows fall in ribbons over the rail and pool in dark blotches on the patchy lawn. Even here, I can smell the strange, heady scent rising off the oozing water.

"I don't—" I start, but she turns toward me and pulls me close, gripping my shoulders hard enough to bruise.

"Don't misunderstand, I'm not angry," she whispers. Her lips move in to brush my ear, and her voice is low and urgent. And then she's gone, flashing past me in a noiseless blur of long skirts and damp hair, vanishing into the cool, sterile comfort of the house.

We keep the windows closed; the breeze coming in still has a bite, raw and cold despite the humid morning. I had imagined Florida as a place that never changed, seasonless and stagnant with no sense of the passage of the months, but the light of the winter sun is ever so slightly different: slender, shyer. Nature is subtle in her shifts here, as quiet about the seasons as her children are loud and proud. In town, there are evergreen wreaths on front doors and obese inflatable snowmen sitting in ironic celebration on lawns that haven't seen a single frost this year. Twinkling lights sway from eaves and balconies; reindeer appear on roofs. It's three weeks to Christmas.

A real Christmas, I think. I have only the dimmest memories of the last one that qualified as "real," the one before my mother died, with a white-lit tree and the *clink* of glass ornaments, my parents laughing as I tore paper from presents. The decorations disappeared somewhere between Nevada and Wyoming, forgotten in an attic or basement, left behind for a family who might actually bother to unpack them and put them up. By the time I started high school, we had officially traded carols and cocoa for Chinese takeout and old movies, or sometimes for the try-too-hard holiday spirit of the pediatric ward, where hyper-happy nurses, exhausted parents, and shuffling kids wearing bathrobes and sick smiles all try hard to pretend that they're somewhere else. Sometimes, like last year, I would wake up to find that I'd missed the day entirely: I'd slept all the way through December 25 after I forgot my inhaler and fainted in a Walmart parking lot when my father, in a rare festive moment, suggested a last-minute run to buy *A Muppet Christmas Carol* on DVD.

But with Nessa here, it would be different. We're a family. A thrown-together one, still taking baby steps toward trusting each other, but a family all the same. Last weekend, my father wordlessly disappeared for three hours and returned with a box of gold glass globes and a synthetic white tree, with scratchy plastic needles and lights already built in. He plugged it into the wall by the living room windows. And in the past few days, as though through unspoken agreement, a small pile of packages has appeared at its base.

Ben is quiet, staring straight ahead as we made our way back out the narrow private drive, the tires thrumming on the endless straightaway of the county road, but now his voice interrupts my thoughts.

"So, I guess your aunt isn't my biggest fan," he says. When I look over, he's giving me a lopsided smile that's halfway between amused and confused. "It feels like a personal failure; parents usually love me."

"Well, she's not my parent," I say, "so I guess your record is still intact."

He laughs, and I feel myself flush with sudden guilt. Like I've betrayed Nessa and marked her as less-than—not my parent, when she's been more there for me than anyone, when she left her entire life behind to help me make one here. Ungrateful. I shake my head, trying to clear the heat from my face, then feel a colder flare of jealousy when I instead start wondering how many other girls' parents Ben has won over.

It must show on my face, because he hastily adds, "Not that I've had a lot of practice. You know, just the odd parent here and there."

I force a laugh.

"Well, you charmed my dad, anyway. I've never seen him so excited. What did you do, memorize flash cards about wind farms and seabeds? Or is this just another thing that you're a random expert in?"

"I happen to find sustainable energy very interesting," he drawls. "It's the future, you know."

"That's what they say." I shrug.

He looks at me.

"You know, it's actually really amazing what they're doing out there? They've got funding, publicity, the best people working on it . . . I mean, your dad is kind of a big deal."

I sigh, and think, *Leave it to me to have a crush on the guy who's got a crush on my father.* I rest my head against the window; the glass is cool against my scalp.

"I know. But I'd rather talk about something other than the fascinating world of sediment."

Ben takes his hands off the wheel just long enough to make an apologetic *okay, okay* gesture, then hits his turn signal and swings the car through an opening in the trees. A small road, that becomes a smaller one, until we're rolling down a dirt drive that's densely shaded by tall, lush trees. Even with the windows closed, I can hear the *click* and chatter of birds, unseen and high up in the tented ceiling of close-knit branches.

"Ben, where are we? I thought you said we had a bio assignment, extra credit or something."

He grins. "I did. Mikah is meeting us here with her camera. But there's something else—it's kind of for you."

I blink and feel a stupid, confused smile spreading across my face. "What's for me?"

His grin gets broader, his nose crinkling behind his glasses. "I think it'll be more fun if I don't tell you in advance."

"Ben!"

"Cal!"

"I don't like surprises," I say, whining more than I mean to, and he laughs. Ahead of us, the dappled denseness of the slender road opens up into a small lot with dry, bleached grass beyond it. Picnic tables sit in the shade of looming oaks; the air is thick with the scent of vegetation. Two spaces away, the door opens on a silver bullet of a car, a sleek, expensive convertible with smooth lines and sparkling paint, and Mikah steps out. Her camera has been outfitted with a lens so long that she has to support it with both hands.

"Ready?" says Ben.

"Ready," she replies. "But if I get a single drop of mud on this camera, it's your ass, Benjamin."

At one corner of the lot, a narrow line of hard-packed dirt leads into the woods and then becomes a trail of wooden slats, curving back and away over the muddy ground, overhung thickly with tall trees and trailing vines. I've stopped asking about our final destination—Ben only grins and shakes his head at my questions, while Mikah clicks the shutter and smiles like a secret-keeping sphinx—and our shoes tap softly on the weathered wood. It's cool back here, soft and damp and shaded. Animals keep startling in the brush. I breathe in as the trees breathe out, and the air tastes earthy.

"All right," says Mikah, breaking the silence. Her voice startles something in the unseen muck beneath us; we hear it rustle away, and her next words are cautious and breathy. "All right, I've got some good stuff here."

"Good stuff?"

She points at the tree nearest us and we all lean into the rail to look closer. The bark is covered with a thin scrim of red-flecked growth, a second living skin that begins at its base and climbs heavenward until I can't crane my neck farther to see it.

"Check that out. Remember, that whole crazy thing with Strong and fractals?"

I think back, and grin. Just before break, Mr. Strong had stood in front of the class and cradled a head of green cauliflower as though it were his infant child, waxing poetic about the predictable, mathematical beauty of its conical florets while Ben leaned in close, tapped me on the shoulder, and whispered, "You know how most people feel about God? That's how Mr. Strong feels about cauliflower."

"Right," I nod, remembering. "An extra point on the final if we can bring him photos of fractal patterns in nature." At the time, I'd silently thought that the assignment was meant particularly for Mikah and her camera.

We hunt our way along the path, pointing to the symmetrical fronds of ferns, the scattered growths of lichen, an exposed log riddled with cracks. Mikah removes the long lens, caps it, and carefully secretes it in her bag.

"It's a stupid, easy assignment, but whatever. I'll take all the points I can get." She sighs. "I've got dibs on the lichen, but I'll send you guys pics of the leaves and ferns."

"You sure you don't want to come along?" asks Ben. She shakes her head and purses her lips nonchalantly, but I swear that I see a look pass from her deep brown eyes to his gray ones, and her mouth twitches in a half-second smile.

"Nah, you guys go. I've seen them a million times."

I watch her retreat back the way we came, a single beam of sunlight sneaking through the trees to glide gently over her shoulder and bounce off the canvas surface of her bag, until the wooden track curves between two thick stands of trees and her footfalls are swallowed by the rustling green all around us.

"Them?" I say, turning to Ben. "What's she talking about?"

He grins back, and then, with just a flicker of hesitation crossing his face, he reaches for me.

"C'mon," he says, and I watch as his hand, smooth and freckled, slips into mine. My heart beating fast, faster, the blood in my ears rushing so loud that it drowns out the gentle sound of the treetops, as we step in silent tandem down the wooden path to the place where the tree line ends and the sun breaks through.

I see why we've come, what he wanted to show me.

I see the long, pale bodies in perfect motion, tumbling over and under each other, a smooth and supple back cresting quietly into the sunlit air and then slipping below the surface.

"It's for you," he'd said.

And it is. They are. The manatees are playful and unself-conscious, suspended in perfect harmony with their underwater world. There's a lump in my throat as Ben says, "I remember you said you were hoping to see one."

I can't tear my eyes away. I can't keep the emotion out of my voice.

"I told you that?"

"At lunch, a month ago," he replies. "It was just in passing, but I remembered." He looks at the ground, and for just a second, for the first time, Benjamin Barrington looks really and truly unsure of himself. Quietly, he adds, "I remember a lot of the things you say."

And all I can do is gulp and nod and squeeze his hand when he squeezes mine.

I am here. Anchored. Tied to this place, this boy, this sparkling winter hideaway with its narrow wooden path, the sweet and musty smell of tree bark when it's damp. He is holding me here, under the green canopy and the dangling gray of moss, and when I part my lips to breathe I feel as though my lungs have dropped into my hips, so deeply and heavily does the air move inside them.

I think, *Wait until I tell Nessa.*

And then, I think, *But I won't.*

Because she knew. Even before he took my hand. Even before Mikah's secret smile. From the moment he said hello, from the moment he stepped into orbit around my life, she knew.

And though I don't want to—though I don't want anything to break the spell of the sunlight, the river, the manatees at play, and Ben at my side—in my head, I hear her voice again. Low and dark as her lips brushed my ear, as she held me close and then let me go.

"Just be careful, Callie," she'd whispered. *"Be careful. This boy will want to keep you."*

CHAPTER 17

BUT NOT AS BADLY, I think, *as I want to keep him.*

There is something happening between us, something thrilling and terrifying, a series of small moments that add up to so much more than the sum of their parts. The rush of pleasure when I catch a glimpse of him by my locker, the way the bottom drops out of my stomach when his arm brushes up against mine. The way he casually says, "We should"—we should do that, see that, try that together—and smiles when I smile at the way we suddenly have a year's worth of plans.

"Have you D-T-R-ed?" Jana asks, then laughs when I look confused. "You know 'discussed the relationship'? You and Benny boy. Don't tell me nothing's happening there."

"I don't know," I say. "I mean, we haven't talked about it." But I'm smiling, I can't help myself, and she rolls her eyes and laughs.

"You're not denying it, either."

On the last night before break, five of us slip into the back left row of the darkening auditorium and watch as the choir files in.

"We should see Jana sing in the holiday concert," he'd said, smiling at me—then caught himself when Mikah cleared her throat and shot him a look. "I mean, we should *all* go. Not least because I'm pretty sure she'll kill us if we don't show up."

I feel the heat of Ben's leg pressed against mine as the music begins, I'm acutely aware of his hand on the armrest between us. I feel it there, even as the harmonies begin to soar, even as Jana steps in front of the humming chorus wearing a dangerously low-cut red dress and launches into the throaty first notes of her solo, even as Corey whispers, awestruck, "Oh my God, she's *amazing*," and everyone lets out low sounds of agreement. When the applause begins, I feel his fingers brush mine.

When he whispers, "Let's go," I realize I've been waiting for him to say it.

We slip out just as the lights come up, darting past the tables piled up for the intermission bake sale, calling, "No thanks!" to the pink-lipsticked mom who drawls, "Wouldn't y'all like a gingersnap?"

He takes my hand and we run through the dim and empty hallways, deeper into the deserted school, the walls of lockers flashing by with exhilarating speed. With no bustle of between-class traffic, the resonant slap of our steps echoes off the walls, the ceiling. When Ben skids to a halt in front of a classroom door, the sound of our rushed breathing is very, very loud.

"In here," he says, and twists the handle.

The art room is thick with the competing smells of glue, paint, rubber erasers, and wood shavings. I've never set foot in it, but Ben strides confidently through the door and then closes it behind me. There's a panel of switches on the wall beside us; he flicks the last one, and at the back of the room, a light illuminates a single wall of mounted work. He crosses to it, and points to a small, single canvas.

"This one is mine," he says. His voice is hushed, though we're the only ones here. My body suddenly feels like it's made of spare parts, and nothing fits together quite right. I cross the room and stand beside him, more conscious than ever of the space between us, of how easily I could close it. I busy myself with examining the painting instead. It's a still life assignment, a standard-looking arrangement of objects on a table; there are other versions of it hanging nearby, done by different students from different angles. But I can see Ben's hand in this one, in the careful attention to light and shadow, the enthusiastic brushstrokes, the way one edge of the table looks hastily painted-in as though he'd grown bored toward the end and wanted to move on to the next thing.

"It's really good," I say.

He steps up beside me, replying, "It's really not, actually. But it serves its purpose."

"What purpose?"

I turn my head. He does the same, looking at me seriously, and the skin between his freckles turns pink.

"Well, there's this girl I kind of like. And I wanted to be alone with her."

I guffaw; I can't help it. In my head, I hear Jana's voice saying, *Soooo, have you D-T-Rrrrrred?*, and wish I could borrow just a sliver of her confidence, the total self-possession that lets her stand on a stage in front of an audience of hundreds and slay the whole room. I have an audience of one, and I feel like I'm dying.

Ben's smile loses some of its strength.

"Okay, that definitely wasn't the reaction I was hoping for."

I shake my head, "No, that's not . . . I wasn't laughing at you. I just—" I look everywhere but at his face, and finally end up confessing to my own feet: "Ben, I really don't know how to do this. Whatever this is. I have no idea what I'm doing."

It's his turn to laugh. "You think I do?"

I shake my head. He doesn't understand. "Yeah, I do. At least, more than I do. You've had a normal life, you just don't know—"

He sighs, and looks away.

"You know what? You're right. I don't know. But," he adds, urgency creeping into his voice, "I want to. I *want* to know. You keep people at a distance, and you probably have your reasons for that. I'm not saying you don't. But then there are these times when something happens, and you let your guard down, and I get these little glimpses of who you are. And all I can think about is how amazing that girl is, and how I wish I could see her all the time. I really do. I don't think you even realize how cool and different you are, in the best way. It makes me angry sometimes. Like, I want to find whoever made you not trust people like this, and punch him in the teeth for ruining things for the rest of us."

Even in the dim and empty room, I feel suddenly, utterly exposed. I know I'm guarded, close-mouthed—of course I know, how could I not?—but to have Ben point it out so casually, to just reach out and deftly, gently pluck off the mask I've been pretending I wasn't wearing. To tell me he's seen what's underneath it, and that it's okay. Until he said it, I never knew how much I wished somebody would.

I keep my gaze straight ahead, staring at the little painting. I focus on the dab of white that represents a patch of reflected light on the curved base of the painted vase. He says he wants to know me, and I will give him what he wants. One piece of my past.

"I've never dated," I say. My voice is surprisingly even. "I've never had a boyfriend. I've never even had a crush, not really. Because I've never been around people enough to get to know one to have a crush on. And my first kiss—my only kiss, actually—was in the hospital, and we had matching oxygen tanks."

The room is very quiet, and we both stand very still. Until, from the corner of my eye, I can see Ben nod.

"Mine was in the pantry during a holiday party," he says. "On a dare. And after we came out, I realized that I'd sat on an open box of Fig Newtons."

I turn my head to look at him. He mirrors me, and shrugs, and smiles. "So, now we both know something new about each other."

"But yours isn't even that bad."

"That's only because I haven't gotten to the part where everyone called me 'Figgy Pudding Pants' for the next three weeks."

A beat passes, one moment for what he's said to sink in, and then I'm laughing. I laugh so hard that it hurts, until tears stream down my cheeks, until I can't breathe. It's not just that it's funny (but it is, I think, because *figgy pudding pants*, and I'm giggling again), but because I'm giddy—with relief, with excitement, and with the realization that despite what I said, he's still here. And so am I.

He moves closer, and I lean into him. When his arms lift and encircle my waist, it's with so much practiced nonchalance that anyone watching us would think he'd done it a million times. That we were one of those couples, so comfortable, so easy, that his hands pressing lightly on my hips was nothing new. Only I can feel the tension singing in his fingers, see the bob of his Adam's apple as he swallows and stares straight ahead.

Only he can feel the way my heart is pounding, thrashing in pulse points I didn't know I had, fluttering in my fingertips and armpits and underneath my jaw. His body is close to mine, the distance between us shrinking to a crack, then a seam, then vanishing entirely.

And then I move my head, trying to see his expression, and it's a mistake, because I'm tall, much taller than him, and my nose is in his hair. I smell his shampoo, lemongrass, and the scent of his skin underneath. It's the scent of him, of a man, warm and human, and the feeling inside me is like a thousand knots pulled tight. For all the times I've embraced Nessa, or pecked my father's cheek, even the moment so long ago when I touched my lips to those of another hospital kid, and smelled disinfectant, and ignored the strange barrier of the oxygen tube that ran beneath his nose, I have never been so close to another person.

I never wanted to be.

I thought I didn't know how to be.

But he doesn't mind. And if he feels the shudder that goes through me, he doesn't say. His nervousness is gone; he's assured enough for both of us. And he looks up at me, his face inches from mine, and smiles. The moment stretches out so long that I can count the freckles on his forehead, the slivers of green and gray in his eyes. I can marvel at the quiet confidence I see there, and wish I had it, too.

He keeps his eyes fixed on my face as he lifts his chin, and leans in. And I can't bear it anymore, I close my eyes—I think, *You're supposed to close your eyes, I remember that much*—and then I feel the whisper of air as he speaks, softly, directly into my ear:

"Cal. You have to bend down a little. I can't reach your face."

And our laughter should break the spell, but it doesn't. It should be impossible to kiss while laughing, but we do. We do. I lean into the warmth and weight of him. I drape my arms over his shoulders. He puts his fingertips against my cheek while his lips press against mine, and the last of my doubts—that it was real, that he meant it, that I'd know what to do—wink out quietly, one by one. The only one left, so quiet it's barely even there, is the unwanted, whispered memory of Nessa's voice, warning me to take care.

But if Nessa thinks it's dangerous, then she doesn't understand. This life is the ship I would go down clinging to. I would clutch it greedily to my chest, I would hold him tight and close. Him and all the rest of it. I want it, want to keep it, so badly that it aches. This place, this boy who grips my hand as tightly as I grip it back.

This is the secret that I whisper, in the dark and drifting safety of my dreams.

My mother, pale and inscrutable behind the floating shade of her hair, shakes her head and disappears.

CHAPTER 18

IT'S THE BUZZING OF MY PHONE that wakes me. Once at first, then in a flurry of vibrations that threatens to shake it off the nightstand. The memory of my dream falls away gently and fades in an instant, losing its vividness, replaced by sunshine and sound, the immediate buzz of messages. There are short ones from Jana, Shanika, Corey—all mass-sent to everyone. Cheerful texts, with promises of a meet up during the holiday break. I scroll through them and grin. I save Ben's for last, and laugh when I open it.

> Cal! You alive? I heard that a career criminal named 'Santa Claus' was doing all kinds of B&E last night.

Merry Christmas to you, too, I text back. His reply comes back so quickly, I'm pretty sure he prepared it in advance.

```
Nooooo thank you. Christmas = creepy. If
that red-suited home invader shows up here,
I will beat him. With a menorah. TO DEATH.
```

I laugh again, and marvel at how easy this is. How effortless. How perfectly he's settled in beside me, how his noisy
exuberance fills in all the blanks. There are so many pieces of
me missing, not just the past I'm not supposed to remember,
but the little social fluencies that atrophied and died after
too many years of quiet aloneness and hospital rooms. Even
at my best, I am still a girl with scars on her body and pills in
her bag. But he can take up the empty space, make up for all
the things I'm missing. Even though he'd be the first to tell
me I'm wrong, that there's nothing missing. He doesn't see
what isn't there.

My phone buzzes again—When can I see you?—and
I begin to answer, typing the words, Maybe tonight, but
then I stop. I don't hit the send button. Even as I feel the
flutter in my stomach that always accompanies thoughts
of him, I suddenly feel as though today is something not
to be disturbed. It's not just the holiday—it's been so long
since Christmas meant anything, it no longer registers on
my internal calendar as anything but another day—but the
air in the room. The house is warm, suffused with the gentle
light of almost-sunshine glowing through the thin curtain of
overcast sky. I look out at the bright, gray morning. I breathe

deeply, and the smell of coffee, fresh and rich, fills my nose. The spiced kick of cinnamon. The dark sweetness of cloves.

Today is different.

There are sounds coming from beyond the closed door, from the kitchen. The clink of china, the *ching* of silverware, the smooth *whoosh* of well-oiled drawers opening, then shutting again with a *clatter*. And something else: voices. Hushed, so as not to wake me, but light, happy. Chatty. I hear my father speak; his voice is low, measured, but strangely musical. I hear Nessa's answering laugh. I hear the sound of the radio, the low harmony of a traditional chorus singing softly under it all.

Today is different.

I can feel bewilderment pulling at my face, widening my eyes, as I step around the corner. The two of them are there, bent together over a pan, peering at the concoction inside. The kitchen is warm, full of the scent of something just-baked, the sterile cold of its unused countertops vanished beneath a collection of bowls, a slowly melting nub of butter, a haphazard sprinkle of cinnamon sugar and flour that begins at one end of the breakfast bar, crosses over the stovetop, and ends somewhere in Nessa's hair. She's grinning; my father is grimacing; his rolled-up shirtsleeves are white with floury fingerprints.

Nessa sees me first, and freezes.

"Uh," she says, and my father startles, too. They stare at me, guilty expressions on their faces, and for a long moment, the only sound is a rich Irish tenor launching into the opening verse of "I Saw Three Ships."

I take a step forward, taking in the scene, then peer over the counter and into the pan. Inside, low and flat, is something covered with a crumbled topping. I look at my family—realizing, with a sense of awe and wonder, that a family is what I'm looking at—and clear my throat. I point at the pan.

"What . . . is that?"

Nessa looks stricken. My father draws himself up to his full height, pushes his glasses up his nose, and reaches for a glass full of something white, thick, foamy. He takes a long drink, sets it down, and grins at me with lips covered in a foam moustache.

"That," he says, "is a Christmas coffee cake made by two people who can't cook and have been drinking eggnog since eight o'clock in the morning."

And then he laughs, and so does Nessa, and so do I, and the music soars around us. In the corner of the living room, the little white tree twinkles as though it's just as amused as we are.

———

In the hour that passes, while my aunt hands me my own small glass of eggnog ("Sip slowly," my father warns, before beginning to giggle again) and the coffee cake is scooped out and remade and baked once more, *with* baking soda, I watch the two of them circling each other and marvel at the ease of it. Is this what mornings are like in the homes of ordinary people, the ones who grew up untouched by tragedy and have no horrors to forget? This effortless waltz, the casual sharing of space, someone pausing a moment to hum along to the music that fills the room. Even as I sense that this began as a grudging effort, the two of them coming together to create this day for me, something has changed. My father smiles more easily, laughs more deeply, responds to Nessa's teasing with indifferent ease. And Nessa, for her part, grows less adversarial, less in search of a fight, cheerfully following his instructions and chiding herself for splattering bacon grease on the stovetop.

And with something like wonder, I think, *This is what we could be.* If we only let ourselves. If we only move forward, and don't look back. If we pretend that the past—the loss, the loneliness, the way the air seeped out of the world as we fled inland, mile by mile—never happened.

Maybe it's best if we don't remember.

—

It's nearly noon when we clear our plates and migrate, by unspoken agreement, toward the couches. Outside, the overcast sky has turned dark, slate gray. Small drops of rain streak against the windows, and in front of them, the tree sparkles and shines all the brighter. I find myself wishing it would pour, wishing that the rain would come down in sheets, obliterating the outside world, erasing everything beyond the borders of this room and its warmth and the lazy, languid spinning of the golden orbs on the Christmas tree.

Nessa swoops in, seizes a package, and thrusts it eagerly into my hands.

"Open mine first," she says.

From the package, I lift a shimmering cascade of deep blue-green fabric, shaking it loose as the paper falls away. I gasp in spite of myself. It's a dress, long and heavy, with tiny iridescent beads stitched into the bodice and cascading in ornate patterns down its layered skirt. I stand up, press it to my body, as the hem brushes the carpet with a whisper.

"Oh my God," I say. I know nothing about fashion, but even I recognize the name on the tag stitched along one edge of the plunging back. The dress in my hands must have cost more than the entire contents of my closet, combined.

"Nessa, this is—I mean, I can't—"

"Not another word," she says, grinning from ear to ear. "I knew the moment I saw it that you had to have it. Every girl needs at least one insanely beautiful, utterly impractical dress in her closet."

I swallow, and look down. "I'm not sure it'll fit," I murmur, but even as I say it, I know it's not true. Even now, I can see how its lines follow my body.

"It will fit you like a glove," Nessa says confidently. "Which you'll see for yourself when you model it later."

"I don't think—"

My father breaks in, his voice exasperated but affectionate. "Callie," he says, "why don't you say 'Thank you,' and you can table your doubts until later."

I gulp again, and blush. "Thank you. It's beautiful."

Nessa smiles and puts her hands together, clearly pleased, and my father nods approvingly—though he casts a sideways glance at her, and mutters, "Where do you think she's going to wear a thing like that?" to which Nessa replies, "Alan, you are completely missing the point."

———

The scarf I give to Nessa is, I'm mortified to realize, nearly identical to the one she's already wearing, but she winds it around her neck immediately and proclaims it perfect. The gifts from my father all come in envelopes: movie passes, gift cards, a crisp hundred-dollar bill.

"It was suggested to me that I should give you presents with more, er, flexibility," he says, knitting his brows together, then casting a sardonic glance at Nessa. "Apparently, my taste leaves something to be desired."

"No, this is great," I say. "Thank you. Um . . ." I lean forward to pluck a small package from under the tree. "Here, this is for you."

I watch him unwrap it, pulling the ribbon away cautiously, slicing the tape with a fingernail so as not to rip the wrappings. The sight of him, so careful and deliberate, brings a rush of memory: my mother, giddy and impatient, whacking him over the head with a tube of wrapping paper, laughing, shouting, "Can we get some urgency, here? The roast is about to come out of the oven!"

When he lifts the object from its box, his expression is so inscrutable, so still, that I get nervous and start babbling, "It's an ammonite fossil. I mean, you probably know that. I thought you could use it as a paperweight, maybe, but I wasn't sure if you had one already, and if you do it's no big deal, I can just—"

"It's terrific, Callie," he says, holding up one hand to silence me as he lifts the gleaming spiral to the light. "A beautiful specimen. Thank you."

I don't tell him that it was Ben's suggestion, one so good I was almost embarrassed to take it. He'd pulled me into

Mr. Strong's classroom before the homeroom bell, dragging me back to the decorative glass case full of preserved skeletons, framed scientific illustrations, unnameable things floating in formaldehyde jars.

"Are you still looking for a gift to give your dad?" he'd asked, and then pointed to a curved object on one of the lower shelves. A doughnut-shaped mollusk, polished to a shine, with scribbly jigsaw-puzzle patterns running evenly over its surface. When he explained what it was—an ancient creature, turned to stone, once alive in the sea but now immortalized by the earth—the perfection of it made me grit my teeth in frustration that I hadn't thought of it first.

"That's pretty," Nessa says, and he hands it to her. I watch her examine it, curious, feeling its weight in her hands. The opalescent patches wink with reflected light as she turns it over.

My father clears his throat.

"I have one more gift for you," he says, and hands me a package, square-shaped and carefully wrapped. He watches me steadily as I begin to open it, and I find myself mirroring him as I peel the paper away, feeling the sturdy outline of a cover—a book?—until I loosen the last folded edge and hold it in my hands.

When I flip the cover open, my eyes go wide and my breath catches in my throat.

"I thought . . ."

I can't finish the sentence.

I thought he had thrown them away.

I thought they were lost forever.

I thought it was better, better, better if I didn't remember.

Nessa leans forward to peer at what I hold in my hands, and the color drains from her face. A look passes between them, but I don't see it, only feel it; I cannot tear my eyes away.

"That's really lovely," she says quietly. "Excuse me a moment, please."

I nod, still looking down.

I gaze into my mother's face as she laughs in her wave-drenched wedding gown and the spray glistens like jewels all around her.

I flip through the album without speaking, reaching the end, returning to the front, tracing my finger over all the memories I thought had long since turned to dust. My father watches me, quietly, until I look up and find my voice.

"I thought you didn't have these anymore."

He looks shocked.

"Of course I had them. Do you mean to say that you thought . . . that you didn't think I'd—" He breaks off, shakes his head.

"Well," he says quietly, "that's my fault."

I look down again at the first photo, the one from their wedding, the one that used to hang on the wall in the house high up on the seaside cliffs. It hasn't changed; the two of them are still there, in crisp black-and-white, holding each other and laughing at their incredible luck to be young and so in love.

My father clears his throat.

"I owe you an apology, Callie. I convinced myself that letting you dwell on the past was wrong, that letting you remember your mother too much could be dangerous. Especially when you started getting sick, I just thought it would make your life even more difficult, that you'd have these painful memories to cope with on top of everything else."

He looks at me; all I can do is nod, but it's enough.

He keeps going: "And when we came here, and you started getting better . . . well, I was afraid it couldn't last. Things had been so bad before, I couldn't believe how well you were doing, that you really are finally growing up just like you should. I was just so fixated on what happened to your mother . . ."

He trails off, looks down at the glass in his hands. I watch him consider his words, watch him steel himself to say them. And then, he does.

"I was wrong. I should have remembered that you're not just your mother's child, but you're my daughter, too. There's as much of me in you as there is of her." He pauses, looks down at the photograph in my lap, and smiles a little. He looks at her face, her hair, her smile, and then at me.

"Despite all appearances," he adds.

I can see him waiting for me to acknowledge him again, to say something. I manage to whisper, "Okay."

"Okay," he replies. And then, in a single, sweeping motion, he jumps up, speed-walks to the breakfast bar, returns with a plate of cookies.

"Not homemade," he says, "but I think we can trust the good people at Entenmann's not to steer us wrong."

It breaks the spell, enough for me to shake away the shock that had begun to cloud my brain, and I reach for the box. We munch in silence, until I realize that I'm dropping crumbs into the binding of the photo album. I brush them away and set it aside.

"Dad?" I say, and realize that it feels like I'm testing the word. I don't say it often; it feels strange on my tongue.

"Yes?"

"What made you—I mean, the photos. Is it just that I'm not so sick anymore, or . . ." I can't find the words to finish my question; all I can do is leave the suggestion of it hanging in the air. I take another bite as my father leans back in his chair and sighs.

He begins, "Doctor Belcher says—"

I can't help myself; I guffaw through the cookie. "Wait, doctor *what?*"

He startles and reddens, looking almost guilty.

"She's my therapist. Psychologist. I've been seeing her—"

I shake my head and swallow, trying to organize my thoughts, feeling warm and confused. I don't know why I want to laugh, whether it's the psychologist's ridiculous name or the fact that he's seeing one at all. My mind conjures the image of my father, lying on a couch, while some woman—a woman with long, gray hair, one of those loose-fitting caftan pantsuits that look like pajamas, and framed pictures of cats on her desk—leans forward, puts a finger to her nose, and drones, "And how does that make you *feel?*"

My father sighs again, and looks steadily at me.

"Callie, I sometimes wonder if you realize. What happened, when your mother . . ." He pauses, searching for the words. "That happened to me, too, you know. I lost her, too. And there are things I need to do, things I should have done a long time ago, but . . . well. You don't need to know the details."

He doesn't have to say it. The thing that derailed him, that kept him from healing, was me. With all his energy directed into caring for his sad, sick child, how could he find the strength to move on?

But I'm not that girl anymore, I think fiercely. I'm not. And if I'm not the same, if I've changed, then maybe the rest of it can.

He shrugs. "But yes, I'm seeing a therapist. You may even want to see her, too, some day. Maybe it would help you."

I feel myself shake my head, *No,* without thinking. He holds up his hands and says, "Only if you want to. But to answer your question, she's the one who suggested that maybe I wasn't seeing clearly, that I was seeing the daughter I expected to see instead of the daughter I have. She seems to think you're a lot stronger than I give you credit for." He pauses. "And I think she might be right."

I venture a smile. "Does this mean I can go to the beach for spring break?"

He smiles back. "Let's take these things one at a time. We'll see."

He stands up. The conversation is over, or nearly. He looks toward the hallway, the closed door of Nessa's room, and grimaces.

"I'm afraid I may have upset your aunt. I didn't think to warn her that I'd be giving you those pictures. I'm going to go apologize," he says. He reaches down and squeezes my shoulder.

———

When I'm alone, I reach again for the album. I flip through it, backward, forward, but my mind is racing, careening down untraveled paths, spurred on by the warm belly-burn of the eggnog, the quiet gleam of the tree, the low baritone of my father's voice, too quiet to make out the words. Today is different.

Maybe the next one will be, too.

Maybe this new life is meant to last. Maybe this is where it begins: a cool, rainy day, a baking mishap, the three of us slowly orbiting each other until we find a configuration that fits. Tentative laughter, no offense taken, everyone taking care. A different kind of life, one where we don't dwell on the past, but honor it. One where it's better if I do remember, quietly, occasionally, comfortably nestled on the couch, gazing at my memories through the safe remove of their clear plastic windows.

I gaze at my mother's frozen smile. I memorize her face, the one I'd been so afraid of forgetting. Quietly, I close the cover.

Tonight, I won't need to dream.

CHAPTER 19

IN BOOKS, IN SONGS, in stories, love is a floating thing. A falling thing. A flying thing. A good-bye to all your little earthbound worries, as you soar heart-first toward a light pink sky and your dangling feet forget the feel of the ground.

Only I know, now: it isn't like that at all.

Love is a sense of place. It's effortless balance, no stumbling, no stammering. It's your own voice, quiet but strong, and the sense that you can open your mouth, speak your mind, and never feel afraid. A known quantity, a perfect fit. It's the thing that holds you tight to the earth, fast and solid and sure. You feel it, and feel that it's right and true, and you know exactly where you are:

Here.

———

In my driveway, in the closeness of the car, his face turns serious. He turns to me. He puts his hands in my hair and tells me he feels like he's falling. And I wish for the hundredth time that Nessa could see this, see us, and see that it isn't wrong. I don't understand why she seems to see something sinister in the way he looks at me, why she narrows her eyes when Ben brings me home after school or on Saturday nights. Sometimes, I've wondered if she knows something I don't.

It's a chilly night, damp and still too cold for comfort, but I hear Nessa's voice somewhere down in the dark by the river. It's an unintelligible mutter that disappears under the sound of Ben's car pulling out, tires peeling back over wet pavement. The headlights cut misty white swaths through the cool of the night. I can see the swirling beads of water in the halogen glow, suspended in air that feels like a damp cloth on my face. I peer into the blackness of the yard as the sound of the motor recedes. It's quiet, now, and if she's there, then she has been for a while; the motion-sensing light on top of the garage is dark, the unlit windows of the house like blank and lidless eyes. There's nothing inside, nobody, not even the telltale blue-white flicker of the television. I'm about to call out when the voice comes back, louder this time.

"*I don't owe you anything,*" she hisses, "I know how much time I have, and I haven't broken any rules. Don't punish me for your poor judgment. I've done everything asked of me, and then some, so leave me be."

It is a harsh and grating whisper, full of restrained fury. The coldness of the night seems to crawl down my throat and curl an icy tail around the base of my spine, and when I let out the breath I've been holding, it lingers like a ghost in the air. The silence that follows fills my gut with dread. Whatever is coming, whatever the next line in this conversation I can only half hear, I don't want to know it. I launch myself forward and shout her name.

"Nessa?"

My movement trips the light and I see her, and for a moment the terror in my stomach clenches tighter still at the specter of my aunt. She is crouched low at the end of the dock, the last fingers of the reaching light illuminating her skin in the same gray and lifeless shade as the weathered wood she perches on. Her eyes are black pits, her face a mask of gaunt hollows, and as she stands with a jerking stagger I take an involuntary step back.

And then she moves forward, enough to bleed the color back into her hair and skin and lips, and the knot inside me unties as fast as it came together.

"Callie?" She trips her way up the dock, her shadow dragging like a cape behind her. "What time is it?"

"I'm not late," I say, instantly defensive, then see that Nessa isn't looking for a fight. She's wrapped in a blanket from the house, and though she no longer resembles the skeletal ghoul that the light first revealed, exhaustion is painted in every line on her face. Her hair is lank, her shoulders are hunched, the skin under her eyes is bruised and drooping. She gives me a wan smile, but her eyes are cold, bloodshot, glassy.

"I know, baby," she says. She shivers against the deepening chill of the night.

"Who were you talking to? You sounded so—"

She cuts me off, shaking her head. "My boss. We're having a disagreement about my leave of absence, that's all. C'mon, let's go inside."

"Are you—"

"Inside," she repeats, placing a hand on each of my shoulders. The movement makes the blanket fall away, and I gasp. There are three angry red welts stretching the full length of her forearm, raised up and with tiny dots of blood beginning to bead like Morse code where the scratch went deepest.

"What happened there?"

"*Hmm?*" She follows my gaze, and I see the briefest flash of anger on her face before she covers the injury with her hand and shrugs. "I must have snagged it on that raw edge of the dock. You startled me, you know. Now let's go. I want some coffee."

"Maybe you should just go to sleep, Nessa. You look . . ."

The smile fades and she cocks an eyebrow. Written over her tiredness, the perky gesture looks painted-on and ridiculous.

"Callie, give it a rest," she says. "I'll have plenty of time to sleep when I'm dead."

Inside, I reset the coffeemaker and listen to my father's apologetic voice mail—something about a dinner with investors that was running longer than expected—while Nessa flips switches, bathing the whole house in soft-lit ambiance. From outside, I imagine, it would look like a box made of ivory light, a glowing object between the trees with the two of us moving behind the glass windows like insects in a terrarium.

There's a *foom* sound behind me, and I turn to see my aunt crouched by the fireplace in the corner of the living room. We'd made fun of it, back in the humid fall—who could possibly live in this climate and still want more heat?—but now, orange and blue gas-powered flames are jumping through the grille and licking up between the fake logs.

"I think it's cold enough, don't you?" she says, and I nod. She settles in on the couch, drawing her blanket in close around her, eyes closed. When the coffeepot stops burping and dribbling, I add cream and sugar to two mugs and carry one to her. She wraps her hands around its ceramic curve and smiles at the warmth of it, sighing as I curl up next to her.

"I'm going to miss this," she says, looking around the room and then looking at me. Her expression has gone serious, and I wonder again when she became so tired. So thin. Her eyes seem much bigger in her gaunt, angular face, and her lips have lost some of their fullness. When the meaning behind her words hits me, I swallow, hard. *So*, I think, *that's it.* Whatever fight she'd been having when I came home, she must have lost it. And though, of course, I'd known that she couldn't stay indefinitely, that Nessa had her own life, a job and friends and maybe even a man, a lover waiting for her return in her pretty town by the Pacific, that hadn't stopped me from hoping. From imagining a life, a home, that didn't feel like it was only two-thirds complete.

"Are you leaving soon? I thought that maybe . . ." I trail off. What I'd thought, that she might just leave her life behind forever in order to join our sad, spare excuse for a family, was too absurd and selfish to say out loud. Who would give up Nessa's life, a carefree existence full of sunshine and surf and bronze-skinned beach bums with six-pack abs, for swimming dates and cereal dinners with a sixteen-year-old girl who had only just recently learned how to breathe like a normal human being?

Nessa sighs. "It's not right away, but yes, it's soon. Another couple weeks. It's time I went back where I belong. I'm sorry, baby. I was hoping I might be able to stay to see you through the school year, but . . ."

She waves a hand in the air, leaving me to finish her sentence inside my head with awful things, hurtful things, the kind of things I know she'd never say but can't seem to stop myself from thinking.

I force myself to smile, and shrug. "I bet they'll be glad to have you back."

She looks at me strangely, her lips curling a little at the corners. "They? They, who?"

"You know," I stammer. "Your friends? Your . . . boyfriend?"

Her laughter is sharp, ironic, and with no humor in it.

"Ha! My boyfriend," she says, and then chuckles darkly. "Ah, yes. Of course. That boyfriend, the one I've never mentioned because he doesn't exist."

She takes a swig of coffee and grimaces, and as I look at her, I realize how little I really know about Nessa. How much of her life is a blank that I've filled in with assumptions, projections, with nothing but the confidence that wherever she was, and whatever she was doing, she was wonderful and happy and fiercely loved. That she was living the life I'd have chosen, if I'd been her and not me. But now, I think back on her letters, so many letters, and try to remember even one in which she mentioned another person's name.

"I'm sorry," I say. "I just thought—"

She interrupts, waving my apology off and giving me a real smile. "No, honey, don't apologize. How would you know? But no, no boyfriend. That's okay. I like having things my own way. I don't need some man to come in and throw his socks all over the place, leave dirty dishes in my sink."

I shake my head, at the image taking shape in my mind—a house standing empty, nobody waiting at the airport to welcome her home. "But . . . I mean, you must have . . ."

"What? Suitors?" she laughs again, genuinely this time. "Oh, you know, there's a guy from time to time. We go out for drinks, maybe we walk by the ocean, and if I like the looks of him I'll take him home with me. But that's that. I don't do commitment. I don't have the time."

I shake my head, unable to believe what I'm hearing. In all the years that I've spent picturing Nessa's life from afar, it never looked like this, a lonely place punctuated by the occasional one-night stand. I know I should stop, that it's not my place to interrogate her, but the curtain has been pulled back and I can't keep the questions from coming. My curiosity is like something big rolling downhill, crushing and unstoppable.

"But why? Haven't you ever wanted to get married, or have kids?"

She pauses at that, staring into her coffee cup as though expecting an answer to appear inside it. Her lips press together and there's a long silence before she answers.

"I've had my moments," she says, finally, wistfully. For a moment, all the bravado and cavalier dismissal of a love life falls away, and I see exhaustion in her face. Maybe even regret. "There was a guy, a few years ago, and I almost . . . but that wasn't meant to be," she shakes her head. "A marriage is a promise that I'd just end up breaking."

I wince at that, at the finality in her voice. She doesn't seem to notice. Still looking down, she continues, "Life has plans for me, and I have to trust in that. I have to let destiny be my guide."

The words are out before I know I'm going to say them.

"I'll never be like that. I don't believe in destiny."

Nessa looks up with concern on her face, and I feel my eyebrows rise up to mirror hers.

"No?"

I shake my head, vehemently.

"My life is going to be about what I choose, not what someone else decides for me."

She considers that, and then nods, slowly.

"I suppose you would feel that way," she says. "After the life you've had with your father, I suppose you feel like you've always been held back by something or someone else." She stops and looks at me, and I nod back, relieved that she understands.

"But even you must realize that life has limits," she says. "All paths aren't open to all people. And even if a path is meant for you, you still have a choice. You can always decide not to take it. Finding your way is up to you. Destiny is just what's waiting for you at the end, if you do."

I try to imagine what my father would say if he could hear this conversation, Nessa's hippie proclivities on full and glorious display, and feel a surge of gratitude that he's not here.

"And if you don't find your way?" I press.

"Then you don't," says Nessa. She looks impatient. "What do you think? It happens all the time. People make decisions against intuition, or against their better judgment. Or they second-guess themselves until they're paralyzed, they get scared, they do what's comfortable and convenient and they never get anywhere. Or they devote themselves to somebody else, a parent, a child, a lover, and they ignore the call of their own life." She sighs. "Mostly, the only thing they miss out on is their own best future, and a lot of them don't even know it."

"But you would know."

"Yes."

"Why?"

She sighs. "Because I'd feel it." She taps her chest. "I do feel it, already. That's why I live alone. It's why I wouldn't marry a perfectly nice guy. It's why I keep my own hours at a job where I never see the same faces twice. It's why I went to the doctor and had my tubes tied at twenty-three."

I gasp at that. "What? But you could have—"

"No," she says, firmly. "I couldn't."

I shake my head, trying to escape the image of my aunt on a steel table, her abdomen laid bare, sleeping peacefully as a man in a white mask neatly snipped off her path to motherhood. I haven't even begun to know what I want from life; how could Nessa, only a few years older than I am now, already know so surely what she didn't?

It's as though she's read my mind. She smiles wryly, saying, "You look horrified."

"It's just—you were so young. Don't you ever worry that you'll regret it? That you gave up that chance?"

Her voice is thoughtful, as she replies, "I don't think of it that way. I like to think of it in terms of what I've gained, by following the path I know was meant for me. However much time I have on earth, I want to use it wisely. There's something magic about being exactly where you're supposed to be. It's peaceful. It feels *right*. Whatever I might have sacrificed, I've been given so much more than I've ever given up. This life has its gifts." She pauses, and looks at me slyly. "Material, and otherwise."

I think of the way people look at Nessa, of the electricity that's always seemed to surround her, of her charm and beauty and eerie intuition. I think of the way she lives, in an endless blur of sunshine and salt water, with nobody and nothing holding her back from doing what she loves every day. I think of her home, the beachside cottage she's described so lovingly in her letters, the one my father has wondered aloud how she managed to afford. I don't have to ask her what she means. She's the only person I've ever seen so content with her life. And yet . . .

"It just sounds lonely," I blurt, and then wince, wishing I'd kept my mouth shut. But Nessa doesn't look offended; she only peers at me over her coffee cup.

"No lonelier than being trapped with the wrong person, married to someone who can never truly understand you, knowing it'll have to end one way or another," she says evenly.

"But if you were really in love—"

"There's more to life than love." She shakes her head, then hesitates before saying, "Did your mother ever tell you about our aunt? She was like me, no husband, no kids. She had a little house on a barrier island, out on the coast of North Carolina."

"Auntie Lee," I blurt, and Nessa looks startled.

"You've heard of her."

I close my eyes and see her, motionless in the photo I've carried with me all these years. The tall woman with her face turned away toward the ocean, her hands reaching out to the two little girls at her side. "I have a picture of her. And you, and my mom; you're really little in it, maybe two. I never knew who she was."

Her tone grows wistful. "I know that picture. Our mother, your grandmother, was gone, and we stayed with Lee that summer while Dad sorted out the divorce. She wasn't actually our aunt, really—I think she was Dad's cousin—but I was too young to really understand that part of it. Now that I think of it, she would have been just a little older then than I am now. God, she seemed so glamorous, back then. She was beautiful, smart, gifted. She could have done anything. But then, there was a man. And she got it into her head that a man was all she needed, and that was that."

"Where is she now?"

Nessa hesitates, and then her expression changes in an instant, from nostalgic to angry. She shakes her head.

"She turned her back on us," she says flatly. "Not just us, on her life. She rejected what she was meant for. It was a mistake. And instead of learning from it and facing what came next, she just turned and ran away. I haven't spoken to her since I was young, but seeing what happened to her, I promised I would never lose sight of myself like that."

Curiosity gets the better of me. "But what did she do?"

"Oh, the details aren't interesting. It was nothing sordid," she says lightly, but in a way that declares the subject closed and makes me feel embarrassed for asking. A moment of awkward silence follows, until Nessa sighs.

"Just don't pity me, baby. I'm not sorry for choosing this life." She grins. "Especially not now, when it's one of the reasons I was able to run out the door to come here and be with you, without even stopping to pack my toothbrush or a change of underpants."

I can't help it; I smile back.

"And you couldn't ignore the call of destiny long enough to even pack a bag?" I joke.

"That wasn't destiny," she laughs. "I just wanted to be with you. I wish I could have done it sooner. But no, I can't ignore it. If I did . . ." She trails off, looking down at her hands.

"What?"

She hesitates again, then says, slowly, "I think some people truly have a purpose. And I think fate gives them chances to take the right path. It tries to guide them home. It shows them the way. But if they don't take it, if they don't listen, I think . . . I think that it makes for so much useless unhappiness."

I think about that for a second.

"Does that make sense?" she asks.

And though it does, sort of, though I have the barest sense inside my head of something untangling itself and beginning to take shape, I can't find the words to say so. It all seems too silly, too deep, too spiritually fraught to be talking about over creamy-sweet coffee with a fakey fire burning.

And so instead, I say, "I'm sure it would make sense if I smoked as much pot as you do," and Nessa blinks in open-mouthed surprise before throwing her head back and laughing, loud and long.

Later, when there's only a half inch of murky liquid left to slosh in the bottom of the coffeepot, I sit with my head on her shoulder and yawn out another question, watching the twisting violet tips of the fire through heavy, half-lidded eyes.

"So how do you even live, if you think everything happens that's meant to happen?" I yawn. "It'll happen no matter what. What's the point of doing anything? Why bother, if you only end up the same place?"

Nessa smiles at me from the corner of her eye. "Are you telling me that the journey doesn't matter, just the destination? That's not very Zen of you."

My thinking has gone slow and stupid, my body trying to nudge me in the direction of sleep. I'm not even sure what Zen means, really, but I'm too tired to ask.

"Your face isn't very Zen," I say, and she giggles.

"Listen," she says, stroking my hair. "We all die at the end. Nobody knows how much time they get. All you can do is use it well."

"Because you can't control the ending."

"Of course you can't." She laughs. "You know, you really are your mother's daughter. Maera . . . she didn't just want a choice in life, she wanted *all* the choices. All at once. She was always looking for a way to have everything she wanted, always bargaining for more, even when it was too much. Even when it was impossible." Her voice has gone soft and small; when she speaks again, it's more to herself than to me. The smile slips a little on her face as she murmurs, "Impossible. But God, for a while there, it really seemed like she'd found a way. She had everything, down to the very last moment."

"Until she just let it go," I murmur automatically, and my aunt springs back and turns to stare at me with eyes as sad and surprised as my own. It was a stowaway truth, one I didn't even know I knew until I felt it on my tongue.

She begins shaking her head, "Baby, that's not—"

"Yes," I interrupt, suddenly wide-awake, and the words begin tumbling out. One on top of the other, as though the first sentence was the loose pebble that triggered an avalanche of hidden pain. These are the thoughts I've pushed aside all my life, telling myself that I just didn't understand, telling myself that when I got older my mother's death would make more sense. But it doesn't, and the realization that it never will is acid in my mouth.

"She might as well have chosen her ending," I spit. "We were miles from land, in the middle of the ocean, and she just slipped into the water and then let go. How could she do that? How could she be that reckless?"

I stop, out of breath, and feel two spots of color rising high and hot in my cheeks as Nessa stares at me with her mouth open in a helpless *O* shape, with nothing to say, because I'm right. She finally presses her lips together, shaking her head in silence. A long moment passes, my heart pounding and my breath coming in quick gasps, until I realize that this is just the kind of stress that Dr. Sharp warned might trigger another attack. I struggle to slow it down, swallowing hard, inhaling deeply and evenly, exhaling in a slow stream through my mouth until my pulse no longer beats furiously in my temples.

"I'll never understand," I say as I let out another long breath. "I'll never understand how she could leave me like that."

Nessa leans forward, puts a hand on my shoulder and another on my knee, until she's so close that I can see the individual pores in her forehead, the exact contours of the worry line that cuts between her brows.

She says, "Listen to me, Callie, and listen carefully: *my* mother left. She left us, and moved back to Ontario, and married the guy who'd been her high school sweetheart. She started over with him, had another baby, and we never heard from her again. She said she was lonely, and that none of us needed her anyway, and the worst part is, she was right. She was so right that we barely even noticed she was gone, that we couldn't even blame her. But I still know what it's like—to have her walk out the door, with a suitcase in her hand, and leave you behind."

She takes a deep breath. "And if there's one thing I know for sure, it's that your mother did not leave you. She loved you. Everything she did, she did because she loved you and wanted to be with you. Your father, too. She loved you both, more than you can possibly imagine. She wouldn't let go. If anything, that was her weakness. It was the one thing she couldn't do."

I shake my head, and she grabs my face with both hands.

"Callie," she says. "Oh, Callie. You know I'd stay with you if I could, don't you? You know I love you, don't you?"

And somehow, the tenderness in her voice hurts even more than the barbed words I've been using to torment myself. I nod, and swallow again, but it's no good. The sadness is swelling and breaking apart and rising inside me, unstoppable as the tide, and then she's putting her arms around me while I cry against her chest.

CHAPTER 20

THOUGH HE HASN'T SAID SO, it's obvious that my father expects the worst: depression, desolation, the kind of weeks-long relapse and brutal, strangling attacks that a change like this would have brought in the past. He's scheduled an appointment with Dr. Sharp for later this week, telling me that it's "for safety's sake." As though the air itself might turn toxic, now that Nessa is gone.

I can feel his worried eyes, looking me over, as I say good-bye to my friends and exit the school gate to where his car is waiting. I force myself to smile breezily and wave.

I wish I could explain to him—tell him that it's my heart, not my lungs, where it hurts—but he wouldn't understand.

The good-bye was hard. For what it had been worth, in the months that Nessa was here, we'd become a family, if a flawed one. At the airport, even my father had leaned in, so stiffly and reluctantly that I half expected his joints to make a creaking sound, and given her a real, actual hug.

"Thank you for all your help, Nessa," he'd said, then grudgingly added, "I actually don't know how we would have managed if you hadn't shown up."

"You're more than welcome, Alan," she'd replied, and then met my eyes over his shoulder and discreetly mouthed the words, *Holy fucking shit.* When she wrapped her arms around me a moment later, I couldn't stop laughing even as my eyes swam with tears.

I thought of the last time we'd said good-bye, the way that I'd buried my face in her skirt and the way that she'd somehow predicted the miserable future ahead of me. *God knows how your daughter will suffer,* she'd said. But this time was different, both of us older, more stoic, bolstered by the promise of future visits on the horizon. When we hugged, the tawny curve of her shoulder came to rest just under my chin.

"I'm really going to miss you." I gulped.

She squeezed me tighter, bringing a hand up to stroke my hair. Out of the corner of my eye, I saw my father cast an uncomfortable look at us—clutching, crying, the kind of sloppy emotional mess he could never quite understand—and feign a sudden interest in an advertisement for tanning

lotion on the wall ten feet away. The sight of him, the knowledge that this would be the sum total of my family with Nessa
gone, made me start laughing again, made me cry even
harder.

"*Shh,*" she whispered, combing her fingers through a
tangle just over my ear. Her voice broke. "Oh, Callie, don't
cry! If you cry, I'm going to cry, and then your father is going
to think we're hysterical and call the police."

"Just take me with you," I joked, still sniffling. "Put me in
your suitcase. Your purse. Your pocket. Anything."

She shook her head, pulling me close with all her strength,
and said, "You know I would if I could."

"Now." She smiled, stepping back to hold me at arms'
length. "Let me take a good look at you. I know you won't
believe me, but you've become a really striking young
woman, you know that?"

I shook my own head in return, wiping my nose on my
sleeve and doing my best to smile. "Yeah, I'm sure I'm pain-
fully sexy right now."

We stood like that, eyes and hands locked together,
until a speaker crackled overhead and a disembodied voice
announced that the flight to Los Angeles was now boarding.
She picked up her bag. She hugged me for the last time.

"I'm so proud of you, baby," she said. "Take good care of
yourself, okay? And that boy—"

"I know," I replied, squeezing her back. "I'll be careful."

"Good," she said, and I could hear the smile in her voice. "But have fun, okay? After all, you already have a perfect prom dress. You wouldn't want to waste the chance to wear it."

And then she stepped backward, a space opening between us. I fought back a fresh surge of tears as I realized it would only get bigger.

"When will I see you?" I asked.

"I'm not sure, sweetheart," she answered, and took my hand. Her face was strong, serious. "But don't worry. I love you, Callie. I'll send you a letter."

"I'll send you one first."

My father drives home in thoughtful silence, both of us sinking into the expensive leather luxury of his SUV as I stare out at the bursts of lush, green growth that seems to have exploded on the roadside overnight. The trees are heavy with foliage, puffed up and thrusting against one another in search of space and sunlight. When the car rolls to a stop, I step out and bypass the porch stairs to cross the lawn, to slip between the trees, down the dock to the water. The sun has dipped away, leaving a pinkish glow in the west and the water shrouded in deep green shadow. In the early evening stillness, the faint, sweet note of honeysuckle appears like a breath on the air and then vanishes before I can inhale again. It's so pretty, a perfect spring evening, and Nessa is missing it.

Bee is perched out on the farthest point, wearing a bright orange-yellow bathing suit with a frilly skirt. She bounces toward me, a tiny golden ball of butter-colored energy, and I smile at her in spite of the sadness blooming in my chest.

"Did your auntie go home?" she asks.

"Yes," I say, dropping down to sit beside her.

"That's too bad," says Bee, climbing into my lap with matter-of-fact affection. I cinch my arms tightly around her, grateful, not even minding the way her weight makes the sharp wooden edge of the dock bite deeply against my thighs.

"It is too bad," I agree.

Bee leans against my shoulder.

"I liked her. She was pretty."

I laugh. "She still is. What are you doing down here, anyway? Playing with Barbie again?"

One chubby hand lifts up, index finger extended. She points down to the glassy surface of the water, to the place where the river curves away.

"I was watching. They left," she says. "They all went down away there, to the ocean."

"Who did?" I ask. And when she tells me, I find myself fighting back tears that sting even more brightly and taste even more bitter than the ones I'd shed at the airport.

"The manatees. They've gone home."

CHAPTER 21

BEN KEEPS APOLOGIZING. He told me that spring came early this year, even for here, that he hadn't thought they would swim downriver again so soon. I told him that it was okay, that it doesn't matter. But on the days I would have gone to see them swim—days that have been given over to the not-unpleasant alternative of rented movies, air-conditioning, and painful burns on both our elbows sustained during frantic make-outs on the living room carpet—I still yearn to see them with a fierceness I can't explain. I had counted on that familiar comfort: the path through the woods, the thrilling first flash of a pale body in the darkness of the water, their peaceful, oblivious tumbling beneath the surface.

The brush of Ben's lips as they graze my ear, his palm splayed on the bare, sweating small of my back, are amazing and exciting, but they aren't the same.

"They might be hanging around one of the beaches or boat basins," he said, the last time I kissed him good-bye. "Maybe we could go take a look."

His hopefulness made my heart swell, made me grin stupidly in spite of myself. He is so intent in his search for a solution, wanting to make it right. It's not that he wants to see the manatees; it's that he wants to see me see them, wants to see me happy. I kissed him again and took his hand, saying, "Maybe." But when I think of the coast, the sand, the endless gulf beyond it, something twists in my gut. Something equal parts fear and longing.

We should wait until you're a stronger swimmer, Nessa had said. And I had always thought that she'd be the one to take me to the sea. I'd imagined us there, maybe even with my father, too, moving forward as a family to look out at the open water. Confronting it, together. It's silly, I know—and impossible, now, with Nessa gone back to her beachside bungalow, hundreds of miles away.

But when my phone lit up this morning with his text message, an invitation to go searching for them, I wrote back: Not today.

Today, I sit with Bee on the dock. The manatees have all gone home, but some good things haven't changed.

"She's so beautiful," she whispers, for what feels like the hundredth time, and clutches at my wrist with one small, sticky-fingered hand. The other one holds tight to the present I've given her, an oversized picture postcard that I picked up at the museum, already dog-eared at one corner from being loved just a little too hard. I look at Bee's hands, her fingernails like grimy half-moons, caked underneath with a mix of dirt and glittery lip gloss, and wonder if I shouldn't have bought more than one. The woman in the picture, her silver fishtail wrapping behind her and over one hip as she combs out a hank of her long auburn hair, seems to be peering at me with an I'm-not-so-sure-about-this expression; unprotected like this, she won't be beautiful for long.

"You might want to put her in a frame, so she doesn't get dirty," I suggest, gently prying up Bee's fingers and trying not to grimace. She's so excited, she keeps pinching me. "Or an album, like mine—see?"

She looks over at my lap, where my mother and Nessa stare up from under their protective plastic veil. Frozen in time, in childhood, with their knees being kissed by the surf.

"I'll be careful," Bee promises, and gently lays the postcard flat on the dock as though it were made of glass. "I'm just looking at her now. See?"

"That's good, that's perfect." I smile at her, and she grins back.

The museum had been a weird, belated rite of passage—
the first time I hadn't brought back a field trip permission
slip only to have my father sigh, and squeeze my shoulder,
and say, "I don't think it's a good idea." Not that I'd blamed
him; even then, I'd known he was right, and didn't want to
go, anyway. It wasn't a good idea, not for me, and not for
the hapless teacher in charge who would receive such stern
warnings in advance that she'd panic and dial the fire de-
partment if I so much as looked like I might cough. But that
girl, the one who never visited the caverns or the slot canyons or hopped the yellow school bus to the Capitol to see
the state Senate in session, is gone. She would have been
startled to see me, the new and improved Callie Morgan,
right there with the rest of my history class, blithely turning
in a signed slip and clambering onto a shuttle bus alongside
Jana and Corey.

She would have been even more shocked when Ben
bounded onto the bus past our protesting teacher and
kissed me good-bye. Deeply, his hand on my cheek, in front
of everyone.

I was still flushed, cheeks hot with surprise and pleasure
and embarrassment, as we pulled away. Jana, grinning in the
seat across from me, leaned over and whispered, "That boy

is smitten with you, my friend. That boy is in *deep smit!*"—and then laughed at her own cleverness for as long as it took the bus to reach the highway.

It had been a beautiful day, too beautiful for anyone to sit still even for the half-hour drive to Tallahassee. By the time we reached the outskirts of the city, a concrete mess of greasy roadside restaurants and storefronts offering check-cashing services, the chorus of teenage screeching and singing and shouting out the windows had reached a fever pitch. Ms. Wilkinson, who had moderated dozens of heated classroom debates without ever breaking a sweat, practically threw a sheaf of study sheets at Corey, yelling, "Hand these out!" By the time we had made our way off the bus and through the museum gates, she was furiously smoking her third cigarette.

"My great-great-great-great-granddaddy is in this exhibit," Jana remarked as we stepped past the registration desk and into a quiet room, the doorway overhung with a red-and-white banner that read, FLORIDA IN THE CIVIL WAR.

"Really?" Corey replied.

"Mmm-hmm. He was a general in the Confederate Army. His name was . . ." she trailed off, then muttered, "Well, shit. I can't remember. I'll know him when I see him."

"Aren't you embarrassed?" Corey needled her. "Being descended from a racist traitor to the Union, and all?"

She rolled her eyes. "If your family had lived in the South back then, you'd be descended from racist traitors, too. It's just your luck that you get to be descended from filthy carpetbaggers, instead."

Their good-natured bickering went on, but I'd stopped listening, hanging back. This was still one topic on which I had absolutely nothing to say. My friends at Ballard came from families with old money, but it was their deep roots, their well-mapped histories, that made jealousy sink its ugly needles deep into my gut. They knew exactly where they came from, who they were; they could trace their ancestral trees back six generations. They had grandparents, great-aunts, cousins, sprawling families with stories to tell. I had none of that. My father's parents, already middle-aged themselves when they'd had their only child, had died before he had made his own late marriage to my mother. My mother's father, too. There was only Nessa, and she was just as adrift without family connection as I was—only she seemed to neither think nor care about anything but the here and now.

Watching my friends trading stories of great-grandparents and long-lost ancestors, walking past walls hung densely with artifacts, photos, papers that held carefully preserved memories of a bygone era, I felt utterly alone. Not the loneliness of an empty room or a phone that doesn't ring, but another kind. Something deeper, the sense of having nothing and no one to anchor me in the vast ocean of human history. No foundation to stand on, no stories to tell. It was as though I'd suddenly turned in time, peering over my shoulder to see where I'd come from, and found nothing but yawning blackness behind.

When Jana spotted her sought-after ancestor on the wall and her delighted shout rang out in the room—"There you are, you old bastard!" she'd cried, loud enough to make heads turn from twenty yards away—I'd quietly slipped out the door, found another room, and finished my note-taking alone.

Corey had found me in the gift shop an hour later, staring at the art print postcard of Waterhouse's mermaid.

"Hey, you okay?" he asked. "We turned around a while back and you just weren't there."

"You guys were having a conversation I couldn't participate in." My voice was snappish, louder than I meant it to be, and Corey's slender eyebrows rose up in alarm. I put a thumb and forefinger to my temples, and sighed. "Sorry, that came out wrong. Are you guys done?"

"Yeah. The bus doesn't leave for a while yet; I think we're headed to Publix for food." He hesitated. "Do you want to come?"

I plucked the postcard from its display, and nodded. "Let me just pay for this."

He peered over my shoulder as the cashier rang me up.

"Huh. Is it for you?"

"The little girl who lives next door. She's got a thing for mermaids."

Corey grimaced, and I laughed.

"What? You're not a fan?"

"No, I was just remembering this thing Mr. Strong said last year about where those stories come from."

"What?"

"He said that most guys would rather claim they were seduced by a beautiful half human, half fish than admit that they got drunk and tried to have sex with a manatee."

I'd laughed, and he did, too. And when we found our way out to where Jana was waiting, I tried to leave the emptiness behind.

But now, with the album of photos open in front of me, with Bee chattering on by my side as she gazes at her postcard, I feel it creeping in again. Even the pictures—of my grandfather in his naval uniform, of my mother as a teenager with gangly limbs and wild hair—feel like faded, tattered mementos in an empty house that's crumbled from neglect. I don't know what they meant to my family; with no one left who cares to tell their stories, I can never know. I turn the page, gaze into the eyes of people who refuse to look back at me. My parents have eyes only for each other, laughing on the first day of their lives as husband and wife. No matter how many times I peer at the shot of Lee, holding hands with the two little girls that my mother and Nessa had been, her face remains turned away.

I turn another page.

And suddenly, I see her.

It's a picture I've skimmed past a hundred times, dismissing it as uninteresting when there were other ones, better ones to look at. The woman in it—a woman I always assumed was my mother, too close up and slightly out of focus, with a paperback book in her hands—peers into the camera from under the hand that she's pushed deep into her hair.

But it isn't my mother. It isn't.

There are silver strands in this woman's hair, and age lines etched deep into her forehead, marks of age that Maera Morgan never lived long enough to earn. It's Lee's deep-set, almond-shaped eyes that are staring back at me, bright blue and piercing. And when I gently pull the photograph from its sleeve, it tells me as much. On the back, lightly scrawled in handwriting I don't recognize, is an inscription:

Lee Morgan Deering, 1999, Beardstown.

CHAPTER 22

IT TOOK A HUNDRED FLIPS through the photo album before I found the photo of Lee, peering over a paperback in someone's kitchen, a moment captured, almost twenty years ago in a town I'd never heard of.

It takes less than a minute to find her in Illinois, staring out from the website of the *Cass County Star Gazette*. I'm sure it's her, even with only the two photos to go on, even though there's only the barest echo in her face of the young woman in my pictures who stood on the North Carolina shore and turned away just as the camera clicked. Her wild hair has gone completely gray, and the years have not been kind. She looks old, so much older than the fifty-something I've calculated she must be. Time has sunken her cheeks, sagged her jawline, taken the fullness from her face and lips. She sits at a table, her expression steely and grim between the smiling people on either side, gazing out at me from beneath a headline that reads, *Fellow teachers bid a fond farewell to Alethea Morgan Deering.*

The small article about her retirement is dated last year. I have time to read it and wonder why she quit so early, before I look again and see the oxygen line snaking under the woman's nose. It's not only time that's put the hollows in her cheeks or the bruised-looking circles beneath her eyes. Alethea Deering is sick. The kind of sick that steals your life away piece by piece, until there's nothing left but you, and a quiet room, and the sound of your rattling breaths, while you wait to take your last one.

But there's no obituary. And there's only one white pages listing for someone named Deering in Beardstown.

I don't stop to think.

The phone rings, rings, rings—endlessly, six times and then seven, until I'm about to give up. And then, midring, it stops. I hear a clatter, a muffled cough, the scrape of something against the receiver.

I clear my throat.

"Hello? May I speak to Mrs. Deering?"

Even in the perfect, crisp space of our connection, the voice that replies sounds like something crawling out from the bottom of an ash pit. It's frictive, painful, scraping like metal on concrete.

"Who is this?"

"My name is Callie," I say, and then, cautiously: "Alethea? Lee?"

But I don't have to ask; I know it's her. I knew it from the first rattle of ragged breath in the receiver. The hairs have risen up on the back of my neck; my skin is prickling. I clear my throat; on the other end of the line, Lee does the same.

"I'm calling from Florida," I say. "I found your number on the Internet—"

The gravelly voice rasps impatiently, "Who are you? What are you selling?"

She's going to hang up on me. I forget about being polite or cautious; I rush to get the words out, babbling, "I'm sorry, it's just, my name is Callie Morgan. My grandfather was Douglas Morgan, my mother was Maera. We're cousins. I mean, you were my grandfather's cousin."

There's a long silence, so long that I'm about to check to see if we've somehow been disconnected, and then she replies in a voice so cold that it sends chills down my spine.

"I haven't heard those names in quite a while."

I don't have time to reply before she launches into another long, rattling spell of coughing. When it ends, she sighs and in the same icy tone, says, "You'll have to excuse me. I'm not well, and you surprised me." She pauses. "And how's your mother?"

It takes me a moment to find my voice.

"She's . . . she's dead," I reply. "Almost ten years."

There's that same eerie silence on the other end, and I find myself thinking, suddenly, *But you knew that. You just wanted to hear me say it.*

I don't know how I know. I've also never been more sure of anything in my life.

"I'm sorry for your loss," says Lee, but her voice is still so cold, so strange. "But I don't know what you think I can do for you."

"I don't know, either," I reply, and kick myself as I realize how true it is; I dialed without thinking, intruded into this woman's life without ever stopping to ask myself what I wanted from her, without ever wondering how she'd feel to answer the phone and find me on the other end. It never occurred to me that I might be someone she wouldn't want to hear from.

Her voice cuts through the silence again. "Well then, Callie, as interesting as this has been—"

"Wait!" I cry, knowing that whatever comes out next will sound pathetic, and deciding that I don't care. "Wait, listen, I have a picture of you. You and my mom, and my aunt, Nessa. I've always wondered about you. About everyone. I don't know anything about my family or where my mother came from. She died before she could tell me. And when I realized that you were still alive, I was hoping you might—"

Lee snorts, cutting me off in a voice that's shockingly sharp.

"And why should I tell you anything?"

I open my mouth to reply, but all that comes out is a weak-sounding *Uhh*. I'm beginning to wonder whether there's a good reason why her name had been buried so deeply in my mother's past that it took more than ten years to surface. Why Nessa had clammed up when I pressed for details, dismissing Lee's mistakes as "nothing sordid" but refusing to tell me what they were. I wonder, with unease, just what kind of person Alethea Morgan Deering truly is.

She's still waiting for her answer. I stammer, "I don't know. I just thought maybe you could . . ." I trail off again, hopelessly lost, hearing the desperation in my voice and hating it.

But the breath coming through the receiver has softened, just a little. There's a sigh, and I hear the creak of a chair as she settles into it, and when she speaks again the hostility has gone from her voice.

"Nessa," she says. "You mentioned Nessa. I guess she'd be in her thirties, now, assuming she's still around."

"Yes." I sense she wants more, and add, "She lives in California. She teaches surfing."

"Married?"

"No."

"Ah," she replies, and I think how strange it is that a single syllable can convey both scornful approval and an utter lack of surprise at once. I wait, letting the silence stretch out, until Lee sighs again.

"I'd like to tell you something. Before you say anything else. Just a little story, but it's something I think about sometimes. On the subject of family history. Okay?"

"Okay," I say.

"There was a young woman, a friend of mine, worked in the office at the high school. Michelle. Probably a lot like you. A little older, of course, but a smart girl, curious about things. She was one of those know-thyself types, always meditating and reading those self-help books about parachute colors, personality types, and whatnot. You know the kind, I suppose."

She pauses, as though expecting a reply. I murmur a yes while she clears her throat again.

"Well," Lee says, "a few years ago, she reads an article about that gene, the one they can test for, the one that gives you breast cancer. Amazing, really, the things they can do with medicine these days. Anyway, she decides she wants the test, seeing as she knows it runs in her family. And next thing anybody knows, she's got a positive result back and she's getting preventative surgery. Just cuts 'em right off, a double mastectomy at thirty years old. And can you guess what happens?"

"No," I say, although something in her voice makes me think that yes, I can. I can guess. I think I already have.

Lee chuckles, a low, mirthless sound. "She gets breast cancer. She gets breast cancer in the breasts she doesn't even have anymore, if you can believe that." She pauses. "What I wonder is, did it do her any good to know? Did she change a damn thing for the better? Or did it just give her some false hope, some stupid idea that she could control what couldn't be controlled?"

"I . . . I don't know."

"Well, neither do I," she says. "And we can't ask her, for reasons you can probably guess. But I wonder about it. And I also wonder whether it all would have happened the same, if she hadn't known. I wonder if she would still have gotten that cancer, if she'd never taken the test to begin with." She pauses to cough again; I cringe at how familiar the sound is. My own throat feels close and dry. "Point is, I never met anyone who was better off for sniffing out all the answers. Not my friend, God rest her. Not me. Not any woman in this family, that's for damn sure. The more you know what's coming, the more you think there's something you can do to change it."

I can't believe what I'm hearing; she sounds like Nessa, babbling about destiny, only harsh and bitter where Nessa is patient and easy. And where Nessa might be prone to New Agey magical thinking, Lee sounds like her grip on reality is shaky at best.

"Look, I think we're having a misunderstanding," I say, exasperated. "I'm not asking you to tell me my future, I just want to know a little bit about who my ancestors were. I don't see the harm in that. Just anything you might know about my grandfather and his parents, where they were from, what they did."

Lee hesitates.

"That's it?" She sounds incredulous. "That's what you want to know?"

"That's all, I swear."

Her voice is still cautious, but she says, "All right." I hear her settle deeper in her chair, and her voice turns more businesslike. "I won't be able to tell you much. Your grandfather was my cousin—his father was my uncle. He married late, and it didn't last. I guess you know that part."

"A little. I know he was in the Navy."

"Yes, a Navy man. Lots of those in the family." She chuckles. "You probably have quite a few more long-lost cousins out there, the way the men in our family go port to port. Sowing their wild oats, if you get my meaning."

This time it's my turn to cough as I fidget and feel my face turn red. My grandfather died before I was born, but I still don't like the idea of him "sowing" a bunch of women during his time in the service. If Lee notices my discomfort, she doesn't say so; she's already moved on.

"His parents, I never knew. His father, my uncle Ethan, died in the Korean War before I was born, very young. Also a Navy man. They all lived in Norfolk back then. Before that, the family was in Wellfleet. New England. They were in the fishing business, and very successful. That was where it started, as far as I know."

"You mean, where the family started?"

There's a long pause on the line.

"That's all I know," she says, finally, in a way that makes it clear that I ought not to ask any questions.

"That's great," I say quickly. "Thank you."

It's not great, of course. It's a pittance of information—but still, I think, a hundred times more than what I had when I called. It's a place to start. In my mind, I trace backward through this new knowledge of my family tree. Stopping briefly in the Pacific Northwest, just long enough to remember the way the horizon looked from our living room windows, then eastward in a great, sailing leap to Virginia, and up the coast to Long Island. To a place I'd never been, cold and raw in the winter, where my family's shuttered fishing boats would have bobbed in a biting gray sea.

"We live on the coast," I blurt. And somewhere, a small, answering voice whispers, *Of course.* Isn't this what Nessa has always told me? That our family hears the call of the ocean, always has, always will. That we live scattered up and down the coasts of half a dozen countries, connected by the seas that stretch between us, listening to a song that only we can hear.

The hardness comes back to Lee's voice.

"Not *all* of us," is the reply, each word bitten off hard at the end. "Me, I've been in Cass County twenty years, and I'll be damned glad if I never see the ocean again."

I don't know why it should feel like a slap in the face, but it does. It's as though the taut, shimmering line I'd been drawing up and down the world's coasts, the spiderweb that linked me back through time to a family I'd never known, had gone suddenly dull and slack in my hand. When I answer, my voice sounds wounded.

"Nessa told me you lived on an island. She said you were very glamorous."

"Did she?" she says, and chuckles darkly. "That was a long time ago. I left twenty years ago when my husband died, and I'll be glad never to go back again. Not that I could, anymore. I'm not well."

I don't have to ask what she means; her ragged voice and wheezing breath in the receiver, the glint of the oxygen tube in the photo are answer enough. I know these things; I know how they mark a life full of lost time and loneliness. Instead, I say, "I didn't know you were married."

"I wasn't married for very long," she replies, and I shudder. Her voice is positively grim.

"I'm sorry."

She sighs.

"No point in being sorry. What's done is done. I made my choices. Coming here with my boy, that was just the last of them."

"Your boy?"

"He'll always be my boy," she says, and I can hear the swell of pride in her voice. "He's all I have. He's a man now, of course. Lives just across town with his wife. They've got a baby now, a boy, thank God."

"That's nice," I say, although an impertinent part of me wants to ask her what's so bad about girls. But I don't. I want to end this call. I want to take what Lee has told me, this handful of raw materials, and plug it into a search engine. With luck, I'll shake something else loose from our family tree.

But Lee isn't finished.

"You know, I remember when your mother got married. She called me up then, a lot like you have. Asking questions, looking for answers."

That gets my attention.

"My mother? She did?"

Lee erupts in a fit of coughing that goes on for ten seconds, then twenty. When she speaks again, the warmth in her voice has disappeared, as though she hacked up and spit out her sympathies along with whatever was clogging her lungs.

"Yes," she says bitterly. "She did, for all the good it did her. She didn't like what I had to say, and clearly, she didn't heed it. But I'll tell you what, young lady: everything costs, and somebody else is fixing the prices. I told your mother that. I told her there's no negotiating. You get your time, and then your time comes, and that's that. Ask for more, and you'll wish you hadn't. And do you know what she said?"

I don't reply, and Lee doesn't wait for me to answer.

"She said, 'I'm not going to make your mistakes.' That's what she called it, a mistake. Oh, your mother always thought she was smart that way. Thought she was tricky. Only I'm still here, and Maera's gone, and she's left behind a daughter as ignorant as her mother was greedy. You really don't have the slightest idea, do you, girl? Nobody's told you a damn thing, have they?"

"I don't know what you mean," I say desperately. And I am desperate, aching, to understand what my mother did to make her so very angry. To know the woman I lost, even if it has to be like this, through memories tainted by bitterness. "Can't you tell me? What did my mother want? What was she trying to do? I don't understand."

She sighs, and hesitates.

And I don't know why she says it—whether it's to hurt me, or to help me, or maybe both at once—but the darkness in her voice sends chills down the length of my spine. I'll still hear it long after I've hung up, a rasping whisper that won't stop echoing back through my mind.

Because when I say "I don't understand," Lee laughs again.

And replies, "Oh, don't worry. You will."

CHAPTER 23

I AM IN THE WATER.

Back and forth in the eight-lane pool, back and forth under the sweeping, silent watch of the lifeguard. Alone, where everything is blue and muted and the only thing that matters is the repetitive rise and fall of my stroking arms, the endless in-out of air in my lungs. I can forget everything down here, drown everything, but especially that rasping echo of Alethea Deering's strange good-bye. The water blunts the memory, takes away its teeth.

Even my father says that it was nothing, only the delusional rantings of an unhappy old woman who was clearly just trying to upset me.

His words had been a surprise, unexpectedly comforting. I hadn't even meant to tell him; I'd only pushed the album across the dinner table and asked, as casually as I could, whether he'd ever met the woman in the pictures.

"Oh," he'd said, recognition instantly crossing his face as he looked at the faded photo. "That's Lee. She was your mother's first cousin, once removed."

"You knew her?"

He shook his head. "No. I never met her. I remember her, though, or remember hearing about her. Your mother had asked her to come to our wedding, but she wouldn't." He squinted at the recollection. "She was awful about it, actually. Really cruel. Maera was so upset, although she tried not to show it. She said she should have known better than to ask."

"Ask what?" I said as Lee's voice echoed back in my head, whispering, *She didn't like what I had to say.* Had this been the source of their argument? A wedding invitation?

My father looked at me, hesitating, then said, "Ask her to attend a seaside wedding. Lee's husband had been killed about ten years before your mother and I got married. It was just one of those terrible things. He drowned, along with her little boy."

I was too surprised to stop myself.

"But her son lives across town from her, with his wife," I blurted, and my father's eyebrows shot up as I realized I'd given myself away.

"She had twins," he said, evenly. "One survived. Now, how did you know that?"

"Uh," I said. "Um. It's just that the reason I was asking is that I talked to her today."

I told him the story, trying to reassure myself as I did that I'd done nothing wrong. People researched family histories all the time, it wasn't so strange, was it?

But I was still floored when he just nodded, and grimaced, saying, "I'm sorry, Callie. I wish you'd told me. I could have told you that Lee probably wouldn't be happy to hear from you. But still, scaring you like that . . ." He frowned. "I should really speak with her."

"No!" I cried out automatically, and then took a deep breath. "Dad, don't. Please. I'm fine, really. If you call, she'll just flip out again."

He looked at me a moment longer, and finally shrugged. "All right. If you're sure."

"I'm sure." I paused. I still wanted—needed—to know the rest of Lee's story, to understand how just hearing from me could make her so bitter, so angry. "You were telling me what happened to Lee."

My father shook his head. "I don't know anything more than what your mother told me. It would have just been one of those freak accidents. A sleeper wave, they call it. They were all on the beach together, just sitting there, and all of a sudden an enormous wave rolled in and carried them all out to sea. The boys were just infants, less than a year old. Lee managed to save one of them, but the other . . ." He stopped and shuddered. His eyes looked wet, and I realized with a pang who he must be thinking of, and how easy it had been for a moment to think of this as the sort of thing that happened to other people. Even after everything. Even though we both knew better.

"I'm sorry, I'm sorry, forget it," I said. But my father just smiled sadly, and shook his head.

"Even I can't imagine what that must have been like," he said. "Not just to lose her husband and her child, but to be there when it happened. To have to choose which one to save. Something like that, it changes you. Not for the better."

I swallowed and nodded, and he patted my shoulder.

And I tell myself that my father was right: this woman, whoever she once was to my mother, has become someone else. I tell myself that Nessa was right, too: that Auntie Lee, the one who stood on the shore with her cousins and turned her face to the sea, isn't around anymore. She disappeared beneath the waves just as surely as her husband and her child, and a brittle, rasping shell of the person she was walked out of the sea in her place.

If I repeat the words for twenty laps, maybe I'll start to believe them.

I surface for breath and dive down again, finding my rhythm in the water. I push myself to move faster. I imagine Nessa waiting for me at the shallow end, calling out encouragement; I imagine that if I just keep kicking, breathing, pulling, I'll feel her touch my shoulder to tell me I've arrived.

But she doesn't. Instead, the hand that reaches down and draws me to the surface is larger, stronger, attached to an arm that feels like sandpaper where the hair has been shaved away.

"Sorry," Eric says as I sputter and swat at my burning eyes. "You okay? You looked like you were about to hit the wall. You were really cruising," he adds, grinning.

I nod wearily and mumble a thank-you.

"Give you a hand?" he asks, and then doesn't wait for an answer before saying, "Up you go!" grasping my wrist, and hauling me up to sit on the coping. Even with water still lingering in my ears and dampening every sound, I can hear the indignant gasp from across the room, the muttering of voices. When I turn around, two dozen eyes bore into me. I lost track of time in the water, enough for the swim team to have filtered in unnoticed while I made my way from shallow to deep end and back again. Their impassive faces over their red uniform swimsuits are all turned my way, and Meredith

Hartman still has her mouth open, her hands on her hips. Next to her, a girl I don't know titters and then whispers, *"Who does she think she is?"* loud enough that the words rocket off the tile walls and echo in my ears. The easy familiarity, the way he reached down to pull me up, the smile. They all think they know what it means. I feel a flare of anger.

"Thanks," I say, looking up at him, studiously ignoring the girls' stares. "See ya."

Moments later, the door to the locker room slams open behind me hard enough to send a tremor through the floor. I've only just managed to pull my underwear on before her voice purrs icily in my ear.

"Would you mind telling me just what the fuck you think you're doing?" Meredith says.

I swallow, hard, and turn to meet her glare, realizing as I do that I have to look down to do it. I'm taller by half a foot, broader in the shoulders and everywhere else, but she doesn't seem to care; her eyes are bright green and blazing, the skin around them pulled taut with anger. Behind her, two other girls in red team suits stand with their arms crossed and lips pressed together, identical in pissed-off support.

"I'm not doing anything," I stammer, and she takes a step forward.

"You," she says, clipping her words so sharply that I can barely hear the long Southern vowels in her voice, "are flirting. With my boyfriend. You have been flirting with my boyfriend ever since you got here. We've all been watching you do it."

My eyes widen in protest. "That's ridiculous—"

"We've been watching," she snaps, "and we've been waiting for you to realize that what you're doing is *rude* and *wrong*."

She looks over her shoulder long enough for the red-suited pair to nod their heads in agreement, then turns back.

"But since that's obviously not happening, and you apparently think you can throw yourself at every guy in the school, I'm just letting you know . . ."

She takes another step in until I can actually feel her body heat on my puckering skin, close enough that I can see that there's no makeup on the tawny expanse of her unblemished forehead, close enough that I can smell her perfume and that my brain can supply the involuntary, idiotic observation that it smells really good. I wonder how this girl could ever be jealous of me. I wonder if, now that she's close enough to see the brief splash of old acne scars on my cheeks and the bloody crack where my chapped upper lip has begun peeling open, she'll realize what a threat I'm not—could never be—and simply leave without finishing her sentence.

But if she sees these things, she doesn't care. Her index finger, with its manicured nail, rises up to punctuate her threat with invisible periods.

"Eric," she says, "is mine. So stay. Away."

I haven't moved when the door closes behind her, I stay rooted to the spot until I hear the sound of the coach's whistle signal the start of warm-up laps.

But something changes.

Something has already changed, is happening right now. The rush of blood grows louder in my ears. My heart doesn't so much beat as thrash, pounding for escape against the wall of my chest. I'm crossing the room, dressed in clothes I don't remember putting on, passing through the corridor and through the door to the pool and brushing wordlessly past the place where Jana has been waiting, as she throws up her hands and says, "There you are!"

Meredith whirls when I tap her on the shoulder. She says something, maybe; I see her mouth moving, I sense the brassy buzz of Jana's snappy retort behind me without hearing the words. The rushing in my ears soars and crashes, like hundreds of tons of water on rocks, and then I hear the voice. It's mine and yet not mine, ice-cold, the words spilling from my mouth as fast as they take shape in my mind. My tongue is flooded with the taste of copper, of salt, of rage and power.

"*You stupid girl,*" I hiss. The sound is harsh, ancient, vicious. It is the voice of something with claws, teeth, sightless eyes like clouded milk that see nothing and everything all at once. It grates and spits in a way I never have, not even when I could barely speak without coughing and woke up gasping for air in the inland night. I want to shut my mouth on it, but I can't stop, it pours forth like acid and echoes back, back, back off the tiled walls.

"*You're nothing. He's nothing. Your shallow, impermanent life means less than nothing. And when you're gone, and it will be soon, nobody will even remember that you were here.*"

And then it's gone. Disappearing back into the void that it came from, taking all the air in the room with it. Meredith shrieks, "Let go, you crazy bitch!" and wrenches away; my fingers, curled like claws, fall away from her shoulder, leaving long lines of red behind. Vaguely, I hear the sound of clamoring voices, rising up around me, as I wheel and fall to my knees. The water on the floor bleeds into my jeans; the tile is cold against my temple. There are shimmering arcs cutting through my vision, dark spots throbbing and blooming in my unfocused eyes. My pulse is fluttering like a trapped and dying animal in my throat.

"Jana," I croak, but no sound comes out, and I hear her answering scream over mine, "Oh my God, get somebody! She's turning blue!" as a dozen bare feet pound away sideways through the arbitrary place where my pupils are pointing. Pain breaks in spiderweb shatters over my chest. There is no air. There is no time.

But the last thought that the touches my consciousness, as I slip down into the dark, isn't about the crushing weight inside of me or the circle of frightened faces staring down. It's that I was right. Meredith Hartman shouldn't be jealous of me.

She should be terrified.

THE SHALLOWS

CHAPTER 24

MR. STRONG IS EYEING ME SUSPICIOUSLY.

"Morgan?" he says. Beyond him, the eyes of the class stay determinedly fixed on their midterm tests—twenty heads bowed in a portrait of concentration, twenty necks resisting the urge to twitch just enough to witness the return of Crazy Callie Morgan, who "had some sort of psychotic seizure" and "said you-wouldn't-believe-what to Meredith Hartman," before collapsing in a twitching pile on the floor of the natatorium. Only Ben, sitting still and unsmiling at the back of the room, has risked lifting his head to look at me, and I wish he hadn't.

Because this part, I know. I know it by heart. I clench my teeth together, thinking that this day will be a success if I can just make it to the bathroom before my throat starts closing and the world begins to spin, if I can just make it home without collapsing. I wait for the disapproval, the

sidelong glances, the silent stares. I wait for the disappointment in Mr. Strong's voice as he quietly shifts my name from
the mental drawer marked "Star Students" to the one at the
back, marked "Freaks and Fuckups."

Only that doesn't happen. Instead, my teacher smiles,
reaches out, and tugs gently on my ponytail.

"Welcome back, kid," he says quietly. "It's good to see
you."

At the back of the room, just as he did on the very first
day, Ben lifts a hand and grins. And though I feel eyes on
me, though I hear whispers falling in behind me as I pass,
the air ahead stays clear. Nobody sticks out a foot to trip me;
nobody glares or gestures. I take a deep breath, feeling my
rib cage expand, wincing only a little at the soreness there.
When I sit down, he swipes my backpack beneath the table
with his foot and pulls out my chair with a smile. He leans in,
slips an arm around my waist.

He presses his lips to my temple, and though two dozen
pairs of eyes are fixed on him, he only looks at me.

"Hey," he whispers, "do you need some mouth-to-mouth
resuscitation?"

They say it's no big deal. That it could happen to anyone.
That it'll all be forgotten, that it already has been. Later,
with the sun high in the sky and beating down on the sizzling

courtyard, I lean against the wall while five concerned voices clamor to assure me that everything is fine.

"Are you sure you should be out in this heat?" asks Ben. He won't stop hovering, and I close my eyes irritably and nod, turning my face skyward. After a week in the dry, cold hospital and the drier, colder bedroom waiting for me at home, I need this. My whole body is slick with scentless sweat that dampens my cotton shirt, the waistband of my shorts. I've been waking up like this every day since the last attack, but Dr. Sharp says that it's nothing new. That night sweats are another side effect of the chemical cocktail he's mixed to fix my body, that if I want to be well then I'll have to be tolerant. I make noises of agreement and don't tell him the truth: that the sweat doesn't bother me, that I like the feel of air traveling the length my clammy arms, kissing its way under my collar and down the curve of my spine. The flaking dryness and rough, raised rashy patches that used to make up the landscape of my body have disappeared, replaced by skin as supple and pale and dewy as a salamander's belly.

When the moist air of the Florida morning moves over me, it feels like my body is breathing. The sunshine is fierce, a physical force against my eyelids, knocking there as though daring me to open them and look directly into it.

"You were gone for a week," Shanika says, her brows knitting together. "I just can't believe you didn't tell us you had this . . ." She gestures, searches, and then gives up on finding a word. She glares at Ben, too. He knew what they didn't, but he kept my confidence, leaving them all in the dark.

"Sorry," I say, but my voice is hard. I look at the faces looking back at me, their wondering, wounded stares, I think, *But I'm not. Not really. And neither are you.* The way they're looking at me now, like something breakable and to be handled with care, is all the reason I needed not to tell.

There's an uncomfortable pause before Jana breaks in.

"All right," she says loudly. "So there's good news, and there's bad news. The bad news is, a certain someone— I don't think you need me to tell you who—is telling pretty much anyone who'll listen that you're a psychotic man-eating whore who's trying to murder her and steal her boyfriend."

The answering laughter is weak, but it's there. She gives the group an approving nod, then continues, "But the good news is, the boyfriend in question told this certain someone that she's crazy, and you didn't do anything, and she needs to chill out and stop being a jealous asshole. And because Eric Keller is a golden god of high school hotness, what he says, goes. And actually"—She pauses long enough to throw an *I'm sorry* look at Ben—"actually, Callie, he's been really worried about you. He asks me every day how you're doing and if I've talked to you."

Ben rolls his eyes at her and shrugs, but puts a hand on my knee under the table. I wince—it's too hot, his palm feels like fire on my skin—but cover his hand with mine anyway. I've been watching him struggling with the urge to touch me since the moment I stepped into bio class. I've been watching him the way they're all watching me: like something curious and other, something they've never seen before. It's been a week, only a week, but despite their insistence that everything's fine, none of this feels familiar. None of it feels the same.

"And anyway," Jana is saying, "the point is, it's no big thing. Okay? Half the kids in this school are on medication for anxiety or whatever. Everyone has panic attacks. So you having one, that's no big deal. Especially when, you know, you just happened to call Meredith Hartman insignificant and shallow before passing out cold and being taken away in a motherfucking ambulance *like a hero*, okay?"

Around the table, people are grinning nervously and tittering. The laughter is genuine now, growing in strength. Ben shoots me an encouraging look; Jana nods eagerly.

"Okay?" she says, again.

"Okay," I say. "Okay."

And they believe it. They believe it because they want to. My friends, who are determined to pretend that nothing happened—or that, if something did, it was funny and forgettable in the same way as any high school embarrassment. My father, who chalks the whole thing up to stress and anxiety over Nessa's departure and only spends a handful of days hovering over me like a worried hummingbird before cautiously resuming a life of late nights and distracted dinners; resisting the urge to infantilize me on the advice, I imagine, of Dr. Belcher. Even Dr. Sharp scowled at the fluid he drained from my lungs but allowed me to go home after only a day, admonishing me to avoid stress and cutting off my questions with curt dismissiveness.

"Of course your voice sounded strange," he'd said, stabbing at my chart with the gleaming tip of his pen. "You very nearly needed a tracheotomy, for God's sake. Frankly, I'm amazed you could manage to speak at all."

And though the echo of what happened isn't entirely gone—people peering at me strangely across classrooms, a boy I don't know giving me a look of spooked recognition as he passes me in the hall, Kimberly Dunn cornering me in the bathroom and whispering, "I think you're really brave," before banging hurriedly out the door—it grows fainter, and fainter still, until the space immediately surrounding my life is as placid and quiet as it ever was. Even if things aren't entirely the same; even though I had to surgically clip away the piece of Meredith Hartman's favorite cinnamon-flavored gum that I found mashed into the frayed ends of my ponytail on my first day back at school. In the end, I'd rather be a freak, be feared and hated, than go back to being the sick girl. To being nobody at all.

"Back to normal," is what everyone keeps telling me. "Now, you can get back to normal."

As though normal was just behind me, waiting for my return. As if I could just find my way back to a place that I had only barely ever touched to begin with.

But life is like a song that I've forgotten the words to; I am out of sync, out of step. The feeling I once had, of slipping effortlessly into a life made just for me, I can't get it back. I don't even know if I want it. Instead, I lie awake at night with the uneasy sense that this place, these people, this life, are perfect . . . for some other girl. It has all slipped right through my fingers. A barrier has come down in between me and it; I feel it shimmering there, invisible, impermeable. I press against it, but cannot break through.

They say nothing has changed, but it has. I have. There is an awareness growing in me now, buried deep, dormant, but I know it's there. I will never forget the feel of it digging in, taking root, something dark and hard and strong. That day at the pool, an ocean opened at my center, black and glittering, wide and infinite and full of rage. It rattled my vocal cords with rasping threats until I gagged and crumpled, but in that moment before I sagged to the floor, I had never felt so powerful.

I'm afraid it will happen again.

I'm afraid that I want it to.

And if it does, no one will herald me as a hero then.

Not if, something whispers inside of me. *When.*

CHAPTER 25

WHEN I WAKE UP with my throat swollen, my breathing shallow, my body hot and stiff and aching, I feel almost relieved.

"It's just the flu," my father says, but his worried eyes tell me that he's trying to convince himself, too. He feeds me three small, brown pills, then nods with cautious confidence twenty minutes later when my temperature drops and I close my eyes.

"Just the flu," he repeats, but continues to hover. Crisis, my father knows. But the flu, just the flu, is unfamiliar territory.

He puts a palm to my forehead. "Do you want me to stay? Maybe I should stay. It would be difficult to work from home, but I might—"

I struggle back toward consciousness long enough to give him a thumbs-up and a weak smile.

"Go," I croak. "I'm fine."

When I fall asleep, it's with gratitude—that for a little while, just for today, I won't have to pretend that everything is fine.

People tell you to fake it until you make it, as though such a thing were possible. As though pretending comes easy, as though you could role-play your way through every day, every minute, and never let the mask fall from your face. I've tried so hard to press myself back into the space where I used to fit, the life that came before that day at the pool. I've spent weeks ignoring the teasing darkness that lurks just out of sight in the corners of my mind. I've pretended that normal is in reach, so close that I'm already there. I've laughed at Jana's jokes; I've leaned into Ben as he strokes my hair and chatters happily about the prom plans he's already making; I've written letters to Nessa, and I tell myself she won't notice that I'm once again holding things back. Even though she hasn't answered. Even though I can feel the lies of omission pressing out from in between the lines, blotting out my words like an ugly, silent stain.

Sometimes, I've even come close. I convince myself that nothing has changed. Sometimes, the hours pass and I feel just like I did in those first golden weeks, just as stable and unexceptionally well, just as anchored in the ordinary life that's all I've ever wanted. But as I sit at lunch or in Jana's car or across from my father at the quiet table, I feel it stir and flutter. I feel myself sink away, inside, and then yearn to sink even deeper.

I hear an old woman's rasping voice, making threats I don't understand.

I hear the crashing of waves.

As I fall into a fevered sleep, my phone begins to buzz. I pull the covers over my head. I sink down, down, down.

In my dreams, I am floating somewhere beneath my life, looking up from a distance. I see my friends, elbowing in the lunch line; my father, eyes glazed and glued to his Black-Berry's screen; Ben, talking about some new song that all of us have to hear. I hear snippets of conversation, trivial arguments, so much chatter that will be forgotten in a matter of minutes. The whispering thing, the voice that is mine and yet not quite mine, whispers encouragements in my head. It tells me that this is the truth of who we are. That these connections are as tenuous and drifting and meaningless as the broken strands of spiderweb that wave in glistening fragments from the trees beside the river. The dark thing creeps out of the shadows, the tide inside me rises, something peels back out of sleep and peers out at the world through my eyes. It laughs at my fear of being different. How, it asks, could I care so much for these small, petty people? How could I have ever wanted to be loved and accepted as one of them? How could I have thought I'd be happy in their laughably impermanent lives, pretending to share their shallow concerns? And even as part of me recoils at my callousness, another part looks out through my unveiled eyes and sees: they are as insignificant in their pathetic rushing as ants carrying crumbs to feed their queen. There is more than this. I am more than this.

I need only let it in, to listen closely, and then I'll understand.

I wonder if this is what Nessa hears, when she talks about hearing the call of her life. If this is what it sounds like, the voice that hammers and demands, so loud and urgent that it seems to be coming from under a trapdoor inside your own brain. I wonder what it will tell me, if I let myself give in.

I dream that I am hurtling through the darkness, clutching my mother's hand, and wake up gasping. I dream that we aren't alone. Shadows chase us down into the deep, pale faces with huge, glittering eyes loom out of the dark below me. A hundred pale hands reach up to clutch me, and someone—some*thing*—rears up and calls my name out of its black and wide-open mouth.

"Callie," it coos, in a voice made of raw meat and shredded metal. "Come down, *come down.*"

My phone buzzes again. I rear up out of sleep to clutch it. There are ten messages, each more worried than the last, asking if I'm okay. Words from the people who would hold me, trap me, keep me close between two narrow walls and make me breathe the stale air. I stumble across the room, gasping, and open my dresser. I shove the phone deep into a drawer.

I close my eyes again.

I drift.

Somewhere behind my eyelids, my mother's voice whispers, *Come down.* I open my arms beneath a starless sky, and tumble headfirst into the crashing dark.

Everything feels wrong.

Everything feels right.

CHAPTER 26

"I'M SORRY," I SAY.

It's not the first time. I reach for him, try to slide my hands over his shoulders and draw him close to me, but he ducks away and stares. His brows are knit together, slanted down. His face is worry, painted over with anger.

"Do you have any idea how worried I was?" he cries. "Not just me, Callie. Everyone! After what happened, we all thought—I mean, you couldn't even text me? You couldn't even answer your door?! I stood out there and knocked for thirty minutes!"

I know.

I heard him.

I heard him, and I hissed through my teeth, and dove back down into the dark.

"It was just the flu," I mumble.

Ben huffs with exasperation and turns away, saying, "I have to go to class. I'll see you later."

He doesn't kiss me good-bye.

He doesn't believe me.

I'm not sure I do, either.

I had woken on Sunday morning with my fever gone, my sheets soaked in sweat, no sense of how much time had passed. I came out of the haze to the sound of my father, tapping at my door, calling, "Callie? Can you eat some soup, do you think?"

I'd guzzled one bowl sitting up in bed, then peeled back the bedclothes and gone for seconds myself. My body felt tired but strong, as though I'd emerged victorious after hours of fighting an unseen foe in the dark.

It wasn't until I passed a calendar on the wall, stopping to pinpoint the date in my head, that I realized I'd lost four days.

"He'll get over it," Jana says, and shoves a plateful of french fries across the table. "And in the meantime, you're gonna eat these and you're not gonna argue. You look like a fucking skeleton."

I smile weakly and look across the courtyard. The rest of the group is huddled protectively around Ben, helping him nurse his grudge. Shanika scowls and makes a show of turning her back, while Mikah shrugs apologetically before reluctantly turning around.

"They'll get over it, too," she adds, reading my mind. "They're just protective of their baby, you know. He's like the kid brother they never had. It's fine. Eat."

The day is overcast, but the rain has held off; everyone has taken lunch outdoors, hedging their bets that the sky won't open. I reach for a fry but don't eat it, staring at one of the brick walls, trying to will back my memory of the last half week. The missed messages. The sound of Ben knocking frantically at the door. The discovery of my phone, inexplicably stuffed deep in my sock drawer, its battery drained to nothing from buzzing with worried alerts. I know I put it there, just as I know that I chose not to answer its insistent noise, just as I know that I lay in bed, half-conscious, and closed my eyes to the sound of Ben's pounding at the door. I know, but I don't know why; if I had a reason, it's been washed from my consciousness, without a trace left behind.

It doesn't make sense, and I say so.

What I don't say, don't tell, is how right it felt.

"You were delirious," Jana says, shrugging, and starts in on the fries herself. "Honey, come on. You can't keep beating yourself up about something you barely remember doing when you were sick as a dog and pumped full of drugs. I mean, I had oral surgery last year, and I was so hopped-up on Vicodin that I called Corey and told him I wanted to take his virginity."

I guffaw. "You did not."

She widens her eyes in mock seriousness. "Did too. You can ask him. I scared the kid to death!" She laughs. "Of course, I also told him I was the Grand High Empress of a roving band of pirates and that I'd been teaching my cat to speak Spanish, so he didn't take it too seriously."

I laugh in spite of myself. Jana nods encouragingly.

"Look, Ben knows you're sorry and you didn't mean it. He's just being a drama queen because he doesn't like admitting you scared the pants off him."

"Was he really worried?"

She laughs. "Like a Jewish grandma." She chortles, but then looks over her shoulder and frowns. "Just hang in there, okay? I know it sucks, but hey, that's just because you guys love each other."

I look miserably across the courtyard again; Ben looks back at me, holds eye contact for a moment, but then frowns and looks at the table.

"He doesn't look like he loves me." My voice sounds dark, harsh, but I can't help myself. "He looks like he hates my guts."

"Pfffft." Jana snorts. "Give him five minutes. Maybe an hour, at worst. I guarantee you, he'll be all over you again by tomorrow."

I shake my head.

"C'mon, Callie!" she cries, exasperated, then shoots me a devilish look. "It'll all be fine tomorrow. You know, *tomorrow?*" Her voice is getting louder, gaining pitch, gaining traction, and she begins to sing: "The sun'll come out, tomorrow, bet your bottom dollar thaaaaaat . . ."

And as she leaps onto the picnic table and begins serenading me, I look across the courtyard once more, and see Ben watching me. His mouth twitches, just a little.

I shrug.

And he smiles.

The afternoon is thick and humid as we cross the parking lot, hand in hand. When we reach Ben's car, he stops and presses me back against the passenger-side door, standing on tiptoe to kiss me.

"Oh, darling. Let's never fight again," he says, putting on a posh English accent and a mock-serious look. I feel a rush of gratitude for this moment, for the empty, unscheduled afternoon, for Ben's professed inability to stay angry at me. Even if it weren't me, I think, he's too forward-looking, too eager to move on to the next thing, to ever hold a grudge.

"All right," I say. I lean in, I let the heat settle over me, I feel his hands climbing my back and feel momentarily self-conscious at the sweat that's soaking my shirt.

When I pull away, he looks disappointed.

"Callie?"

"Sorry," I say. "I'm kind of . . . it's really hot."

He looks at me, worry falling like a shade again over his brow, and swallows.

"Look," he begins, and then pauses. I watch him gulp again, and realize that I'm watching him ready himself to ask a question he suspects he'd rather not know the answer to.

"Look," he says, again, "can you just tell me? I mean, was this another panic attack thing? Is that why you wouldn't talk to anyone, why you didn't want to see me?"

I feel a surge of irritation and try to cut him off. "I told you, it was just—" But he doesn't stop.

"Because you need to know that nobody cares about that. And even if they did, I wouldn't care about it. But if we're going to be together, you can't shut me out like this."

He stops, looks at me for reassurance. I wish I had more to give, wish I had a better explanation.

"I was just sick."

He looks at me, and I see hope flicker in his eyes before getting pushed away—by realism, by intelligence, by his inability to fool himself. His shoulders slump.

"It's not just this time," he says, quietly. "You've been different ever since that day at the pool. Things just don't feel the same, and I didn't say anything, because I didn't want to push you. But if you don't want this, or if this is about something I did, I'd just rather you told me—"

"No," I break in, so sharply that he falls silent. I grab hold of him, to reassure him, except it feels more like I'm trying to steady myself. To convince myself.

"No," I say, my voice softer. My face has grown hot, there are knots twisting in my stomach. I don't know how to tell him, I *can't* tell him, that when I look at him, everything feels exactly the same and yet utterly, horribly different. That the sight of him makes me feel like I'm being ripped in two.

But I try. I try.

"I do want this," I whisper. "But sometimes, it's also like I don't. I feel like I'm not supposed to, like it's not right, somehow. And it scares the shit out of me. You, and this relationship—it's like it doesn't belong to me, and I know it, and someone is going to make me give it back."

In the moments that follow, I watch him watching me and feel my heart racing at double time, feel the tension arc out from my center and send tremors through my lips, my fingertips, my knees. I've spoken the truth out loud, and I've never been more terrified.

He reaches up to stroke my hair.

"Okay," he says. "Well, I'll tell you what. Maybe it's not meant to be. Maybe you're not meant to ever have friends or a boyfriend or anyone, ever. Maybe fate wants you to die alone, surrounded by thousands of cats." He pauses, and smiles, but his eyes are serious. "But I'm telling you right now, I don't believe in fate. And furthermore, if that's what fate has in mind for you, then it can kiss my ass, because I've got better ideas."

He reaches past me to open the car door, and I sink into the passenger seat at the gentle pressure of his hand.

"Now, you and I are going on a date. Anywhere you want, as long as we can be back before Alan Twaddle, PhD, freaks out and calls the police. Okay?"

And as he looks at me, as I gaze back at him, I feel it.

The breath of a shadow of a remembered dream, the strange mix of fear and longing and sudden, reckless want.

The air moves with a sigh over my body. My breath comes to a shuddering standstill in my throat.

And inside me, the sleeping thing buried under my heart stirs just a little and whispers, *Yes*.

"Okay," I say.

"Tell me."

I do.

Now, says the voice inside, purring and settling deeper in. *Now, you are beginning to see.*

CHAPTER 27

THE CAR IS FULL OF NOISE as we roll southward, with the wind tugging insistently at my hair, the sky looming low and heavy with cloud cover. Ben's eyes keep darting in my direction, but he doesn't try to talk, only looks at me like he's hoping I'll speak and then looks at my hand like he wants to hold it. I close my eyes and feel grateful and guilty all at once.

I reach into my bag, feeling for the edges of the paper I retrieved from my locker, the one I've already covered halfway with hurried scrawl. I'll finish it when we reach our destination, I think. It'll be the reminder Nessa needs that I'm still here. That she needs to remember me, to write me, to not leave me all alone like this with a growing chasm at my center and things falling apart all around me. This letter, she won't be able to ignore.

Not when she sees what's on the page. Not when I tell her that something is happening, had already happened, that

I've heard the call of my life, like she said, and I'm afraid of what it might mean.

Not when she sees the telltale scatter of sand that's sure to find its way into the folded, careful creases on the page.

When she left, I'd almost believed that I'd never get there. That as close as we'd come, the stretching sands of the Panhandle coast would still be just beyond my reach. Not without Nessa there to guide me, not with my father still telling me, *No, not yet, be patient.* Not when I couldn't bring myself to defy him. Alone, I was a coward.

But I wasn't alone. Fate had delivered a surprise gift; it had given me a boy who cared for me, cared for me so much that he'd take me there, and hold my hand all the way to the water's edge.

What was it that Nessa had said? When destiny wants you badly enough, it gives you a way to get there.

The first tease of longing inside me has become a steady throb of want: the growing, insistent urge to find my way to the coast, to sprint with him over the cakey sand, to not stop running until the water breaks in lace-tipped waves over our burning feet. I feel that something is waiting for me where the ocean meets the shore—even if it's only memories, longing, my own desperate desire to get back a piece of what I've lost. To understand what my mother and Nessa seemed to know implicitly, without a doubt.

During those three fevered nights, I lay awake and snatched at splintered fragments that came floating out of the past, from the days before my father took us inland, trying to form a picture that makes sense: the sunlight on the water, Mama's legs draped long and white over the edge of the boat, the way her hair fanned out around her as she lay in the arms of the sea. How many times had I seen her like that? In my memory, she doesn't look like a woman who'd abandoned herself to the dangerous whims of the waves and current. She doesn't look like a woman at risk. In my memory, my mother's face is serene and smiling, comfortable and happy. The water breaking against the hull sounds like delicate laughter.

And why not? She was always in the water. And she had always found her way back to the boat, to me, to our house high up on the coast.

Nessa told me once that the sea had a voice. Could it have called out to my mother, too? Could she have believed that it would keep her safe?

My focus dissolves when Ben makes a grunting noise; there's a lurch and thud of a pothole beneath the tires. I force myself back to the present and gaze out at the passing land-scape. The car has slowed; the wind has lessened. The high-way has narrowed to a winding stretch of pale, white road, pocked here and there by deep holes filled with stagnant, filthy water. Trees crowd in on both sides, palms and pines that are hidden at their bases by a crush of close-knit green. On the right, a hand-painted sign advertising BOILED PENUTS points to a brief opening in the trees; I see the flash of a road curving away before the forest closes up and obscures it.

"Hey, boiled peanuts," he says, speaking for the first time. "You've probably never had those. Should we stop?"

I force myself to smile. "No thanks. Maybe on the way back."

He smiles back, and this time, he does reach for my hand. I watch him pick it up, seeing my fingers intertwining with his as though from a distance, as though the hand he's holding belongs to someone else. Even the pressure of his freckled fingers seems to be lightweight and far away. For a moment, our destination is forgotten. I bring myself back to this little anchored life. I close the empty space inside of me, I cover it over with promises of sunshine and conversation and lazy Saturday dates with this boy, who sees something in me and refuses to give up. Who loves me, I'm sure of it, and who will keep loving me—no matter how strange or how sick I get, no matter how uncertain my future. I focus on the weight of his hand, the heat, the remembered sensation of his lips against mine. *I could choose this, too,* I think. *This could be my life.*

I come close, so close.

But then he drops my hand, he says, "We're here," and the trees fall away from the road and the wind grows stronger again and the car is rolling to a stop while my breath dies to nothing in my throat.

From somewhere below us comes the sound, one I know from my memory and from my dreams. And in my head, the lines of my mother's hidden poem emerge to beat their rhythm against the inside of my skull.

Water, sucking the hollow ledges.

Even here, in the protected shallows of this Gulf Coast beach, I know this place. The smell of salt, the sound of water. The sea unfurls as far as I can see in every direction, an undulating blanket of blues and greens and browns, until it all blends together and then breaks, vanishing at the far-off meeting where the sky dips down to kiss the earth's curve. Even here, where the waves are not the crashing beasts of the Pacific coast but delicate, tentative overtures against the sand, it is as deep and endless as I remembered.

Tons of water, striking the shore.

It's not until I feel Ben's hand on my shoulder that I realize I'm no longer in the car, that I've fallen to my knees in the sand. Through swimming eyes, I see the pale ovals of strangers' faces turned in my direction.

"Let's take a walk," he says.

I don't answer, but let him take my hand. My eyes stay ahead, focused on the horizon, as my heart opens wide, wider, bursting in all directions and vanishing into the rush and whisper of the never-ending surf.

What do they long for, as I long for, one salt smell of the sea once more?

CHAPTER 28

WHEN I GAZE OUT at the sprawling surface of the ocean, the light ripple of that undulating blue answers back like a thousand tiny, waving hellos. I press my eyes open against the wind, brace my palms against the rough wooden platform under me, lean forward to feel the salt spray in the air and on my face. How could I have forgotten the way this feels? This was how we sat, tangled together in the afternoon sun, my mother's chest against my back and our legs splayed ahead in identical Vs. She'd held me close as we watched the ocean flirt its way up the smooth brown beach, kissing our feet with playful foam and then burying our heels in the sand. She would hold me there for hours, letting the water lick high and higher, laughing with me when the rising tide began to run up the insides of her thighs, shrieking and scrambling to hold me aloft when a big wave came rushing up to slap us and knock us down.

Behind me, there's a grunt as Ben moves to sit beside me. He's trying to brush away the grains of sand that are clinging to his feet, beating at them with his peeled-off sock. His toes are knobby and bone white, sprouting here and there with wiry red hairs that grow in a line toward his ankles.

"I guess this would be a good time to mention that I'm not actually much of a beach person," he says, giving up and tossing the sock aside. I look at him—glasses smeared with salt spray, the part in his hair already reddening with sunburn.

"I'm shocked," I say, and he smiles. When I turn my eyes back to the gulf, he moves up to sit beside me, letting the length of his leg press against mine. I had taken his hand and let him lead me here, while I kept my gaze on the sea and felt the sand shifting underfoot. The broad, flat beach, and the people on it, are out of sight beyond the coastline's curve; we're alone here, back from the water and with a cluster of tall pines at our backs. The sand is littered with cones and needles. It's not until I see a condom wrapper, half-buried and with one torn corner wagging in the wind, that I realize: this sheltered wooden platform with its peaked roof—a structure that might have once served as a lifeguard stand but now sits abandoned and covered in graffiti—is a make-out spot. A couples spot.

I feel frightened without understanding why.

I look up, sharply, to find Ben staring at me. He's waiting for an answer to a question I didn't hear him ask.

"Sorry?"

"I asked if this was anything like the ocean where you grew up. The place you told me about." His tone is casual, but his eyes flick sideways, and I feel a sudden surge of impatience with this game—the one where he hints but never asks, where he tries to draw me out like a skittish cat.

"It was rougher there. And rockier," I say. "There were cliffs."

Beside me, he nods and resumes brushing at the sand that clings to his feet, his arms. The grains are stubborn; for every one that loosens and scatters, ten simply shift positions, transferring themselves from his arms to his hands and then back again. I watch him for a moment, then turn my gaze back to the sea. My lips curl back in a wry smile, and when I speak again, it's more to myself than to him.

"That's the same though, anyway," I murmur. "No matter where you are, the sand gets into everything."

And I would know. Oh, I'd know. I think of Nessa's letters, spilling California earth from their dog-eared creases. Or her car, the one with the salt stains on the seats, the gritty upholstery. I remember the entrance of our onetime house, the dark, warped floorboards that creaked hello, and the way a hundred sweepings couldn't stop the ever-present sprinkle of sand. Nobody's feet could stay calloused for long when we paced back and forth across that threshold, burnishing our soles on the stray remains of the beach until the grains turned small enough to sift down through the floorboards.

I remember thinking that all that sand would grow there, under the house, sprinkle by sprinkle. Small bits of shell and rock, fish bones and driftwood, piled millions upon billions until the foundations were buried and the house sat atop its own dune, and until the dune became its own beach. That one day, we'd be able to fling open the door, leap, and slide—down, down our own self-made hill of sand, smooth and steep and soft, down and down and down to the place where the powder-fine earth met the sea.

I remember.

Something rises up, suddenly buoyant, breaking on the surface of my mind so swiftly that my vision swims before me.

I remember.

Because sometime in that year before she died, something had changed. Our long afternoons at the beach became less frequent, sporadic, then stopped altogether. Instead, my mother would press her finger to my lips—*Shhhh, it's our secret, I'll be back soon*—and leave me in front of the television while she vanished for hours on end. And not long before the day she disappeared forever, there had been a day when my mother banged into the house at a sprint, and hauled a never-before-seen vacuum cleaner from a closet under the stairs. I remember it: the way her hair hung water-logged, coiling on her neck. The frantic pass of the whirring hose with its gaping plastic mouth, back and forth, back and forth, over the crunchy floorboards. The way her dress clung to her body, soaked and sheer and clutching at her legs, until she suddenly stripped and flung it aside, letting it smack heavily against the floor. Her skin, taut and pale, puckered with the sudden cold like a plucked goose, and there were marks on her body: slender welts that must have stung when they touched the water, three long lines of hurt that rose from her thighs, her back, from each forearm, and that she ignored even as they flared an angry red. Her eyes, darting to the wall clock and back to the floor, as she cursed the intractable sand and then turned, grasped her dress, and fled up the stairs, with water pattering down behind her. She never saw me standing there.

She never even looked.

I remember the way that the windowpanes in my bedroom tapped and clattered in their moorings as my father's voice scraped down the hallway like cold, gray steel. The wind on the coastline is tricksy and sly; in our house, it bounced our would-be private dialogues up the stairs and around corners, keeping us from keeping secrets.

"You left her alone again," he said.

"Don't lie to me," he said. "I know you did. I always know. Did you hurt yourself again?"

I couldn't hear her, only him. Only that metallic, emotionless drone, the voice that was a solid dam through which no emotion could pass.

"How can I trust you?" he said. "After the last time, you promised me! You promised me you'd stay with Callie! And then the moment my back is turned . . ."

The sly wind buried Mama's voice, but his came back stronger than ever.

"You're goddamn right, I don't understand! This isn't just about you! Maybe the harm you do to yourself doesn't matter, but don't you realize you're putting your child in danger? *Our* child?! Now give me your word that you'll stop this, Maera!"

The wind stopped, then. It rushed against my windows and died in a drawn-out sigh, a low note that sounded like sobbing. And in the silence that followed, I heard my mother's anguished cry.

"I promise," she'd sobbed. "I promise, I promise."

And my father began shouting, then, but I heard her scream, all the same.

"I still have time," she cried, in a voice that wailed like the wind beneath the eaves, ragged and raw, and full of terror.

"But you have to promise! Swear it, Alan! Swear that you won't ever, ever go down there!"

"What are you thinking about?" Ben asks. He's moved closer to me, his leg set firmly against mine and his fingertips creeping around to grip my waist. I can feel his breath close to my ear, dry and hot. I can feel him pressing into the shrinking space, obliterating the distance in between us. And when he does, I think, he's going to kiss me, and pull me down in the sand. His want is as loud and unignorable as the shrieking of the gulls that glide and swoop overhead and scream for scraps from the far-off crowd.

"Nothing," I say, and sigh. I turn to let my lips meet his. I lie, and lose myself in the taste of his mouth.

I've gotten good at keeping secrets.

She kept her secrets too, my mother. But my father knew. He knew the way that people who love you always know, the way that makes them dangerous. Because there is no hiding, when your lover is the sea. It leaves its scent in your hair and its taste on your skin. It tiptoes after you, following the salty trail of your footsteps, spilling behind you through the door, and nestling in the floorboards. It is too big, too bold, too changeable and brash to keep a confidence. And though somewhere, a girl named Callie Morgan is being kissed, and kissing back—though her pulse is racing at the touch of his lips, though she sighs and puts her hands in his hair and lets gravity pull her down—I don't hear his whispered words. I don't hear the rustle of fabric under eager hands. I don't hear the beating of my heart, or his, or anyone's.

My head rolls to the side, my open eyes look out toward the wind-tossed, churning water. My ears are full of the sound of breaking waves. They will crash against this place forever, never changing, never ceasing, while people live and love and die here on the shore. And somewhere, even as my voice whispers its own response to the promises of a love-struck boy, I know better than to believe myself. Nessa was right: there's more to life than love. So much more. How could I not realize, when the true meaning of forever is right before my eyes?

CHAPTER 29

INLAND, THE VOICE OF THE SEA GROWS DIM. It dies away, in your ears and in your heart, replaced by the breath of the arid wind, the skittering chorus of grasses that plant their feet in the sun-cracked earth, the soothing hum of machines that live indoors. The air turns dry and thin, the ground is hard underfoot.

Inland, far from the crash and spray and squall of the coast, the voice of the sea fades away. You forget how it sounded, forget that it even had a sound. You look out your doorway and see land. Forested, rocky, mountainous, or just simply there, flat and dull and solid, stretching like a yawn out to the place where the sky touches down. Inland, water is a thing to be contained: in sewers and reservoirs, in hoses that lie untouched during times of drought. Water is what you bathe in; what you drink; what sits, still and dull and flat in a glass vessel or gleaming pipe, patient and under control.

You forget that somewhere out there, the earth becomes soft and then disappears, dissolving under the lacework edges of the waves.

But it does. Seventy-one percent of the earth is covered by water. Start out in any direction, and if you go far enough, you will come to the end of the landlocked world. You will step off the edge and find yourself swallowed, up to your ankles, your knees, your neck, by the pliant mouth of the sea.

And out there, beyond the breakers, when land has faded from a gray mass in the mist to an outline in your memory, you'll remember. You'll look to all sides, and see only ocean. Directionless, endless, everywhere the same. And as you slip below the surface, as you leave no trace behind, you'll remember: that the sea has a voice. That it whispers, laughs, roars.

That if you let it, if you trust it, it will hold you in its arms.

I lie back in the water.

When the waves lick at my ears, it sounds like laughter. It sounds like a love song. It sounds like they're saying my name.

The kissing had gone on and on, until my shoulder blades and elbows began to ache where they pressed against the platform. How long, I didn't know; I kept losing focus, gazing out at the tossing sea and letting my mind drift away, only to suddenly surge and slam against the immediacy of his mouth, his hands, the feel of his leg pressing down between my own. I was sweating again, and my lips had begun to swell.

"Hey," I'd said, pressing him back, and then pushing again when he ducked in to kiss me again. The muscles in my shoulders tensed with strength that surprised me, and him too; he lost his balance, rolled back, his hands tightened and gripped against my skin. One at the small of my back and the other gently grazing the strap under my T-shirt that wouldn't budge any lower, no matter how he pulled and pulled. Instead, he'd pressed his hands against my back, pressing his body harder against mine, moaning softly against the skin of my neck. I felt unexpectedly grateful for Nessa's decision to buy me a one-piece bathing suit, thankful to the firm elastic for being its own barrier and sparing me from having to say yes or say no, for letting me say nothing at all. For saving me from having to think, speak, decide, when the thing I wanted, the only thing, was what I'd come here for.

"Come on," I said.

"Come on where?" he'd asked. His plaintive voice felt like a splinter, scraping at a raw spot I didn't know I had, and I shook my head and stood.

"Callie, where are you going?"

"In."

I hadn't waited. I couldn't wait. I'd left him two steps behind me, then ten, twenty, peeling away my shirt and jeans and stepping into the water. It snapped at my ankles, colder than I'd thought, until the next moment when the gooseflesh disappeared from my body and I didn't think it cold at all. Air bubbles flecked in the narrow lines between my toes, freed themselves and disappeared. I looked at the place where my legs stopped and then started again, broken in two refracted pieces at the shins, feeling the waves rise and fall like colorless silk on my skin. Behind me, Ben had given up on asking me to be reasonable, given up saying "Hang on" and "Wait, are you sure?" He groaned, and began shedding layers.

"There were warning flags back at the beach, you know," he muttered. "But I guess we don't care about that."

I'd turned around, and looked at him with eyes that didn't feel like mine. The black presence opened wide, danced into the foreground, moved to press itself against the windows of my eyes. For a moment, I saw him from two perspectives. One clear and bright, thrown into sharp light-and-shadow contrast as the sun broke briefly through the clouds and blazed briefly on his face. He smiled, with familiar sweetness, and for a fleeting moment I thought of stepping out of the water, of leading him back to the platform, of lying with him as the sun went down and our naked bodies were blanketed in shadow.

And then, as I watched, the view changed. Darkened. A shade had fallen, over the sun and inside my head, and I saw him again—the unseemly glare of his white ankles against the sand, the ungainly splay of his legs, the way he grunted as he dug through a backpack for his swimsuit. Small and slow, and not worth waiting for.

As if any man was worth waiting for.

As if any man could be.

I had turned my back on him and thrown myself into the waves.

Ben calls my name again, and I look back in irritation. I am jealous of this moment; I don't want to share it with him or with anyone. The sea changes directions and slaps my face, gently, teasing me. I close my eyes against the spray and drop below the surface, pulling myself through the dancing, shifting light that pierces the deep green world below, leaving the shore behind. Over and over, I dive and drift and surface. My body is sleek and perfect in the water; I slice through it like a knife. Why should I look back? There is nothing there for me to see.

There is nothing there for me.

Somewhere, I hear Ben splash and splutter as he tries to keep up. Somewhere, a distant voice that sounds like mine whispers, *You should turn back. He's not a strong swimmer.* But that voice is far away, muffled, barely even there. Like someone shouting underwater from the shallows by the far-away shore. It's easy to ignore her. Easy to forget him.

It's easy to forget everything. I understand that now. What she felt, my mother, when she stripped the sails and slipped over the side. I lie back again in the salt embrace, treading lightly, feet pedaling and pushing against the end-less azure nothing below. She used to tell me that it was so lovely. So light. That the sea is like a cushion, a bed made out of sun glimmer and spray. That one day, someday soon, I would be old enough to swim beside her. That we would dive down together, cutting the water like quicksilver, our hands reaching for the deep and our feet tipped toward the surface. Fluttering like pale wings in the sun-dappled blue. Swimming down deeper, down into the dark, until it all turned black. She said I couldn't imagine it, how wonderful it feels.

I close my eyes.

But I can imagine, I think. *Mama, I can.*

The splutter has turned into a shout. The sound of Ben's voice tears the fabric of my thoughts, breaks through the mesmerizing babble and murmur of the waves, and I startle, disoriented, my eyes peeling away from the sky overhead and seeing for the first time just how far away I am from the shore. Just how far we've drifted down the beach, and out to sea, and how the peaked roof of the old lifeguard stand is only a silhouette in the distance. Just how tiny Ben looks surrounded by the water, a small, scared face peering out from between the waves. The water is growing rougher, the wind stronger. Overhead, columns of rising clouds are clustering on the horizon. I swim a few strokes back toward land and feel my muscles strain against the moving sea. We are caught in water with a mind of its own, with a destination somewhere far out in the gulf. In my head, I hear Nessa's dreamy voice warning of rip currents and undertow, saying, "We should wait until you're a stronger swimmer."

But I am. I am stronger, I am strong. I pull harder, and the water pushes back, until I realize that I'm swimming in place. That I can equal the strength of the current, but not overcome it. That my only hope is to let myself drift, follow it where it leads me, and hope that the sea lets me go. And it will, I think. I only have to wait, only have to be patient. I have the strength to make it back to shore; I only have to save it.

But Ben doesn't. I look at his face, and the guilt hits me with near-physical force. He's not a beach person, not a sea person, not a sailor or a swimmer. Ben hasn't learned

Nessa's lessons—about trusting the water, letting it hold you. He will fight it until he drowns. Why did I let him follow me? Why didn't I turn back?

"Callie!" he shouts again, only this time the shout is a scream. Raw and bright and unfiltered. The sound of a person who's abandoned all pretense of being brave, a person who's scared and in over his head, who cries out at the feeling of panic climbing atop his shoulders and digging its claws in deep.

I stare back at him in horror.

Ben is scared.

Ben is struggling.

I have led him out too deep.

I knife my hands into a breaking wave and pull, kicking furiously, closing the distance between us. The sea is drawing him away from me even as I charge against it; I can see his arms floundering, can see the water trying to sneak in at the corners of his mouth.

"Stop!" I yell, and his head snaps around to look at me. What I see makes my stomach turn: not just fear, but exhaustion, painted in purple half-moons underneath his eyes. He is struggling, growing weak, and has been for a while. Maybe even since the moment we began to swim. I can see it in the quiver of his mouth, the way that his lips have gone purple and his teeth have begun to chatter. How can he be so cold in the same water that feels like blissful nothing against my skin? How can his voice be hoarse with effort, when he's barely even spoken?

"We're too far out," he says weakly, and tries to stroke toward the shore. He can't even lift his arms out of the water, and it seems to mock him in response, throwing up a white-capped eddy that strikes the back of his head and then shoves him back even farther. The beach has receded, the sunbathers are anonymous specks scurrying for their cars. One stands at the water's edge and looks out toward us, toward the horizon, shielding both eyes. A storm is coming, and we will be alone in the water.

"Listen," I say, and my voice breaks. I try to remember Nessa's words, try to make my reassurance firm and low like hers. For all the terror in Ben's eyes, my heartbeat is slow and my mind is clear. I still believe, I realize, that everything will be all right.

I ignore the voice inside me that whispers, *Your mother was sure, too.*

I can save him, I can help him save himself, I only need him to trust me. I kick closer, treading water.

"Ben, stop pulling. This is a riptide, you can't swim through it. We're going to move"—I lift a hand above the surface, point at a barely there angle across the water in the same direction as the current is pulling—"that way. We'll make our way back a little at a time, do you understand? We can't swim through this, we have to swim *with* it, okay? And we'll stop to rest whenever you get tired."

The weak laugh that bubbles from between his lips makes me more nervous than any panicked scream.

"Oh, sure," he gasps between kicks. "We'll just lie down . . . on that sofa . . . you brought for the occasion, right?"

I close the distance between us and reach out to grab his arm. I can feel him trembling under my hand.

"I'm serious. You get tired, then you lie on your back and breathe, okay? You can stop and float any time you want. And if you can't, you can hang on to me."

I can tell that he doesn't believe me. I decide not to give him a choice. I turn, saying, "Let's go," knowing—hoping—that he'll follow my lead. He'll see that I'm right. And everything, everything will be okay.

I feel a rush of relief as I take one stroke, then another, kicking behind me with legs that feel like well-oiled pistons. Swimming this way, without fighting the current, the water is a gentle support instead of an impenetrable obstacle. It'll be fine, easy even, and I call over my shoulder to tell him so.

"See?" I yell. "It's not bad, it'll be fine."

He doesn't answer.

I turn to say it again, and the words die on my lips.

Behind me, the sea ruffles indifferently in the strengthening breeze.

Water, gray and grim and unbroken in every direction.

Ben is gone.

I scream and plunge forward, down, spreading my arms wide and pulling with everything I have into the deep blue-green world below. The light is weak, but I see him immediately, his skin cadaver-white against the murk, drifting deeper even as he struggles in waterlogged slow motion. He kicks and waves his arms, useless, going nowhere but down, his chin straining toward the sky and eyes bright with terror. I reach for him, and his fingers close around my wrist. A cascade of bubbles pours out of his open mouth and fly upward; I feel them dance along my body as they chase each other toward the surface.

His next breath, if he takes one, will not be made of air.

I keep my grip and try to flip my body lengthwise, to use my legs and kick us both to safety, even as his weight pulls us both down. Mentally, I calculate how long it's been since I dove; how long since that last breath streaked silver out of Ben's lungs. Too long. Too long. I heave his body upward as I snap my legs closed.

I feel air on my face, hear the cough and heave beside me as he drags air into his lungs.

His hand disappears from mine.

The roar of water in my ears subsides long enough for me to hear the wind, the screaming of the gulls. And something else: shouting. A white speck veers sharply toward me, growing bigger, becoming a small boat with a man waving frantically from the helm. My shriek for help, metallic and tearing out of my throat so hard that my eardrums rattle, tastes like salt.

A wave slaps my face, hard and angry, shoving me underwater. I don't see Ben. I don't see anything. I'm not being swallowed by the sea, I am being smothered by it. Chewed. Eaten alive by the frothing water with the sounds of screaming coming from somewhere nearby.

The waves push me down again, and this time, I cannot fight back.

There's no weightlessness, no serenity, only pain and panic and no air and my body, too heavy to float.

And then I see him.

I see him for only a moment.

Ben is suspended in the water. Mouth open in a wordless shout, eyes on me. It's only when he reaches for me that I know, for sure, he's still alive. I stretch my own hands toward him. The distance between us closes, and I feel my fingers brush his. I want to tell him to fight, to kick, to get above water where help is coming. I want to tell him that I'm sorry, that I was selfish, that I should never have dragged him into my life or into the sea. I want to press my mouth against his, and fill his lungs with whatever air I have left.

And though I can't say any of it, though my voice is silenced by the weight of so much water against my lips, his eyes widen as he looks at me. As though he understands. As though my thoughts are loud enough to travel through the shifting shades of green between us, to find their way to him.

For a moment, I still believe it all will be all right.

And then something moves past me, quickly. I feel it brush my shoulder. I feel it touch my face. My hair swirls over my eyes, and behind it, I see shifting shapes, a flash of movement, the slow curl of something dark.

There is something in the water.

There is blood in the water.

And from somewhere, a sly voice that sounds so very much like mine whispers, *Breathe*.

I open my mouth, and the sea rushes in.

CHAPTER 30

MY ROOM IS FULL OF DOCTORS. Doctors who look like doctors, faceless nameless bodies wearing stethoscopes and knee-length coats. One of them looks at me, and then looks away just as quickly. Sharp is here somewhere; I hear his voice stabbing through the air and his pen jabbing at my chart, but everything is out of focus. Bleary, dreamy, drifting. I open my eyes, then open them again not knowing when I closed them, not knowing how much time has passed. The light in the hospital never changes. It is always bright, white, blaring.

They say that I came close, so close, to drowning. They say that when they pulled me out, my lungs were like wet paper bags in my chest, my skin like ivory ice. They don't say anything about the boy, the one who was with me, the one who vanished before my eyes and left his blood in the water.

My father stands away from the bed, cold and motionless among the whirring machines, and doesn't look at me. I can feel his anger, though—feel it humming through the floor, up the silver length of the IV stand, down the translucent tube that disappears into the bruising crook of my elbow. It shimmers in the air and makes the bed tremble, makes me shiver so violently that the nurses think I'm cold, bring me blankets, and tuck me in up to my chin. His face is gray, grave, motionless. I ask if he's called Nessa, if she knows that I'm here; he shakes his head and looks away.

I ask if Ben is here, if he's all right, if I can see him.

When I say Ben's name, the nurses exchange glances and press their lips together. I ask again, and again, begging, until my breath begins to wheeze and whistle and my father steps out of the background. He fixes his obsidian glare somewhere just over my head. His voice floats out from between teeth clamped hard together.

"He's alive," he says.

"There was something in the water," I say.

The nurse says, "It's the drugs. She should rest."

My bed tips back of its own accord, my eyes roll back toward unconsciousness. Away from the hissing and beeping, away from the vibration of my father's disappointment, away from the too-bright lights that never turn off. And they let me.

Nobody demands that I tell them the truth.

Nobody wants to know if I remember what happened there, under the churning sea.

And it's just as well, because I won't tell. Not this time. I won't hammer at their indifference, won't insist on being heard. I will keep this secret, the one whispered to me from the black space within, the purring awareness that opened wide as I sank into the water.

Because in the movies, drowning is the most undignified of deaths. Flailing, panicking, thrashing, and fighting. It's a victim caught under the surface, a frantic Saint Vitus's dance in the deep, one that goes on and on until there's no air left. No choice but to try to breathe, and then to die trying. It's terror, torment, a mouth open forever in a silent scream.

But that's not how it happens at all. I knew then, and I know now. And when I slip down into the dead warmth of sleep, I feel my lips curl in momentary bliss. Because this is how it happens. A slow descent, and then a moment of darkness.

In the silence under the tossing waves, it feels like going home.

Somewhere, a machine hisses and beeps; somewhere, two people mutter quickly in conversation. Their voices cut through the fog: tragic tones, but blurred at the edges by breathless excitement. Something terrible has happened. Terrible and thrilling. I close my eyes and focus on their words.

"A shark?"

"We thought so, at first . . . the boy's wounds . . ."

The boy. There was a boy. Behind my closed eyes, I see his pale face, his open mouth. I see the crimson spread, drifting dark in the undersea currents, curling like spilled ink. I try to say his name, *Ben*, but my lungs sear with pressure and pain and nothing comes out but a croak. Unconsciousness swims up around me and I collapse back into it, thinking, I'll try again when I wake up. When I wake up, it all will be okay.

The muttering is moving. My eyelids are too heavy to see who it is, to follow them where they're going. The voice drifts near to my bed and hovers in the darkness.

"Watch her," someone says. "Something's not right."

When I wake up, nothing will ever be right again.

CHAPTER 31

IT TAKES THEM THREE DAYS to expel me from Ballard.

The headmaster folds his hands in front of him and gazes at me. His mouth pulled down at the corners, his eyes glazed over with shallow disapproval. We've met once before, when I first enrolled, but I can tell that he doesn't remember. It doesn't matter now. I can see him looking at me and seeing something else. Not a person, just a problem—trouble without a name, just one more kid who broke the rules and doesn't belong. My file is open beneath his palms; he keeps looking down at it, frowning, as though he expects it to explain what happened. As though somewhere, among the yellowed transcripts and my last semester's grades, there was a hidden prophecy of terrible things to come.

Beside me, my father presses two fingers into the place between his eyebrows, and sighs into the cover of his palm. The headmaster looks at me but doesn't see me; my father doesn't look at me at all. In the hour that we've sat here, side by side in stern chairs, through discussions and debate and then this—the decision that will see me out of this office, through the front door, armed with a black mark on my record and a warning never to return—I have seen him only in profile.

The headmaster clears his throat, and I watch the sound as it travels through his face. He's a tall man, built thick through the shoulders and neck, with skin that wags and sags beneath his disappearing chin. It quivers when he coughs, and he glances down at my file again, then up at the clock on the wall. Wanting it to be over. Somewhere behind the tired eyes and grimacing mouth, I can see shades of the athlete he might have been once, back before the passage of time and a desk-bound job padded his body with flesh, before exhaustion and the endless parade of troubled teenagers through his air-conditioned office made puffy, sallow pouches underneath his eyes. Somehow, I know that once we've left, he will pull a nearly full bottle of brown whiskey from its hiding place in the corner of his desk drawer, press his lips around its small, round mouth, and drink until the memory of this meeting goes fuzzy around the edges.

He spreads his hands—the ones he says are tied in this matter, bound up by protocol and procedure, zero tolerance, no exceptions—and says, "I'm sorry, but in cases like this, our policy is to expel the student even if no criminal charges are brought. We have to be consistent."

My father's voice is cold and tired. "I assume we have the option of contesting this decision."

The man clears his throat again, looks again toward the clock, looks longingly toward the drawer that holds the bottle.

"There is an appeals process," he says, and coughs nervously. "But, sir, if I may—I think it might be advisable if you don't, er, what I mean to say is, the boy's parents have suggested that it would be best for everyone . . ."

"If Callie doesn't come back," my father finishes flatly.

The headmaster spreads his hands again, and for a moment, he looks almost sorry.

"Let's just say that David and Eliza Barrington aren't the type to let something like this stand. I know Callie may not be charged, but there could still be a civil suit."

I cough, and his gaze settles on me. He shifts uncomfortably in his seat, the apologetic look disappears, the flat mask of disapproval returns. But before it does, I see it: I see him see me, and just for a moment, I see fear. I watch it flash in his eyes, dilate his pupils, press his lips into a taut, tense line.

And then it's gone, and he looks out at me again from within the safe cocoon of his authority, his place as disciplinarian, his power to make me go and never come back.

He says, "And frankly, Ballard isn't an appropriate place for someone with your daughter's . . . tendencies."

"I didn't hurt him," I say, and my father sighs. "Callie, please be quiet."

The headmaster looks at the drawer again, and this time, he licks his lips. I watch his pink tongue dart out once, twice, and think about leaping across the table, reaching into his mouth, and tearing it out at the root.

He says, "You don't really expect us to believe that."

When we stand to leave, he opens the door to his office and then puts it between himself and us as my father leads the way out. One more barrier, one more inch of distance, one more vestige of separation put between me and a world that believes the worst. My friends are gone, my messages go unreturned. They all think it's true, too. In the hallway, Eric Keller and Meredith Hartman are coming around a corner when I pass. They see me and stop short, breaking off midsentence as suddenly as if an invisible shield had come down between us. She whispers quickly to him, and they step back in wary unison, hugging the wall. She meets my eyes and smirks; he keeps his gaze glued to the floor. If he was on my side once, he isn't anymore.

When they think you've tried to kill someone, nobody wants to get too close.

It was the Barringtons who marched into my hospital room, swooping down like black-suited birds of prey, turning a hushed conversation between my father and several doctors into a squawking melee. I woke to the sounds of chaos, the doorway to my room crammed with people, an explosion of clutching hands and shouting mouths, so many people at once that I could see only body parts, hospital scrubs, somebody's watch cracking hard against the doorjamb. With my vision swimming, I had tried to remember which hospital this was, thinking desperately, *Where am I,* until my frantic brain reeled backward and I found myself believing that this was Laramie, that we had never left, that I had slept too long in the dreamless, drugged-up sleep of Dr. Frank's pediatric ward. That the raised voices and rushing feet all around me were the nurses, rushing to the side of someone who had coded in the night.

And then the flickering awareness, that nesting, purring blackness, came awake inside of me and the memories slammed home.

You know where you are, it said.

And then, so slyly and quietly that I wondered if someone had crept up behind to whisper it in my ear: *And you know what's coming, don't you?*

When the couple in black broke through the crush at the door, I felt my guts twist like coiling ice. Everything else in the room disappeared; it was only them and me, the man glaring down as I shrank into the thin bedclothes, his wife by his side. I knew without asking that I was looking at Ben's parents. I could see him in their faces, in his father's pointed chin and deep-set eyes, in his mother's patrician brow line, her auburn hair, her forehead dotted with freckles. But it wasn't their familiar features that filled me with dread; it was the familiar way they were knit together, full of the anger and exhaustion I'd seen in the faces of so many hospital parents. The same tired skin around the eyes, the same deep lines carved by worry and fear. I knew without asking that they'd been here for days, sitting by the bedside of someone they loved, sleeping in shifts on two chairs pushed together and struggling not to break down when the doctors used words that they didn't understand.

Ben was alive, that was what they'd told me.

For the first time, I wondered what they hadn't.

When I moved to sit up, the woman raised her hand to stop me. I watched her fingers float into the air, saw her wristwatch slide down a delicate, small-boned arm toward the wrinkled cuff of her shirt. It had been rolled up hastily, but I could see the coffee stains peeking out here and there, the product of shaky hands and anxious pacing in the hospital cafeteria.

"So you're Callie," she said, quietly.

"You're Ben's mom," I said, the words tumbling out. "Aren't you? Please, tell me, is he—"

She raised her hand again, this time a soft request for silence. For a moment, she only stared at me, breathing softly through her mouth and swaying ever so slightly on her feet. I had the time to peer toward the floor, to wonder if she was still wearing heels or if she'd already made the hospital parent's pragmatic decision to wear only soft-soled shoes, the kind that didn't *click* angrily against the linoleum and wake up the resting patients. I had time to imagine her in a chair, stocking feet tucked beneath her, leaning forward to hold Ben's limp, cold hand as he slept in a bed just like mine.

Above me, Eliza Barrington's lips curled in the barest suggestion of a smile. She leaned forward, gripping the rail of my bed.

"I thought you'd be prettier," she said, and spat in my face.

My father appeared then, a firm hand coming up and over the woman's shoulder, whirling her to face him with teeth bared and mouth contorted in rage. Raised voices echoed in the close space as I reached up to feel the slick wetness on my cheek, as all eyes in the room turned to the jumbled

cacophony of competing shouts and someone dialed secu-
rity and a passing nurse appeared in the doorway saying,
"What in the hell?" then gawked, turned, and ran. For a
moment, their angry voices were a wall of sound, nothing
but froth and nonsense syllables—and then, suddenly, fragments began to break loose and make their way to my ears:

"—attacked our son—"

"—you've got some nerve—"

"—witnesses said—"

"—mean to press charges—"

"—don't understand—"

"—have to question her—"

"—been searched for a weapon—"

—Until somewhere, inside my head, a terrible understanding began to take shape. An image that was clear and
bright and horrible, that made no sense and at the same time
seemed like the only answer, the only possible reason that
these people could be here and be so angry. The shouting
rose to a crescendo, and I thrust my hands over my ears and
screamed.

"Stop it!"

In the silence that followed, I could taste blood on the
back of my tongue. My voice was like nails on slate, echoing
back off the walls and windows and scrolling screens of the
monitors. Someone gasped and the knot of people by my

bed stopped moving, stopped speaking all at once; all their black eyes, in all their pale faces, turned to look my way. When I spoke again, it was half whimper, half hiss.

"I didn't hurt anyone," I whispered, and felt my voice break. "I didn't mean to swim out so far. I was helping him get back to shore. Ask Ben, he'll tell you! I know he'll remember!"

Ben's mother appeared again, stepping forward to the side of my bed. She looked at me and laughed, a high, hysterical giggle that twisted her lips into a sneer. Her voice, low and smug, floated out from between her teeth.

She said, "Who do you think told us what you did?"

But it's not just Ben; the men who pulled us from the ocean all agree on what they saw. They say that they slowed the boat at the place where the water still rippled, peered into the churning depths where Ben and I had disappeared, that they looked through an ocean like clouded glass and saw a swirling mess of blood and hair and limbs. They say I was clawing at him, pulling him down, that I glared out from the curtain of my drifting hair with eyes gone cold and angry. That when they reached for him, I grabbed him by the ankle and tried to drag him with me, down into the airless, drowning deep. That when they hauled him up and away and onto the deck, they wondered whether they shouldn't just leave me. It was only one man, whose conscience couldn't take it, who saw me drifting there below the surface and decided to reach into the water once more. He pulled me out by my hair. My scalp has swelled in the aftermath, with plum-colored bruises blooming just under the surface and bald patches near the crown where the hair ripped out at the root.

On the morning that they released me from the hospital, as we drove to the meeting where the headmaster would tell us that I'd been expelled from Ballard, my father handed me a shopping bag with a scarf in it and said the first words he'd spoken to me in nearly two days: "Put this on."

Now, he slams the car door and twists the keys in the ignition. He stays silent as we pass out of the parking lot, around the single lane that circles the oak tree, under the dappled shade of the leaves and the gentle, swaying overhang of Spanish moss. He takes the turn with precision, his hands in perfect ten-two position on the wheel. We take one road, and another, until the school is long gone behind us and a red traffic light commands the car to stop. It's only then that he looks at me, and I realize that he's been steeling himself for this moment. Working up the nerve to turn and truly see me, sitting here. I shudder at what I see: something beyond disapproval, something even more cold and removed than the smug authority of the man who called me a liar. I thought he'd be angry. This is worse.

"Dad, please believe me, I didn't—" I begin, and I see a muscle twitch in his jaw. He shakes his head so hard that I hear the bones pop.

"I don't care whether you did it or not," he says, and his voice makes my hair stand on end. "All this time, I told myself it was going to be okay. I told myself you were okay." He shakes his head, and his voice breaks. "I told myself you hadn't inherited whatever it was, whatever made her so reckless, so obsessed. God, I'd even started wondering if the problem was me! If I was being too overprotective!"

At first, I don't know who he means; my mind casts out in search of the woman he didn't want me to become, and I think, *Nessa?* But inside me, the darkness is awake and whispering. It's there all the time now, eyes wide-open, curling like a snake against the warm, close curves of my mind. And though I fight against it, though I struggle not to know what it knows, I feel another name rise unbidden to my lips. I press them together in horror, in protest; I think, I won't say it, you can't make me say it.

And I don't. I don't have to. He does it for me, turning his eyes back to the road as the light turns green, as we roll away through a landscape of strip malls, tire warehouses, check-cashing storefronts blinking neon in the late-morning sunshine.

"But I was wrong," he says. "You're just as sick as she was. It's my fault. I should have seen it before. It was a mistake to bring you here, Callie. I should have known better."

"Dad, please, just listen! I didn't hurt him, there was something there, there was something in the w—"

He cuts me off, slamming his palm against the window so hard that I'm afraid it will shatter beneath his hand. His composure vanishes. He beats the window and screams, "GOD-DAMNIT, CALLIE, STOP IT! THERE WAS NOTHING IN THE WATER!"

He shudders and shakes his head. Breathes in, breathes out. I see his composure return, see the roiling emotions settle again in their place beneath the surface. He keeps his gaze straight ahead. He has gone back to not looking at me, will keep on not looking at me all the way home.

He says, "You'll need to start packing your things. We're going back to Laramie just as soon as I can make arrangements. I've already called Doctor Frank."

I open my mouth to speak. Nothing comes out. And for once, it's not my lungs that betray me; my throat is wide open, my breath coming fast and easy. For once, it's my mind that has gone silent, stopped by the suffocating glut of incomprehension. My thoughts resolve not into words, but a strangled croak, and I grip the door handle to steady myself.

Laramie.

Where the earth freezes solid in winter, where the only moisture in your skin seeps up through the spots where it cracks in the cold. Where my lungs will seize and crumple in the dust-dry inland desert. Where I will wake up, night after night, in an airless hell that scrapes my throat like sandpaper claws.

Far from the seaboard, far from the sound.

My father keeps his eyes on the road. He lifts his chin, with its three-day stubble, and swallows down the last of his reservations.

He says, "I couldn't stop your mother from taking her own life. But I'll be damned—I Will Be Damned—if I let my daughter do the same."

When he pulls the car to the side of the road, I fling myself onto my hands and knees, straddling the faded white line of the curb, and vomit until there is nothing left.

CHAPTER 32

I HAVE NEVER BEEN SO ALONE. Day after day in the empty house, staring at a phone that rings only when my father wants to test my promise not to stray beyond the property lines. As if I had anywhere to go, as if anyone wants to see me. I didn't even argue when he took my cell phone; it's one less way for people to get at me, to sling their accusations. It makes it easier to pretend that none of it ever happened. The last text message I got was from Jana, only three short words, but each one of them like a knife: *I trusted you.*

The first day home, I wrote Nessa a letter, telling her everything. It's signed and sealed, sitting in my dresser drawer. I should send it, but I can't. Not yet. As long as she still doesn't know the truth, somehow it seems less real.

Before, I spent my days in solitude and never knew what I was missing; now, I find myself turning on the television just to hear a human voice. I'd forgotten how time blurs and blends when you're alone, how the days and dates grow meaningless until you simply stop keeping track. Whether it's Monday or Thursday or Sunday only matters if you have somewhere to go, someone to see. Schedules are pointless with no one to care whether or not you keep them.

The only appointment I keep now is with the whispering blackness inside my head, and the woman who waits there to meet me. I find her there behind my eyes and follow her down into the dark. I won't believe that it could be true, the terrible thing he told me. I will not think about the way he looked at me when he said, "You're just as sick as she was."

Everyone else has abandoned me; I will not drive her away, too.

Some mornings, I wake up clutching my mother's book in one hand, Nessa's necklace in the other, and wonder whether I'll have to leave the dreams behind when I go. Whether it's truly just the effect of Dr. Sharp's miracle drugs that opened the door and let her in, or whether it's something about this place, this house, the proximity of water. Whether something from the sea has found its way upstream, to us, to me. Whether it will miss me, a week from now, when it searches the dark and finds me gone.

Or whether this, the very thought of it, is just more evidence of the same dark madness they say took hold of my mother, that they say is now blooming inside of me, too.

On the morning I left the hospital, Dr. Sharp had pressed a new bottle of pills into my father's hand.

"This is slightly higher than the dosage we discussed," he'd said, in the low tones reserved for the private conversations in public places. He thought I wasn't listening. "But in light of the family history, I think—"

"Thank you," my father had said, and took the bottle. Later, when I asked him what they were, he shook his head and said, "It's not important, just swallow."

Later still, I hid in bed with my laptop and slowly, quietly typed the name from the bottle into a search field. I scrolled results long enough to read the word a dozen times, *antipsychotic*, then closed the computer and turned off the light. I breathed deep in the safety of the darkness. And then, urged on by that small, strange voice inside that I've begun to trust more than my own, I plucked the pill out from under my tongue and crushed it to powder against the wall.

CHAPTER 33

ON THE DAY THAT THE PHONE FINALLY RINGS, I no longer know what day it is.

The interior of the house is frigid as I cross the kitchen floor, feeling my sweat-slicked skin tighten against the chill. Without Nessa to sabotage the thermostat, my father has kept the air conditioner high and the blinds shut tight, blocking out the view of the river and keeping the humidity locked outside. If he could, I realize, this is how he'd live: in a narrow place with no windows, bathed at all hours in artificial light and air controlled by a digital dial. Everything orderly, everything tamed. The sun has gone down, but nobody comes to answer the ringing phone; he must be still at work, which means that it must be a weekday. As I reach for the handset, I watch my own shadowy reflection in the windows of the den. Tall, broad-shouldered, with wild hair spilling over my shoulders, down my back, brushing the waistband of my shorts.

My heart aches with familiarity.

I've seen this body before. It used to hold me close as the tide rushed in, used to plunge feetfirst into the shallows and haul the daysailer ashore, used to whirl around our living room and fall in a breathless, laughing tangle into my father's lap.

Sometime in the months since we came to the gulf, my mother's silhouette has become my own.

When the ringing shatters the silence again, I jump and scream.

"Hello?"

"Callie."

The strength goes out of my knees. I slide down against the counter, clutching the receiver, pressing my cheek to the cool of the wall.

"Ben."

His name comes out as a sob, and there's a long silence on the line. I can hear him breathing: fast, shallow, hitching and uneven. I hear him gather himself, hear the small *click* as he swallows hard and steels his nerve. I do the same.

"Are you okay?" he says.

"Are you?"

"Pretty much."

For a while, that's all there is. The two of us breathe together in silence as I struggle to find the right words. In the end, he's the one who speaks first.

"I'm sorry," he says, and his voice is full of pain. "About the hospital, I heard that my parents—I mean, my mom—"

"It's okay."

"It isn't, though."

"They thought that I'd hurt you."

"Yes."

I take a deep breath, and feel grateful, so grateful, that it glides smoothly in. My body won't betray me this time, not now.

"Ben, I swear I didn't "

I hear him swallow again. And again. And then his voice comes, thick with emotion, dragged down a full octave by regret.

"I know." He pauses, and then he's talking fast, the words tumbling and crashing into each other as they spill into the receiver. "Callie, I tried to tell them. I woke up in the hospital, I was confused, everyone wanted to know what happened, and I knew—I know you wouldn't hurt me, I swear to God, I knew you couldn't have . . . but I was so confused, they'd pumped me so full of drugs I could barely think straight, and they kept asking and asking, and I just . . . I just . . ."

There's a strangled sound from somewhere deep in his throat; he coughs and falls silent.

"You told them it was me," I say. "You told them you saw me, in the water."

"I . . . because I did. But I don't know . . ."

He trails off. I swallow, hard.

"Ben?"

"I'm sorry." He clears his throat. "Callie, I just can't remember. I'm sorry. I know you wouldn't hurt me, I know that, but . . . I don't know what I saw."

I don't push him. I won't. I can feel it, how badly he wants to tell me what I want to hear, and how much he can't unless he lies. I will not make him lie to me. I will not make him lie for me.

There's another long pause, another minute ticked off by the glowing green numbers of the clock on the stove.

"I'm so sorry," he says. "I hate doing this on the phone. This bullshit, my parents threatening to press charges. I told them I absolutely won't. I'll find a way to see you as soon as I can."

I sigh, and fight back tears. "If that's what you want, you'd better do it soon."

"What are you—"

"I didn't just get expelled. My father is sending me back to Laramie."

I pause, and then say out loud the thing that I've trusted to nobody. The one thing that, until this moment, I've left unspoken in the hopes that it will go away.

"My dad says I'm . . . sick. Mentally. He says my mom was, too. He told me . . . he told me she killed herself."

When he answers, the tenderness in his voice is so heavy, so intense, that for a moment, I don't understand what he's saying.

And then I do. I do, and I want to scream.

"Callie," he says. "She did."

My hands are shaking as I hunt for Nessa's number, as I jab my finger against the phone's buttons so fiercely that my nail bends back, snaps off, brittle as a long-dead twig. I've never felt anger like this, the kind that spikes out from my center, vibrating down my spine, drawing the blood to my head so fast that my hands and feet begin to buzz and tingle. The article, the one dated ten years ago and on a day I'd spent shivering in the hospital with ointment greased over my sunburned skin, is still open on my laptop screen. Not that I need to look at it. I have already memorized the words. I'll remember them for the rest of my life.

A massive search failed to recover the body of Maera Morgan, who is now presumed to have left her boat with the intention of drowning herself. Alan Twaddle, her husband, told authorities that his wife had struggled with depression for years but that her condition had worsened in recent months, exacerbated by ongoing family conflicts.

In all the years I'd spent with only the computer for company, all those nights tumbling alone down Internet rabbit holes when I was too sick to sleep, I had never thought to read the news accounts of my mother's death.

And why would I? I think, bitterly. I had seen her vanish into the blue. I had heard her cry out over the rush of the waves. I had known, better than anyone, that she called my name, and the sea opened wide, and then the wind blew softly across the glassed water as though she'd never been there at all. It had been over in seconds, but even in that last glimpse, she hadn't looked like a woman who wanted to die.

But she did. It's here, right in front of me, and Nessa must have known. They'd been close—too close for her not to know, too close for her never to suspect that my mother had climbed out of the boat meaning never to return.

My mother left me.

And Nessa had lied.

"I'm sorry," Ben had said, over and over, as I stared slack-jawed at the words on the screen. I barely heard him over the rushing of blood in my ears, the first wave in a tide of rage and hurt. That my father had kept this a secret, I could at least understand. It was like him, to try to shield me, to think that I was better left in the dark. But Nessa, I had always thought I could trust. I thought that when I asked if my mother had chosen her ending, I would get the truth, instead of something dressed up and distorted, just to make it hurt less.

Ben was still stammering, "I'm sorry, I'm sorry. I thought you knew! I thought . . ."

Even to my own ears, my voice was low and lifeless.

"How did you know? How could you know, when I didn't?"

"I . . . I googled your dad," he stammered.

Of course you did, I thought, and the voice in my head sounded like a sneer. Ben, who is interested in everything. Ben, who could never let a subject go unresearched. Ben, whose interest in my father's history would have drawn a direct line from his eager questions to our family tragedy.

"I'm sorry," he said again. "I thought you knew it was suicide. I thought that was why you never talked about it, or about her."

"How long have you known?"

"Awhile. That first Saturday, at your house, I knew then."

I sucked in my breath, and my voice turned sharp. "That was months ago. How could you lie to me like this? You never even asked about it!"

He cried, "Jesus, Callie, I was trying to do the right thing! You think that was easy for me? Knowing what happened, and pretending I had no idea? How do you think I felt, sitting there at the beach with you, knowing that the last time you'd even been to the ocean was probably the day your mother drowned herself?!"

"That . . ." I trailed off, suddenly lost in the memory of the water licking at my ankles, my knees. Remembering how it felt to drift there, in the hidden pull of the riptide. I had been thinking of my mother in that moment, and yet, I'd felt no fear at all. "It wasn't the same."

"Maybe not to you," Ben had said. "If it had been me, I'd never want to go near the water again for the rest of my life."

I said, "You have more in common with my father than you know."

Nessa picks up on the fourth ring. I don't bother with hellos, I spit the words out hard and fast before she even can finish saying my name.

"When were you going to tell me that my mother committed suicide?"

There's a sharp intake of breath. In the long pause that follows, I begin to wonder—to hope—that I was wrong. Maybe she has an explanation. Maybe the words aren't coming because she's working so hard to choose them. Maybe, maybe, maybe.

Finally, she speaks. "Is that what you think?"

At first I wait, thinking she'll say more. When she doesn't, the full force of what she has said, no denial, no explanation, my question answered with one of her own, has the impact of a physical blow. My vision swirls and swims, my knees buckle under me.

"How could you keep this from me?" I cry. "After everything we talked about? How could you sit there and not tell me the truth? You lied! You looked me in the eye and told me she didn't leave, that it wasn't her choice!"

"Dammit, Callie! Do you think this is easy for me?" she shouts back, and she sounds so much like my father that the next accusation I'd planned to fling at her seizes and dies somewhere in the bottom of my throat.

"You're not the only one who lost something, you know," she cries. "I've made the best of it, I've done my best for you, but do you think this is really what I wanted? We were supposed to be—"

Her voice breaks, she catches her breath, and whimpers, "We were supposed to be together. That was why my father wanted another daughter, so that we'd always have each other, so that it wouldn't be so goddamn lonely. But it wasn't enough for her." She stops. I think she's stopping for good, but then she laughs, and I hear bitterness seeping into her words, poisonous and thick. "She thought she could have more, that she could control everything if she played it just right . . . but not even Maera could get her way on that one. She tempted fate and it called her bluff, and she was a fool to think it wouldn't. She actually had the nerve to mock me for the way I lived, telling me that if I just tried harder I could have what she had. The husband, the child. But she was wrong, and it cost her—"

She stops, bites back her words so quickly that I can hear her teeth click together. But not quick enough. The last thing she said hangs in the distance between us, settling in, hideous and heavy with meaning.

"It was because of us?" I ask quietly. "That's why she wanted to die? Because she married my dad, because she had me?"

There's a long pause, and I can hear the air hiss through Nessa's teeth as she takes a long, apologetic breath. The energy is gone from her voice; whatever took hold of her a moment ago has passed and left her shaken, deflated.

There's a tremor in her words as she says, "Baby, I wish I could comfort you. I wish I could tell you all this in a way that would make sense to you and make it hurt less. But I can't. You have to make your choices, like I did. Even like your mother did. It's part of the deal, and no matter what, it hurts. If not you, then someone else."

Nessa pauses, and breathes in deeply.

"You asked me if your mother, my sister, wanted to die, and the answer is no, she didn't. But she made a choice about how she would live her life, and yes, she knew that choice might have consequences. She might have wanted to believe otherwise, but she knew. Because that's how it works, Callie. That's how it's always worked, and if there's a way out . . . well, it's for you to decide if you want from life what it wants to give to you. I can only tell you to do the best you can with the time you have."

A white-hot flare of rage explodes somewhere inside me. I cry out, "Are you seriously telling me that same useless crap about destiny again, and thinking it's going to help? My father says she killed herself. He says so. He says she was crazy. And he says I'm just like her."

Nessa sighs. "And he wouldn't be the first man to say that to a woman in this family."

"Because it's true?"

"Because it's easier than the truth. And you know that, even if you don't know yet that you know it. I'm sorry, Callie," she says. Her voice breaks in two when she says my name. "I'm sorry. Please, don't be angry. I have to go, and I don't want to leave things like this."

I could ask for more, at this moment. I could demand that Nessa stop speaking in platitudes and give me a direct answer; I could ask myself whether she's right, whether I know enough not to need one. For a moment, I even feel it, as though if I sit still for one more moment, the truth will crash over me like a wave.

But I am not still. I am not patient. I am angry and sick, abandoned and alone. I have nothing left, nothing but bottles of pills, and broken promises, and a plane ticket that will take me away too soon and forever from the one place in ten years that has felt like home, and nothing Nessa says or does will change it.

I snap back, "Oh, don't let me keep you. It's not like you can help me anyway."

She's crying hard, now, her words turning to mush. I listen to it, the sound of her blubbering, and feel a jolt of revulsion. I cling to it, grab hold. I reel it in close. In that moment, I hate her.

"I'm sorry, I'm sorry," she sobs. "I'll send you a letter. Okay? I'll send you a letter."

"Fuck your letter," I say, and hang up to the sound of her weeping.

When my father comes home, I grunt a hello and push past him, outside, down across the lawn and out to the farthest reach of the dock. I'm afraid he'll catch a glimpse of something in my face, the high, angry flush in my cheeks or the clench of my hard-set jaw, and know that something has changed.

The air has turned gray, tinged with violet, still hazy, damp, heavy. The world holds its breath, waiting for night to come and lace everything with dew, for dark that will break the heat into pieces. I sink down through air the color of smoke and reach my bare foot for the water. In the trees, the night songs have begun; I see a heron, stark white in the last of the evening light, step gently from the shadow of a cypress island and take to the air without a sound.

I do not want to leave.

Maybe if I were more like my mother, I could find a way to stay. But no matter how I shuffle my options, no matter how many paths I envision, they all lead away from this place. For all the choices I might have, there's not one that lets me choose this.

I breathe in, relishing the feeling of the liquid air as it slides down deep in my lungs, loving the long, slow glide as I release it through my lips. I wonder if this will be taken from me, too. If I'll return to Laramie and find that wheezing, tired girl waiting for me, ready to slip back into my body and take my breath away. I look out across the water and make a promise: if she's there, that girl I used to be, I will not let her in. I will wrap my hands around her neck and squeeze until blood-flowers bloom in her lifeless eyes.

The pounding of my heart has subsided to a dull patter, and the light is nearly gone. I tuck my damp feet under me, and stand to watch the last of the day dim down behind the trees. I walk backward up the dock, gaze across the languid surface of the river, hoping for a last glimpse of the heron, the first sweeping arc of a bat across the purple sky.

I stop.

There is something in the water.

I peer out, widening my eyes, racing against the failing light to see what's floating there. For a moment I think I've imagined it, I'm about to turn away, and then I see it again. A long, pale body, drifting just below the surface.

One of the manatees, swimming slowly back upstream.

Even today, even after everything, the sight of it makes my heart lift.

"Hey," I whisper, and smile, and take a step forward. "Hey, there you are."

I watch the animal's slow progress through the water, barely swimming, barely moving at all. It's smaller than the ones I'd seen this spring—a baby, I think, maybe lost by mistake in the maze of the gulf's sprawling coastal waterways. It seems unhurried, maybe even confused. As the pale shape drifts closer, I take another step forward, wondering if it'll come near enough to touch. I wonder if it might be sick. It's so small, so thin.

Too thin.

Something isn't right. The too-lean body, its stillness in the water, the long, thin arms that drift down and forward as I watch. They're nearly disappearing in the dark; I can see only the suggestion of its fingers splayed like pale stars in the murk.

Fingers.

I shake my head and let out an embarrassed giggle, glad there was no one to see me talking to an imagined phantom. This isn't a manatee. There is no manatee. This is a trick of the light, shadows playing on the water, a piece of sun-bleached wood trapped in the river muck just so. I step back out to the farthest reach of the dock, peering into the lingering twilight at the strange shape below the surface.

It's still there.

It lifts its head.

Even in the growing darkness, I can see its eyes. Glittering, black, peering out and unblinking.

Its eyes are fixed on me.

The *thud* of rapid footsteps behind me makes me jump and shriek. I turn just in time for Bee to catapult herself against my body, her sticky hands reaching around to clasp the sides of my legs. I cough, feeling my heart thud wildly and then settle, feeling the gooseflesh on my skin sink back and smooth over. I force myself to laugh, only it sounds like a shriek, high and hysterical and looping away into the night.

"Bee, you scared me to death!" I scold, willing myself not to look over my shoulder at the pale form in the water, dropping down to smooth the little girl's hair. I straighten the hem of her dress and wince at the way the fabric bites against her arms. It's at least two sizes too small.

Bee isn't paying attention. She points out at the water, eyes wide, voice barely a whisper.

"Did you see?" she says. "Did you see?"

"Did I see what?" I ask, quietly, but I already know the answer. I follow the line of her finger, and shudder, the hair on my neck rising stiff and stark as darkness closes in all around us.

"She was out there. The one I saw. The mermaid."

I pull her close. I let myself take comfort in the weight of her small body against mine, in the heat of her chubby hands, in the smell of mild shampoo rising up from her tangled hair. I stare out at the river, and when I speak, it's as much to it as to the little girl beside me.

"There's no mermaid," I say.

There isn't.

When I look across to the opposite bank, the water is empty, and the unbroken surface is as still and smooth as glass.

CHAPTER 34

NESSA'S PHONE RINGS AND RINGS. Yesterday, I left another message. I've left more apologies than I can count in the dead space that follows the beep, begging for her to forgive and call back. Today, a recorded voice tells me that the voice mailbox of the person I'm trying to reach is full.

I check every day for her letter, but I know she won't send one. My cruelty and anger pierced her through the heart from three thousand miles away, punched a hole through the middle of what we'd had. I think of the things I said to her, and regret rips through me anew. I deserve this loneliness.

In the days that have passed since that phone call, I've cried, screamed, pleaded. Begged for another chance, begged to stay. Nothing changes. No one answers back. Not my father, not Nessa. And not the river, dark and thick and keeping secrets, the water oozing slowly by and with nothing ever peeking out from underneath the surface. I've sat with Bee every night at the edge of the dock, holding her hand as the evening creeps in, both of us keeping watch. I was sure, that first night, that we'd see it again, and that it would turn out to be nothing. That she'd cry out, and I'd follow her pointing finger, and the thing I'd seen—that we'd both seen—would be only a buried branch nestled in the waving weeds. Or an alligator, the kind with the mutation that turns them white, hiding in the thick of the lily pads. Or nothing at all, a ghostly afterimage from the late-day sun, playing tricks on the slow-moving surface.

Instead, the water stays empty.

Inside the house, the air is heavy with unspoken words. My father has taken a leave from work to make the arrangements and pack my things, and we pass each other in the hallways or kitchen like silent ships in the night, his eyes skating opaquely over my face the same way they do over the furniture. It makes me think of an evening, not long ago but before everything turned sour, when he and I sat side by side, reading books in companionable quiet. The only sound had been the insect-wing flick of a page being lifted, the low cough-swallow-sigh of him clearing his throat.

The silence we share now is different. Cold, flat, empty. It is the silence of one person pretending that the other is no longer there.

—

On the last Saturday morning, with forty-eight hours until our flight, Ben finds me sitting with Bee on the dock. I watch him walk toward me, moving with a stiff, awkward gait that I've never seen before, his hands jammed in his pockets. For a moment, I almost wish the restraining order were still in place, just to avoid this terrible good-bye.

"Bee, I need to be alone with my friend for a little while," I say softly. There must be something in my voice; she doesn't even argue, just throws her arms around my neck and then skips away down the dock.

Ben watches her go, then drops down beside me.

"That is one rotund child," he says. Neither of us laughs. When he reaches out to take my hand, I hear Nessa's voice like a warning in my mind. *Be careful, Callie. This boy will want to keep you.*

If only he could.

If only we could hide away together, forget everything, reemerge into a world where none of this had happened.

"Can I help you pack or anything?" he asks.

"Everything's already done."

The pause stretches out forever, and then he leans in, swallowing hard, and folds me into his arms. I put my face in his hair. I breathe deep for the last time.

Away behind me, I hear the sound of a door opening; when I look back, my father is on the porch, arms folded, staring a warning across the yard at the boy who brought me to the water's edge. Ben coughs and moves away, hands returning to his pockets.

"Sorry," he mutters.

"It's okay," I say again, and swallow down the ache that's begun to rise in my chest. If I let myself cry, I won't be able to stop.

"Callie?"

I manage to look at him.

"We could stay together," he says. "I just can't stop thinking that this doesn't have to end. We could make it work. I'll be done with school in a year, and then I could come be with you. I mean, maybe . . ."

His voice is full of hope, and this time, I do start to cry. For a moment, I nod, and blink, and allow myself to dream on that "maybe." Maybe he could. Maybe we could. Maybe it would even be better that way, to reunite far from this place, with all its fresh, awful memories. Maybe when enough time has passed, we can find a way to start again. He has forgiven me; perhaps I can forgive myself. With enough time, enough effort, maybe I can wipe out the memory of how blithely I led him into harm's way.

And then the moment passes, and another dream takes its place. Only it's more than a dream. It's a memory, something borrowed in the darkness of a fevered sleep from a past that wasn't mine. The memory of a woman, tall and broad-shouldered, with long, tangled hair and almond-shaped eyes the color of deep, cool water. The memory of two baby boys, all chubby thighs and dimpled smiles, so sweet and sleepy, in matching hats to protect them from the sun. And of a man, tall and strong and with so much love in his eyes as he turns to look at her. I see them. I feel them. I reach for them.

And then they're gone in a crush of froth and spray and salt, and I scream, and scream, and scream.

"Callie?"

I swallow. My eyes are dry. My head is clear. There are no daydreams, only the sense, sudden and sure, that I know what must be done. I remember Nessa, nudging me gently in the direction of a truth she said I already knew.

I remember the rattle of an old woman's breath in the receiver as I cried out, desperately.

I don't understand.

I remember her long, low laughter.

You will.

I turn to him.

I don't know I'm going to say it until the words are already out.

"I love you."

At first, he smiles. He reaches for me. And then he sees my face, and he stops. I watch the smile fade; I watch understanding dawn in his eyes. I watch him swallow, and nod, and say, "Oh."

This is the moment where my heart breaks.

He stands, and so do I. He looks at me, glances backward as the porch door slams and my father disappears inside. He steps forward again, quickly, scoops my hand from where it hangs by my side, and presses it to his lips. I stand still. I don't breathe.

And he doesn't move at all. He's staring intently beyond me, behind me, at the boards beneath my feet—and then staring down, just as intently, at his own outstretched forearm.

"Oh," he says, again, only it's different this time. The sadness and understanding in his voice is gone. He only sounds curious. Confused.

And scared.

And then he's gone, and I kneel down, and gasp.

The lines are long and unbroken, standing out in stark relief. Deep, slender furrows in the wood, side by side, as even and perfect as if they'd been made by a machine. Marks that could have been made by anything, anything at all—except that I've seen them before.

Lines like the ones on my mother's body, as she stripped off her dress and sobbed, not seeing me, and fled up the stairs.

Lines like the one on Nessa's wrist, angry and red and fresh.

Like the ones on Ben's own forearm, standing out in sharp relief against his freckled skin. The ones they thought were my doing, souvenirs of his struggle as I'd tried to drag him deeper below the surface.

Lines like the marks of long-nailed fingers, a signature raked into the wood that I run my hand over, again and again, until I can't doubt that it's real.

One. Two. Three.

I am the one to break the silence.

"Ben has scratches on his arms," I say. I keep my gaze steady. I won't blink, won't break, until my father looks at me.

When he does, his eyes are glazed and glassy. In the week since I was expelled, he's taken to drinking scotch at night, keeping company with a glass that seems to always be two sips shy of empty. When he sighs, the smell of his breath holds the high, sweet note of whiskey.

"Nessa had them, too. And there are more, on the dock. Down by the water."

He shakes his head.

"Please, Callie. Let's not do this."

I take a deep breath.

"And Mom. Mom had them, too."

I don't know what I expected. A gasp, maybe, as realization dawned on his face that perhaps I was telling the truth. Or even just curiosity, blooming somewhere under the flatness of his convictions, enough to make him look at me with fresh eyes and an open mind. But I didn't expect him to laugh, and that's what he does. Bitterly, darkly, with his fingers pressed down on either side of his nose and his mouth drawn down in exhaustion.

"I'm surprised you remember that," he says. "And what do you think that means, Callie? Can you put two and two together?"

"Dad, I'm telling you, there was something—"

"STOP IT." He swirls the glass again, swallows deeply, and I realize that he's drunk. He shakes his head and looks at me with so much sadness that I flinch and turn away.

His voice is low.

He says, "Your mother had been hurting herself for months before she died. She'd go down there by the beach and carve herself up and then try to tell me she didn't know how it happened, even after the doctors had told us both that it was obviously self-inflicted."

The memory swirls up, overwhelming me.

You were down there again. Did you hurt yourself? I know. I always know.

I open my mouth to speak, but nothing comes out, and he smiles ruefully.

"She used to leave you," he says. "Do you remember that part? I'd come home, no wife, no lights on, and you'd just be sitting on the floor in the dark, all alone while she was down there doing God-knows-what. Never mind her baby, crying alone in a dark house. Never mind her husband, who loved her."

Something heavy and cold untwists in my stomach, and now it's Nessa's voice that I hear in my head: *She's the one who thought she could have it all. The husband, the child.*

I try to imagine the moment that it changed, when everything my mother wanted became everything she wished she'd never had. When she disappeared down the steps to the water, opened her veins, and bled against the stinging of the surf. I imagine her sinking into the deep on the day she died, the weight of her life, my father and me, like a stone albatross around her neck. I imagine her giving up, saying yes, drifting down into the dark.

The air conditioner kicks on in the silence, chilling away the lingering heat of my father's words. I watch him deflate in his chair, shoulders sinking down, the color draining away where it had surged high and bright in his cheeks. Only his nose stays red.

My voice is so quiet, I barely recognize it as mine; the words feel like somebody else's.

"Dad, please believe me."

He doesn't look up. His words are slurred and husky. He speaks them not at me, but into the glass cupped in his hands. He's lost in his memories; I don't think he's even heard me.

"I thought I was the luckiest man in the world. She could have had anyone she wanted, but she picked me. I thought I was so lucky. But that's how it works, isn't it? Perfect wife, perfect life. And then you find out that it's not enough. The life you gave her, the life you have together, it's not enough. Not when there's all that darkness inside and she won't let you in, or tell you how to fix it. Not when she shuts you out and she won't even try."

He swirls the dregs, drains them in a single gulp, sets the glass gently back on the table.

"And now she's gone," he says, quietly. "She's gone, and I'm left with—"

He stops, abruptly, and looks up. His eyes focus on me. He coughs, stands, stumbles away from the table.

"You should finish packing," he says, and disappears down the hall.

His sentence, the other one, stays unfinished. But in my head, I hear its ending loud and clear.

All he has is me. Her carbon copy, her spitting image. Reckless, wide-eyed, stupid.

And crazy.

All that darkness inside, he'd said, *and she won't even try.*

And as I lie in the humming chill of the darkened house, I feel it. The familiar sensation of the thing inside, stirring, stretching, opening its cold and curious eyes. Suggesting, in its casual purring way, that I could know more, be more, *have* more, than what I see before me. Than what he wants for me, from me. That there are other things, greater things, than the small and temporary life that was stolen from one frightened man.

I think of my mother's face, sun-kissed and serene, in the moments before the end. I think of the way I felt, under the waves, when that voice that was mine but not-quite-mine whispered, *Breathe,* and the sea pressed against my lips and flooded its way inside. I think of the words she left behind for me, in a book passed down through the years.

And as I drift down into sleep, I think: my father tells me my mother succumbed to the darkness.

But I think she welcomed it in.

CHAPTER 35

I AM IN THE WATER.

Not the inky liquid nothing where sleep always found me before, but above, over, skimming the surface in the nighttime air. My upturned eyes take in the world, green and black and silver, drenched in the light of a pale, high moon that makes shadows of the trees. I tilt my head back and gaze at its face; it glares back sightlessly, swollen and cold.

I have been here before. I know the creeping silhouettes of the cypress trees, the pale snake of the dock as it stands sentry in the dark. I am floating in my own backyard. The river is motionless in the moonlight, waiting and oh-so-still, the current slowed to nothing as the night world holds its breath. I have no memory of waking, or crossing the lawn, and its quiet expanse is shrouded in shades of gray. The motion sensor is silent and dark, no glow shows through the windowed walls of the house.

No lights tripped by a sleepwalker, none lit by a wakeful father, no alarms raised up at the sound of midnight foot-falls.

It's a dream, only a dream.

I breathe and trail my fingers through the water, and watch as they sink into nothing.

There is no panic, not this time. This is only more of the same, a world inside my head and behind my eyelids. Just another midnight meeting, the only appointment I care to keep. One more memory to follow me inland, one last chance to swim in the mouth of the sea.

One last night to search the depths, and find her waiting there.

When I see the pale body rise up in the water, I smile and whisper her name.

She is different in this dream, in the moonlight, in the shallows. More here, more clear, as I watch her swimming closer. Her skin is silver-white and cold, hairless and slick. I feel long limbs sliding past me, a hand like silk on my back. I catch hold of it as she glides by, and we turn slow circles in the water. She tenses, but doesn't pull away. There is some-thing stretched between her fingers, a gossamer membrane too slippery to grasp. The oval nails are longer now, skinless, gray, thick, and hooked and glistening at their points. There are fewer of them than I remember.

If I pressed them down against my skin, they would pierce it in three perfect lines.

The high rise of her forehead breaks the surface, water beading on the ridges where her eyebrows used to be. Eyes like black marbles peer back at me, lightless and shining, with no whites at all. The water has washed her features, smoothed them, narrowed them, but her face is still my mother's. Her hair floats up and fans out all around her, and I think again of Bee scribbling on the dock. Drawing her mermaid, that green-black tangle of hair like reeds, the reaching arms, the body a long, gray bullet. A body made for diving down and cutting through the deep. A body seen in shadowed glass, as I gazed at my own reflection.

Even now, we look so alike.

There is no warmth in the arms that reach up to embrace me, no heat from her body as she pulls me close.

"Mama," I say, my voice scraping the night.

My daughter, she says, with no voice at all.

She rests her face against my throat. Together, we go down.

I can see the moon, swimming and distant, licking like mercury somewhere above. We never break the surface. There is no need to breathe in a dream. I lie on my back and kick, kick, grazing the weeds with my fingertips. My mother's body mirrors mine, moving with silent strength through the black. Her legs are pressed, seamed together; they move as one, long and powerful, her feet curved like scythes in a dancer's point. Moving like a liquid, river-born thing, flipping and tumbling through the weeds. She sees me watching her, and the slit of her mouth seems to smile.

How did you find this place? I ask her. *How did you find me here?*

You called out to me, and I came, she says, and before I have time to ask her how, the words roll away into blackness. She reaches out, she takes my hand, and I feel a massive, painless jolt as my consciousness opens wide. I am in the water and in her head, caught up in a memory that isn't mine, dragged into its whirling center and slipping into its depths. I feel the river shifting around me, opening, deepening. I am someplace vast and endless, a sea inside my mother's mind, the ocean of her memories.

If not for the water, I'd gasp and cry out at what I see.

Because I am here. I am her, seeing the world through her eyes.

I am sinking beneath the shimmering waves, staring up at the belly of the boat that holds my child.

I am alone in the infinite blue of the bay, drifting on currents that run deep, strong, and fast.

I am floating in froth where the waves toss and toss, gazing up at a high cliff whose name I could have said out loud, but I have no words, and no voice to say them.

I am down, way down, in the darkest depths, where we all have sharp teeth and eyes like lamplight, and the sun's dancing beams do not reach.

I am home, but I still yearn for what was left behind.

I long for it, look for it, this thing that I've lost. I search, while the sun rises and sets in the faraway world and the tides go out and in again. My anguished voice calls out to all corners and echoes back empty-handed, as I drift and drift in the dark. I am looking for something in this wide-open place. It never stops. Something dear, something lost. I have cried out for it so many times that the words have lost their meaning. I don't know why, or how long I have looked, only that I want it. I need it, this thing that is mine.

My daughter, my daughter, my daughter.

I am the thing she couldn't let go, the only thing she took with her. The sea has worn away her memory as much as it has molded her body, sharpened her senses, washed away all the remnants of her years on land. She is as worn down to the core as the sea-glass necklace, tumbled smooth and essential by the breaking waves. I search her memories for more, for answers, and find only the endless stretch of days, months, years in the blue underworld with its ridged, barren landscape of shifting sands.

Do you remember the house? I ask her. *Our house?*

She answers, *I remember you.*

Do you remember the places we used to sail?

I remember you.

Do you remember your husband? Your sister? Our family?

I remember you.

Ten years, and more, she had looked for me here. All while I lay coughing in inland beds, in a landlocked world where her voice could not reach. Choking on nothing, putting lies in my letters, while she called out in search of her child. Always seeking, never finding. Until that day, when the voice of the sea made a long-distance call, and we came back to the edge of the earth.

Until the message of longing came back with an answer, a faraway whisper sent through miles of water. A heartbeat carried down the river and out to the open sea. A beacon, blood-thick and made only for her, a connection not even ten years could sever.

Here, it said, softly. *Here.*

———

The images are sharper, now, honed by a knife's edge of anger and need, as I follow her forward to now. I am hurtling through the blackest deep, guided only by instinct, feeling the pull grow stronger. I am in the green murk of the marshy shallows, where the water flows warm from a narrow mouth. I am hiding in the shadows of the great, gray trees, safe at my journey's end. There's a light through the swamp, a box made of glass, with small figures moving inside. She is there, but I cannot reach her.

And then the light changes, and I can.

She is here, in the water, so close I can feel her pulse. I am watching from under the whirling waves as she kicks with the current. A girl, tall and strong, arms slicing and pulling, moving like silver on the tossing surface.

But she isn't alone. There's another one, a boy, following, calling. He kicks and sends up spray, he struggles against the will of the water. He flounders, goes under, eyes white all around. Pale-skinned, red-haired, splashing and thrashing. He is trying to reach for her hand.

I can hear his heart, I can feel his desire, and the sea is seething, raging, wanting. She is mine, she is ours, this dark heart beats for her as it beats for all of us, and he cannot have her. We will tear him apart. We will show him she does not belong to him.

My daughter, my daughter, my daughter.

CHAPTER 36

THERE IS GRAY LIGHT FILTERING IN through my curtains when I wake, tangled in sheets so soaked with sweat that they're chafing my skin where they touch me. The phone in the kitchen is ringing, insistent, shattering the silence of the sleeping house. My hair is stuck in sodden curls to my neck, my back, my chest. I groan and throw off the heavy bedclothes. My feet tangle in them and I curse. My body is stiff and aching everywhere, my mind still fogged with the remnants of my dream, as the answering machine clicks on and whoever it is hangs up.

When the phone begins ringing again, shrill and insistent, I kick off the sheets with a final thrust and swing my feet to the floor.

What I see makes me gasp.

There are streaks of mud at the end of the bed, gray and gritty. There's more between my toes, and curling up my bare, white legs. My skin puckers in the chill of the room, and panic begins to stroke its crawling fingers up and down my neck. I'm naked. Dirty. The pajamas I'd worn to bed last night are in a crumpled heap on the floor.

I struggle to remember if I locked the dead bolt, realizing at the same time that even if I could, even if I stride up to it now and find it still in place, that it could mean anything and nothing. I tell myself that it doesn't matter. I tell myself rapid stories, one after another, trying to untie the knot in my gut. The dirt could have come from anywhere, could have been carried in unnoticed on the bottom of my feet. My hair tastes salty with sweat, not brackish river water. I must have grown hot sometime in the night and cast aside my clothes, peeled them off in half consciousness and then falling back asleep. And even if I walked last night, even if I did, that doesn't mean my dream was real.

Inside me, the sly voice whispers back, *And even if you didn't, that doesn't mean it wasn't.*

The phone shrills again, and I rush to cover myself at the muffled curse and dull *thud* that follows as my father's feet hit the floor. I listen to his path: the whiff of an opening door, heavy steps receding down the hallway, the clatter of sleepy hands lifting the receiver. I hear his grunted hello. I hear him ask the caller, whoever it is, if they have any idea what time it is. I look to my bedside table, and stare.

It is five o'clock in the morning.

Something is wrong.

This time, we won't play pretend with coffins. There will be no trip to the coast. No singing or reading, no open grave, no handful of dirt to throw down in memory. Nessa left instructions, careful and explicit, as though she knew there would be no body. Far away, on the California shoreline, the handful of people who knew her best—who hardly knew her at all—are gathering in awkward silence to have a small memorial service.

Here, nothing changes. There's no ceremony for saying good-bye, just the hollow place inside me where I know she'll never be again. It feels unfinished. A conversation on permanent pause, nothing but silence on the line. With the exception of the lawyer who calls just after nine, the phone rings only once; a man with a name I've never heard tells me that he had loved her, a long time ago, and is sorry for my loss.

"She talked about you all the time," he says.

I think, *She never mentioned you at all.*

Nessa always said that relationships were just promises you ended up breaking. I wonder now if she did it on purpose, if she always knew that she wouldn't be staying. I think of the way her voice broke as she sobbed, "I have to go. I don't want to leave things like this."

And I think of Lee, coughing bitterly, saying, "You get your time, and then your time comes."

They found her surfboard washed up on the shore, broken in two jagged halves where it had slammed on the breakwater and with seaweed tangled around the leash. Some people remember seeing her on the waves, at dawn or maybe midday, riding with her hair like a wild thing and her long, tawny legs flashing bronze in the sun. Catching the rise, paddling back. Moving as smoothly and freely as the water under her feet. She was beautiful and alone, confident and easy even as the waves grew high and fierce.

"I didn't know her," is what they said. "I just noticed her there."

And of course they did. She was too beautiful. Even in her carefully constructed life with no connections, no one to know her name as they watched her surf, nobody could fail to notice when Nessa was there.

But nobody, nobody at all, noticed when she wasn't. She left her life behind as quietly and completely as the sun winking out in the western sky. No trace, no good-bye, just gone.

In an article this morning, a coast guard official expressed hope that a body might still be found. That's the word he used, "hopeful," as though it were something to look forward to, as though we should all cross our fingers that Nessa might still wind up on a beach somewhere. Facedown, ravaged, an empty horror-show shell for somebody to see, to point at and scream.

But we know better, all of us who've been left ashore before. The ocean doesn't give back its dead. It doesn't give anything at all. And there is nothing left for me in her house by the sea, not even the start of a last scribbled message.

In the afternoon, my father picks up his briefcase and heads for the door, speaking to me over his shoulder as he goes.

"I have an appointment. I'll be home late. You should be in bed before I get back. You're packed, I hope?"

I stare at him. He sees my look, and sets his jaw.

He says, "We need to be at the airport by six a.m., no later. What happened to Nessa is terrible, but it doesn't change anything. You're getting on that plane tomorrow."

When I'm alone, I close my bedroom door, open Mama's book of poetry, and roll the words around in my mind and in my mouth. Nessa is gone, and the emptiness is sharp and pure and so very real. Everything that came before it seems pale, thin, transparent. Was it only eight hours ago that I woke in my bed, naked and drenched with dirty feet? Was it this morning, this year, this lifetime? I'm no longer sure that it happened at all, and if it did, it doesn't matter. I don't care if I walked last night, or even where I went. The things I saw in that dream-woman's memories can't be anything but the desperate churning of my sick subconscious, a story I told myself while I walked around in my sleep looking for somebody to love me.

Exhaustion is draping itself over my body, making my head ache, forcing my eyelids shut.

I think, *I should check the mailbox.*

But there won't be a letter. Not now, not ever. Nessa's final wave has taken her home, and I am alone on the shore.

The slam of the car door wakes me. I hear my father's heavy steps, stumbling and uneven up the wooden stairs. There's the metallic *cling* of a key ring, a louder jangling noise as he drops them. I hear him curse once, fumble, twist the key savagely in the lock, then groan aloud when he steps through the door.

My lips peel back in the dark. I turned off the air conditioner hours before, letting the watery heat drift in through the windows while the crickets sang me into a fitful sleep. The strange, heady scent of the river is thick in every room.

If I have to leave this place, then I want to take it with me, let the dampness sink into my pores, drip from my clothes, settle in stagnant pools in my shoes and at the bottom of my suitcase. Or better yet, I wish that it would take me with it—that it would swell and rise and swallow the whole world, creeping across the lawn, drowning the house's stilted legs, and pouring in through the windows. In the minutes before sleep took me, I'd pictured my father coming home not to a house but an aquarium, green and glowing with the soft lights still ablaze, a pale creature with glittering eyes and long, long hair drifting silently past the glass walls.

I hear the *thud* of the briefcase, the *clink* and *clatter* of heavy-bottomed bottles. He's pouring himself a drink. Not his first, I think.

In the low light, hunched protectively over his glass of scotch, he looks small and tired and petulant. There are brown shadows in the pits of his sallow cheeks, and dark sweat-stain circles blooming in his armpits. The briefcase is open in front of him, a sheaf of papers and folders splayed out across the tabletop. When I step through the doorway, he startles and hastily pushes the pile aside, then looks at me with narrowed eyes.

"You should be asleep," he says. "And why the hell isn't the air conditioner on?"

I gaze back coolly.

"I like the heat. And I live here."

He shakes his head, and glances at the clock. "For another four hours, yes, you live here. Now go back to bed."

I don't move.

"What is all this?"

He glances at the pile and says, "Nothing. Work. And some things from Nessa's lawyer, for whenever they make it official. She named me executor of her estate. God knows why."

The grief in my belly sinks lower, gets heavier. For Nessa's last words, last wishes, to be left in the hands of a man who so utterly failed to understand her feels like a final insult to her memory. Why would she choose him?

"Have you looked through it? Is there anything . . ." I stop. I don't even know what I'm asking; as if there were anything that could explain this, that would make it all okay.

He doesn't look up. "Nothing."

I step forward and reach out, asking, "Can I—" and he swats my hand away.

"No!"

I look at his eyes, shaded and evasive, and the darting of his tongue against his lips. I look down at the mess on the table. I see a lot of fine print, business stationery, forms . . . and something else. The barely curling corner of an envelope, a white point against the tabletop. Not crisp and professional like the rest, but worn and frayed as though it had been passed through many hands. He sees me see it, he reaches for it at the same moment as I do, but I'm faster. My hand flashes out like lightning and I pull it free, feeling the familiar weight of the folded sheets inside, feeling the places where grains of sand have indented the paper like Braille.

It is my name on it, just mine, in Nessa's familiar swooping script. I clench it tightly, press it to my chest, and look up at the man across the table. There is no hiding the guilt in his eyes. When I speak, the words uncoil from my mouth as smooth and deadly as a snake.

"You were going to keep this from me." It isn't a question, and he doesn't give an answer, only sighs and turns away.

"You were going to keep this from me," I say again, louder this time. "You had no right to keep this from me."

He turns at that, and fires back, "Actually, I have every right. Not only that, I have the responsibility. It's my job decide what's best for you. And yes, if I'd had my way, that letter would have gone straight into the fire."

The rage rises up in a white-hot instant, and my hands curl into fists.

"How could you?" I cry. "This could be important, there could be something—"

He sees my face, my trembling hands, and slowly shakes his head.

"You can relax," he says. "I'm not going to take it away from you. But whatever it says in that letter, you need to understand, it doesn't change anything."

I look at the way he's looking at me and feel the last sliver of hope leave my body—a tiny, glimmering thing that I didn't even know I'd been harboring until the moment it disappeared. Tears prick at my eyes, and I take a step forward.

"Dad, would you just—"

"This is not a discussion," he says, cutting me off.

"It's never been a discussion!" I cry. "When have you ever given me a voice in any of this? When was the last time you talked *to* me instead of about me? You never asked if I wanted this. You never asked me anything! You never even asked me what happened at the beach that day!"

He smiles, but there's no humor in it.

"You're right, I didn't. I can't. I can't stand here while you tell me another lie, and I wonder where I went wrong that I couldn't see this coming." He shakes his head. "No, honey. All I can do now is try to get you the help you need, and hope it's not too late."

He stands, pressing his palms against the table, and looks at me mournfully.

"I'm not asking what you want because you are too young, and too sick, to make decisions for yourself, and every word you utter about staying here makes me that much more sure that I've made the right choice. I'm your father, and I'm going to make sure you can't hurt yourself, or anyone else, ever again."

I swallow twice before I can find my voice.

"What are you talking about?"

I watch him slump, watch his jaw soften, as he thrusts a hand into his hair and grimaces. His face is full of pain and pity. Our eyes meet, and he holds out his hands.

"Callie," he says, and peers into my face. His voice is pleading. "Do you really not understand? Did you think that you'd just go back to school in Laramie and it would be like none of this ever happened?"

I don't answer, but I feel pink patches of shame coloring my face and neck, my stupidity and shortsightedness suddenly thrown into sharp, painful focus. In my mind, I'd thought of this as a step backward. Back to the barrenness I'd lived before, back to hospital stays and loneliness, my life like a flower that bloomed briefly and then closed, shrank, and grew backward into the ground.

But that's not the way it works, it's not. There's only forward motion, the next thing, another step and another. Whether you want it to or not, life only moves in one direction.

My father's composure is back, his voice as even and assured as if he were speaking to a board of directors. He says, "It's a facility for children like you, who suffer from mental illness and who need to be monitored. It's not far from the university in Laramie, and Doctor Frank has agreed to oversee your entry. Your intake is on Wednesday." He spreads his hands, and looks at me helplessly. "I'm sorry, Callie, but I have no choice. I can't take care of you. I can't watch you all the time, I can't deal with the lying and the hiding. Christ, I can't even make you take your pills."

I startle at that and watch him nod, sadly. I can see it in his face: that he knows he's caught me, that he wishes he hadn't.

"You learn from experience. Your mother didn't take hers, either," he says quietly. Then he looks at me, his jaw set, hard. "But I'm not going through that again. I can't. Not with you. You'll enter this program, you'll take your medicine and do whatever they tell you. I can't lose you to this, do you understand? I don't care how long it takes. You'll stay there, where you're safe, until you're well again."

I listen to the cadence of his voice, growing more confident by the minute, and realize what I'm hearing under the sadness: relief, the guilty kind that comes from handing off an unsolvable problem to someone else. And I realize something else, too: this was always the plan, even if he won't admit it. All my life, he's been observing me, waiting, watching for signs of the sickness that took my mother. Fearing it, yes, maybe even hoping against it, but certainly still expecting it. No matter what the doctors, the therapists, said. And when those first hints of darkness appeared, he was always going to do with me what he wouldn't, couldn't, with my mother: hand it over to professionals, put it in capable hands, spare himself the pain and effort of watching history repeat itself.

But I see the grief in his face. Raw, churning, desperate, the grimace and twist of his features at feelings flayed down to their core. My father has never liked to relinquish control, to admit defeat. I see that it hurts him to give up this way. I see that he believes he's tried, and failed, and it's killing him. I see that he wants to save me like he couldn't save her, but he doesn't know how, he never did.

Because he wanted an answer. A solution he could hold in his hands, hard and tangible and unchanging. He wanted solid ground and sure things, pills and promises, a ten-step plan that would flush the dark spots from my mind and leave no room for error. He wanted to pluck the madness out in pieces, close his fist around it, and pull, pull it free, pull it out by its deep purple roots.

He wanted all these things, never understanding that he could no more take hold of what's inside me than grip water in his hands. That sometimes, the more you try to grasp a thing, the more it slips slyly between your fingers, until you open your fist and find nothing there but the place where you've cut and bruised your own skin from trying too hard to hold on.

And in that moment, like a dam breaking, my anger cracks and shudders and then splinters, shattering, drowning in a surge of forgiveness and pity and cool, deep understanding. Because he doesn't know, of course he doesn't, that there's nothing crazy in what I feel. He has never felt this longing, this pull. He could never understand the comfort of that restless water, the lullaby *shush* of the breaking waves, the way that all the small and petty sorrows of little human lives turn to nothing in its cold and endless depths. He has never seen the joy in the embrace of a capricious and powerful lover, the one who could kill you, but doesn't, and that's how you know it's real. He tried to understand. He couldn't.

But I do.

The sea is everywhere, in my mind, in my veins, crashing unseen on the rocks in my Pacific memories, kissing the Panhandle coastline that I'm meant to leave behind. It surges inside me with whispers and promises, rushing, hushing. It is full of comfort, knowledge, peace. It's the dark and patient consciousness that moves beneath my heart. It's the quiet voice that speaks to me, speaks through me, so old and so cold, a voice I can hear but my father cannot, no matter how hard he listens.

And I forgive him for it.

I pity him for it, the way my mother must have.

He nods, taking my silence for acquiescence, and says, "Get some sleep. We'll discuss this tomorrow. I'm sure you have questions, and I'll answer them as best I can."

I blink away tears, letting my gaze drift over his back, the empty glass, the cluttered tabletop. The envelope in my hand is hot, crumpled. I smooth it against my hip and back away.

His voice follows me back through the shadowed house.

"Just don't expect any answers from her, Callie. I didn't get any from your mother."

CHAPTER 37

Dear Callie,

Fate has a way of believing in people, whether or not we believe in it. By now, I trust you understand.

Yours does not have an infinite reach, and there are places, places like the ones you've been before, where it cannot touch you. You can hide there, if you choose to, and live as best you can. But remember this: a thing that cannot touch you also cannot nourish you. You know better than anyone what it will cost you to turn your back on your destiny.

Every choice has its cost. These are lessons everyone learns, and we learn them harder than most. It isn't fair, I know. But this is what it means to be loved,

deeply and powerfully and all your life, by something
much larger than either of us. We are privileged to
know that love, and to let it guide us home.

I hope you'll be happy, Callie, wherever you are. I
hope I will see you again.

The scrawl on the paper is thoughtful, even, with none of
the usual sloppiness or swirling, extravagant flourishes.
Nessa wrote this letter slowly, and took care with every word.
And my father is right: it contains no explanations, no apologies, not even a good-bye. There are no answers here.

What he doesn't know, doesn't understand, is that I don't
need one.

Nessa used to say that the sea had a voice. And when I call
out in the dark of my dreams, I hear it answering back.

I hear it.

I have always heard it.

It tells me it's time to come home.

THE SEA

CHAPTER 38

I WANT TO TELL YOU A STORY.

You'll think you've heard it before, because you know the way it begins. Once upon a time, there was a daughter of the sea, a beautiful girl from the watery world who fell deeply, terribly, tragically in love with a man who lived on land. And though she watched him from the shallows, and he watched her from the shore, they knew that they could never be together. And the girl grew pale and lonely, watching as the man she loved lay in the golden sunshine, on the earth she could not reach or touch.

But the sea loved his daughter. He hated to see her suffer. He wanted to give her everything. And so, despite his misgivings, he brought her to the surface, and pushed her to shore on a gentle tide, and drew back as her lungs filled with air. And when her eyes opened and she saw what he had done, she threw herself into the surf and thanked him, thanked him, thanked him. And for a time, the world was full of light and laughter, as the daughter of the sea and the son of the earth were together at last. They walked together in the surf each morning, and slept each night in a cabin on the shore. And when the young wife of Earth's son bore her husband children, they brought them to the shallows and bathed them in the sun-warmed pools on the incoming tide.

But that is only the beginning. The sea is a changeable thing, never still, never satisfied. Its moods can turn as subtly as the tide, or with the wailing thrashing fury of a summer's sudden storm. And though the sun warms its surface, its heart is deep and dark.

I want to tell you another story.

This one, you won't have heard before. A story of women, swept up by the same impossible yearning, all heeding the call of a voice that only they could hear. All reckless, all wild, all believed by the ones who loved them to be in the grips not of fate, but of madness.

Women who live alone by the seaside, guarding their hearts against all others, finding pleasure in their solitude. Women whose boats are one day found abandoned, empty of the captains who steered the course. Mothers who swam out at sunrise and never came back to shore, daughters who dove with arms outstretched from high seaside cliffs, who fell into the churn and froth below and simply disappeared. Women who went for evening walks on the sand at low tide and never came home; women who vanished, car and all, on winding coastal roads and causeways where the surf nips at every passing traveler's heels.

And others, the ones who turned their backs and ran, who built their houses inland, who languished and shrank in landlocked beds. Who struggled to breathe on their borrowed time, who grew small and weak and sallow as the dried-out years passed by. Women who were loved by men, in sickness and health, but mostly in sickness. Women who, in their final hours, grew delirious and desperate, begging to be taken to an ocean they'd never seen, to be bathed in waters they'd never touched. Women who gasped their last in narrow rooms, surrounded by miles of dirt and forest, dry-drowned in the broth of their own sodden lungs.

I want to tell you the story of a man who the waves had not awakened, and the woman who thought he was perfect and safe. A defiant, wild, idealistic woman who believed that she could sidestep fate by refusing to fall in love. A mother, a wife. Haunted and breaking apart at the seams, losing herself in pieces, until her time ran out, too soon. A woman who tempted her jealous fate and lost, for loving her little life too much.

And I want to tell you the story of a girl who lost her way and lost her breath, while everyone forgot her name. Who grew up lonely and empty, until she came to a world full of water. Who peered into a river that led to an ocean and found something waiting for her there.

A path.

A choice.

A chance to walk out and grasp hold of her fate, to finally go home.

I wait two hours in the dark, feeling the house grow icy and quiet, as the steam on my windows disappears. I wait, sitting at attention, rubbing my hands over my long arms, my broad shoulders, my smooth, sweat-slicked skin. I am wearing the swimsuit that Nessa bought for me, her necklace rapping lightly against the smooth, black fabric that stretches over my chest. The voice inside me has gone quiet, but I know it's there. Only barely moving, lapping gently at the corners of my consciousness, as still as an impatient thing can be. It doesn't speak, but its will is like a heartbeat.

Go, go, go.

This is what my mother felt, begging, yearning, needing her love. A voice, insistent and growing louder. My father thought it was madness, slinking and crouching in circles around the close, warm walls of her brain. But it isn't. It can't be. Is it?

It isn't.

Go.

When I step into the hallway, my feet make no sound against the carpet. The door swings open on silent hinges. The boards of the porch stay still as I move over them, no creak from the stairs as I take them one by one. Only the motion-sensing light blares out, awakened from sleep by my passing shadow, a silent alarm in the deep blue of predawn. Nobody stirs inside the dark house, no surprised light casts a warm glow. No animals startle out of the brush as I pad barefoot across the lawn, down the white wooden track of the dock that rises like a phantom path from water shrouded in mist. A cloud has seeped in low along the riverbank. My feet kick through a swirl of ghost-cold gray as I stop and crouch down in the dark.

The cover of the boat slips off as smoothly and silently as a stocking. The motor starts at a single pull, purring loud enough to wake my father, wake the neighbors, but it doesn't. It won't. It won't let them catch me, I think. It will keep me safe, keep my secret, it will shush anyone waking back down into sleep. I've listened carefully and done everything right. I've made no mistakes, said no farewells, save the one. Just one, just one *I love you,* and it will let me have that.

CHAPTER 39

THE SKY IS STREAKED WITH PINK and red as I make my way slowly south, under clouds like reaching fingers in the lightening sky between the trees. The cypress loom out of the dawn like gaunt, gray sentries, dangling moss like a ragged cloak. Sleek lilies, still sleeping, bob gently on the little boat's wake. An alligator, indifferent and half-submerged in the shoreline weeds, fixes one amber eye on me as I pass. The air is cool against my bare skin, cooler as the boat picks up speed, and I wish without thinking that I'd brought a sweater.

Then I do think, I think of where I'm going, and laugh.

It's not difficult to steer the boat. The water is like glass. Nobody runs out to investigate the sound, nobody shouts at me to stop. Minutes pass, five and then fifteen, and the trees begin to thin and pull back, shrinking from the land too salty to sustain them. I pass an early fisherman, throwing off lines on his own little boat, a thermos of coffee already sitting in the stern. I slow, so as not to rock the boat, and he peers at me and waves. I lift a hand in return.

Hello.

Good-bye.

When the marshlands appear on either side, I throw my head back and breathe in deeply. The grasses are yellow-gray in the early light, the smell of mud and brine is everywhere. Miles away, on a wind-burnished outcropping, a lighthouse winks in the pale breaking dawn. I pass down the narrow inlet, between the flats with their fluttering grasses and pale fringe of sand. Ahead of me, the land sinks low, lower, and peels away. I hear surf rushing gently against the coastline as I pass through, out of the river shed, out of the mouth, and into the open sea.

When I finally slow and kill the motor, the land behind me has all but vanished. It's there, but barely—only an outline, a memory, a long and indistinct shadow between the water and the sky. The wind has died to nothing, only barely moving in my tangled hair. I peer over the side of the boat. The sea-glass necklace dangles between my fingers, its chain a coil in my palm. I watch it swing gently above the blue. When it slips through my fingers and into the water, it doesn't make a sound. I watch it sink down, out of sight, and look out across the waves.

There is something in the water. A shadow, long and strong and sinuous. It slides along under the gray of the waves, moving fast, an opaque patch that surges forward and slips under the keel of the boat on one side, as sleek and silent as it was all those years ago. And now, as then, there's no splash. No sign. No portent cloud come to cover the sun.

The boat rocks and tips as I slip over the side.

For only a moment, I wonder if I should have stayed. I lie back on the surface, letting the water hold me, feeling the rise and fall of my chest. So smooth and even, so effortless. I could still turn around, go back there, inland, and find a way to make peace with that landlocked life. Take my medicine. Share my feelings. Make them believe that they've cured the illness inside my head, even as my body grows weak and soft and the air grows harder to breathe. I could live as best I can in a place with narrow walls, locked doors, bars on the windows, and pills by the bedside, and pray that when they let me out, I would find him waiting to meet me. I might even discover that they were right. That she was sick, and so am I. That the voice I hear, the desire I feel, is crazy after all. That each whispered urge to come home, come down, is only madness, delusion, a delirious death wish that bloomed like a dark flower in my imbalanced mind and spread its roots down through my veins. Not magical, just chemical, and easily washed away.

I pull the straps down over my shoulders, slip the swimsuit over my legs. I watch it bob briefly, air caught somewhere inside, then disappear below the surface. For one last moment, one last breath, I lie naked in the water and feel the bare heat of the sun, cresting on the horizon. Day breaking over my body. Early morning light paints the sky.

In the movies, drowning is the most undignified of deaths. But that's not how it happens at all. The air leaves your lungs, your body grows heavy, and you slip out of sight without a sound.

It's so quiet, down here in the blue. I exhale and sink, down past the sun-warmed waters near the surface, down into the twilight depths below. The surface of the sea is alive and restless above my open eyes, playful, shimmering, teasing me with bits of sunshine and refracted sky. But I don't want to go back there, to that petty, noisy world. I don't want the passing fancies of earthbound life, small dramas and shallow loves.

I don't want to become like Lee, atrophied and bitter, clinging to a man who might love me but can never truly understand. And no, I don't want to try my own hand at my mother's reckless gambling, the kind that breaks promises and hearts. This is what I want. The deep, endless and unexplored, full of secrets. I want to be held, forever, in the arms and heart of this cold, dark home and the cold, dark people in it.

I want to see my mother again.

My lungs collapse painlessly, one, then the other, as the last of the air bubbles in silver streaks from my lips, flying away toward the surface. I watch them, all the way to the end. I do not need to blink. I do not need to breathe. There is gossamer webbing between my fingers, as fine and translucent as an insect's wings. There are arms wrapping around me, there are songs inside my head.

I am here. We both are. We all are.

And it is so peaceful and beautiful, down here in the blue, where the sounds of the world fade away to nothing, where I can go anywhere that the currents take me, where my body moves with so much effortless grace. And I feel her long limbs cradling me, and I hear her voice all around me, full of love so fierce and wild that it could fill a hundred oceans, could flood the whole world.

My daughter, she says. *My daughter.*

And together, we go down.

INLAND

CHAPTER 40

THE WINDOW IN MY ROOM LOOKS TO THE WEST.
Every evening, I can watch through its small, steel-reinforced panes as the sun goes down behind the hills. Beyond the hills, the desert. Beyond that, miles and miles away, the restless sea. The week after they moved me in, I found a road atlas in the patient lounge and tracked my journey inland. The route from this room to the beach where they found me is exactly one thousand miles.

The first week, in the unchanging blue-white light of the hospital, I never knew what time it was or how many days had passed. Just like before, so long ago, I'd awoken in a strange place, strange bed, to questions and curious stares. There was the same beeping of the monitors, the same endless parade of question-askers. The lines in my father's face, though—those were new. Harder. Deeper.

Just like before, she was gone, and I had been left behind.

"Please tell me, Callie," my father said, after the last police officer had left. "Just tell me the truth."

"What makes you think I haven't?" I said, and turned my face to the wall.

The story I told is the one they told me. It was obvious, of course: that I'd left, run away, because I didn't want to be sent to Wyoming. That I'd been gone four weeks, which I spent hitchhiking and hiding, stowing away in the backs of trucks and keeping out of sight. They knew what had happened, they said; all I had to do was fill in the blanks. They told me not to lie.

I didn't. I told them I didn't remember the names of any driver who'd picked me up. I told them I didn't remember the make and model of a single car. I told them that if I did, I wouldn't tell them anyway. I made angry faces and rolled my eyes whenever they pressed for more, but they didn't press hard. Not for a run-of-the-mill rebellion, just some dumb, troubled, selfish teenager who was not just diagnosed schizo-affective, but already had a room ready and waiting at the asylum. I was just another runaway, angry and scared and crazy, who was lucky to turn up alive on a beach instead of dead in a ditch somewhere.

They'd heard the same story enough times before; they were glad to congratulate themselves that this one had a happy ending.

—

But this is not the end.

Sometimes, on visiting days, I catch my father looking at me like I'm someone he doesn't quite recognize. Sometimes, he swallows and clears his throat like there's something he wants to say. And sometimes, I wonder if I should tell him a story. A strange one, and sad, about a girl who only wanted to go home, who really thought she could. I'd tell him about how it felt to be loved, deeply and surely and fiercely and forever, in a place so cold and faraway that not even the sun could touch it. I'd tell him about the way she held me in the deep, and how we shine in the dark like starlight. I'd tell him that he shouldn't cry for me, for any of us, when there's so much beauty waiting just beyond the edges of the earth.

I'd tell him the truth: that I don't know why they found me on that rocky beach at daybreak. I don't know why I was left behind. But I'll take my pills, and I'll talk to the doctors, and I'll be good, so good, such a very good girl, if only they'll let me go back.

At night, the wind that blows across the desert is as dry and airless as a tomb.

My breath is turning ragged again. It's only a matter of time.

EPILOGUE

IT IS NOT YET SUNSET when the little girl slips barefoot out her door. She steps carefully across the street, across the empty driveway, through the unmown grass. She passes down the long dock that leads to the river, one hand stretched in front of her to clear the way. The spiders, emboldened by the lack of traffic along the wooden walkway, have taken to stringing their webs between the posts.

When she drops to her seat and dangles her feet in the water, the green glass pendant on its long, golden chain lays heavy and cool against her thigh.

Nobody believed her when she told them where she'd gotten it. Three different policemen had taken turns, asking her where and how and when, frustration showing on their faces as the day wore on. They reminded her that this was serious, that her friend's father was very worried, and urged her to be honest.

They said, "We're not angry, nobody's angry, we just need you to tell the truth."

She must have told the truth a hundred times, her story always the same. Eventually, they'd stopped asking. That was when she heard one of the men saying that he didn't think she'd seen Callie at all—that she'd had the necklace all along, that she was lying because she'd stolen it.

But it wasn't stolen. It wasn't. She'd told them that a hundred times, too, until they threw up their hands and left.

One of the policemen, the one with kind eyes who patted her shoulder and told her after everything that she was a very good girl, had pulled her mother aside on his way out the door. He'd kept his voice low, but she heard all the same.

"It's not her fault," he said. "Kids this age, they're just not reliable witnesses, even when they do know something. And between you and me, the way these things usually end . . . it might be best if she doesn't remember."

But she did.

She does.

She remembers, and always will. She remembers that the sun was going down, the sky all painted in pinks and purples, when she'd wandered down to the river. And that it was even later, the last of the light leaking out of the sky, when she bent down and reached out with one small hand to receive the beautiful present. She had looped it around her neck and promised solemnly to take the very best care of it, as the night creatures began to sing.

She would pretend to forget, like they wanted her to, but this was how it happened.

The moon was heavy and full in the sky as she sat with her friend for the last time.

"I'll miss you," she said, and the older girl smiled, and silently kissed her cheek. She turned to where the others waited, arms outstretched. They went. She followed.

Her skin had gleamed like silver as she swam down into the dark.

ACKNOWLEDGMENTS

Inland was born at a kitchen table in the world's most charming Wicker Park apartment, where Jessi Lansgen made a pie while I talked about mermaid myths, missing mothers, and a story that I wasn't quite sure how or whether to tell. This book was not the most amazing thing to come out of her kitchen that day (that would be the pie), but I'm so grateful for that conversation, and all the other ones, too.

Thanks to Yfat Reiss Gendel at Foundry Literary + Media for her tireless work, steel nerves, and excellent hysteria-calming skills. Thanks to Julie Strauss-Gabel for insightfully guiding this story from "sloppy" to "creepy." Thanks to Tara Fowler, Melissa Faulner, and everyone at Dutton for bringing this book together from the inside out.

More thanks: to my father, who was a valuable source of information about hospital settings and medical conditions that might have (ahem) aquatic implications. (If it makes sense, it's thanks to him. If not, it's definitely my fault.) To my mother, who sent me every article under the sun about *gills*. To Mardie Cohen, who answered all my questions about Floridian culture, and then some. To Amy Wilkinson, who listened to me fret about revisions more than any human being reasonably should. To Olivia Tompkins, who graciously read anything I threw at her and answered all my questions about What the Kids Are into These Days. To Mary Dorn and her camera, the most amazing lifesavers in a photo-related pinch. To Noah Rosenfield, who was always up for a discussion of family drama and watery graves.

And to Brad Anderson—beloved husband, most trusted reader, maker of delicious steaks, and all-around best guy in the world. Thank you for everything.